TWENTY-ONE STORIES

Graham Greene was born in 1904. On coming down from
Balliol College, Oxford, he worked for four years as sub-
editor on *The Times*. He established his reputation with his
fourth novel, *Stamboul Train*. In 1935 he made a journey
across Liberia, described in *Journey Without Maps*, and on
his return was appointed film critic of the *Spectator*. In 1926
he had been received into the Roman Catholic Church and
visited Mexico in 1938 to report on the religious persecu-
tion there. As a result he wrote *The Lawless Roads* and,
later, his famous novel *The Power and the Glory*. *Brighton
Rock* was published in 1938 and in 1940 he became literary
editor of the *Spectator*. The next year he undertook work
for the Foreign Office and was stationed in Sierra Leone
from 1941 to 1943. This later produced the novel, *The Heart
of the Matter*, set in West Africa.

As well as his many novels, Graham Greene wrote several
collections of short stories, four travel books, six plays, three
books of autobiography – *A Sort of Life*, *Ways of Escape*
and *A World of My Own* (published posthumously) – two
of biography and four books for children. He also con-
tributed hundreds of essays, and film and book reviews,
some of which appear in the collections *Reflections* and
Mornings in the Dark. Many of his novels and short stories
have been filmed and *The Third Man* was written as a film
treatment. Graham Greene was a member of the Order of
Merit and a Companion of Honour. He died in April 1991.

ALSO BY GRAHAM GREENE

Novels

The Man Within
It's a Battlefield
A Gun for Sale
The Confidential Agent
The Ministry of Fear
The Third Man
The End of the Affair
The Quiet American
A Burn-Out Case
Travels with my Aunt
*Dr Fischer of Geneva or
The Bomb
Party*
The Tenth Man
Stamboul Train
England Made Me
Brighton Rock
The Power and the Glory
The Heart of the Matter
The Fallen Idol
Loser Takes All
Our Man in Havana
The Comedians
The Human Factor
Monsignor Quixote
The Honorary Consul
The Captain and the Enemy

Short Stories

Collected Stories
The Last Word and Other Stories
May We Borrow Your Husband?

Travel

Journey Without Maps
The Lawless Roads
In Search of a Character
Getting to Know the General

Essays

Collected Essays
Yours etc.
Reflections
Mornings in the Dark

Plays

Collected Plays

Autobiography

A Sort of Life
Ways of Escape
Fragments of an Autobiography
A World of my Own

Biography

Lord Rochester's Monkey
An Impossible Woman

Children's Books

The Little Train
The Little Horse-Bus
The Little Steamroller
The Little Fire Engine

GRAHAM GREENE

Twenty-One Stories

VINTAGE BOOKS

London

Published by Vintage 2001

10 9

Copyright © Graham Greene 1955, 1963, 1969,
1970, 1974, 1975

First published in Great Britain in 1954 by William Heinemann

Vintage
Random House, 20 Vauxhall Bridge Road,
London SW1V 2SA

Random House Australia (Pty) Limited
20 Alfred Street, Milsons Point, Sydney,
New South Wales 2061, Australia

Random House New Zealand Limited
18 Poland Road, Glenfield,
Auckland 10, New Zealand

Random House (Pty) Limited
Isle of Houghton, Corner of Boundary Road & Carse O'Gowrie,
Houghton 2198, South Africa

Random House Publishers India Private Limited
301 World Trade Tower, Hotel Intercontinental Grand Complex,
Barakhamba Lane, New Delhi 110 001, India

The Random House Group Limited Reg. No. 954009
www.randomhouse.co.uk/vintage/classics

A CIP catalogue record for this book
is available from the British Library

ISBN 9780099286165 (from Jan 2007)
ISBN 0099286165

Papers used by Random House are natural,
recyclable products made from wood grown in
sustainable forests. The manufacturing processes
conform to the environmental regulations of the
country of origin

Printed and bound in Great Britain by
Cox & Wyman Limited, Reading, Berkshire

CONTENTS

THE DESTRUCTORS

1

IT was on the eve of August Bank Holiday that the latest recruit became the leader of the Wormsley Common Gang. No one was surprised except Mike, but Mike at the age of nine was surprised by everything. 'If you don't shut your mouth,' somebody once said to him, 'you'll get a frog down it.' After that Mike kept his teeth tightly clamped except when the surprise was too great.

The new recruit had been with the gang since the beginning of the summer holidays, and there were possibilities about his brooding silence that all recognized. He never wasted a word even to tell his name until that was required of him by the rules. When he said 'Trevor' it was a statement of fact, not as it would have been with the others a statement of shame or defiance. Nor did anyone laugh except Mike, who finding himself without support and meeting the dark gaze of the newcomer opened his mouth and was quiet again. There was every reason why T., as he was afterwards referred to, should have been an object of mockery – there was his name (and they substituted the initial because otherwise they had no excuse not to laugh at it), the fact that his father, a former architect and present clerk, had 'come down in the world' and that his mother considered herself better than the neighbours. What but an odd quality of danger, of the unpredictable, established him in the gang without any ignoble ceremony of initiation?

The gang met every morning in an impromptu car-park, the site of the last bomb of the first blitz. The leader, who was known as Blackie, claimed to have heard it fall, and no one was precise enough in his dates to point out that he would have been one year old and fast asleep on the down platform of Wormsley Common Underground Station. On one side of the car-park leant the first occupied house, No. 3, of the shattered Northwood Terrace – literally leant, for it had suffered from the blast of the bomb and the side walls were supported on wooden struts. A smaller bomb and incendiaries had fallen beyond, so that the house stuck up like a jagged tooth and carried on the further wall relics of its neighbour, a dado, the remains of a fireplace. T., whose words were almost confined to voting 'Yes' or 'No' to the plan of operations proposed each day by Blackie, once startled the whole gang by saying broodingly, 'Wren built that house, father says.'

'Who's Wren?'

'The man who built St Paul's.'

'Who cares?' Blackie said. 'It's only Old Misery's.'

Old Misery – whose real name was Thomas – had once been a builder and decorator. He lived alone in the crippled house, doing for himself: once a week you could see him coming back across the common with bread and vegetables, and once as the boys played in the car-park he put his head over the smashed wall of his garden and looked at them.

'Been to the lav,' one of the boys said, for it was common knowledge that since the bombs fell something had gone wrong with the pipes of the house and Old Misery was too mean to spend money on the property. He could do the redecorating himself at cost price, but he had never learnt plumbing. The lav was a wooden shed at the bottom of the narrow garden with a star-shaped hole in the door: it had escaped the blast which had smashed the house next door and sucked out the window-frames of No. 3.

The next time the gang became aware of Mr Thomas was more surprising. Blackie, Mike and a thin yellow boy, who for some reason was called by his surname Summers, met him on the common coming back from the market. Mr Thomas stopped them. He said glumly, 'You belong to the lot that play in the car-park?'

Mike was about to answer when Blackie stopped him. As the leader he had responsibilities. 'Suppose we are?' he said ambiguously.

'I got some chocolates,' Mr Thomas said. 'Don't like 'em myself. Here you are. Not enough to go round, I don't suppose.

8

There never is,' he added with sombre conviction. He handed over three packets of Smarties.

The gang was puzzled and perturbed by this action and tried to explain it away. 'Bet someone dropped them and he picked 'em up,' somebody suggested.

'Pinched 'em and then got in a bleeding funk,' another thought aloud.

'It's a bribe,' Summers said. 'He wants us to stop bouncing balls on his wall.'

'We'll show him we don't take bribes,' Blackie said, and they sacrificed the whole morning to the game of bouncing that only Mike was young enough to enjoy. There was no sign from Mr Thomas.

Next day T. astonished them all. He was late at the rendezvous, and the voting for that day's exploit took place without him. At Blackie's suggestion the gang was to disperse in pairs, take buses at random and see how many free rides could be snatched from unwary conductors (the operation was to be carried out in pairs to avoid cheating). They were drawing lots for their companions when T. arrived.

'Where you been, T.?' Blackie asked. 'You can't vote now. You know the rules.'

'I've been *there*,' T. said. He looked at the ground, as though he had thoughts to hide.

'Where?'

'At Old Misery's.' Mike's mouth opened and then hurriedly closed again with a click. He had remembered the frog.

'At Old Misery's?' Blackie said. There was nothing in the rules against it, but he had a sensation that T. was treading on dangerous ground. He asked hopefully, 'Did you break in?'

'No. I rang the bell.'

'And what did you say?'

'I said I wanted to see his house.'

'What did he do?'

'He showed it me.'

'Pinch anything?'

'No.'

'What did you do it for then?'

The gang had gathered round: it was as though an impromptu court were about to form and try some case of deviation. T. said, 'It's a beautiful house,' and still watching the ground, meeting no one's eyes, he licked his lips first one way, then the other.

'What do you mean, a beautiful house?' Blackie asked with scorn.

'It's got a staircase two hundred years old like a corkscrew. Nothing holds it up.'

'What do you mean, nothing holds it up. Does it float?'

'It's to do with opposite forces, Old Misery said.'

'What else?'

'There's panelling.'

'Like in the Blue Boar?'

'Two hundred years old.'

'Is Old Misery two hundred years old?'

Mike laughed suddenly and then was quiet again. The meeting was in a serious mood. For the first time since T. had strolled into the car-park on the first day of the holidays his position was in danger. It only needed a single use of his real name and the gang would be at his heels.

'What did you do it for?' Blackie asked. He was just, he had no jealousy, he was anxious to retain T. in the gang if he could. It was the word 'beautiful' that worried him – that belonged to a class world that you could still see parodied at the Wormsley Common Empire by a man wearing a top hat and a monocle, with a haw-haw accent. He was tempted to say, 'My dear Trevor, old chap,' and unleash his hell hounds. 'If you'd broken in,' he said sadly – that indeed would have been an exploit worthy of the gang.

'This was better,' T. said. 'I found out things.' He continued to stare at his feet, not meeting anybody's eye, as though he were absorbed in some dream he was unwilling – or ashamed – to share.

'What things?'

'Old Misery's going to be away all tomorrow and Bank Holiday.'

Blackie said with relief, 'You mean we could break in?'

'And pinch things?' somebody asked.

Blackie said, 'Nobody's going to pinch things. Breaking in – that's good enough, isn't it? We don't want any court stuff.'

'I don't want to pinch anything,' T. said. 'I've got a better idea.'

'What is it?'

T. raised eyes, as grey and disturbed as the drab August day. 'We'll pull it down,' he said. 'We'll destroy it.'

Blackie gave a single hoot of laughter and then, like Mike, fell quiet, daunted by the serious implacable gaze. 'What'd the police be doing all the time?' he said.

'They'd never know. We'd do it from inside. I've found a way in.' He said with a sort of intensity, 'We'd be like worms, don't you see, in an apple. When we came out again there'd be nothing there, no staircase, no panels, nothing but just walls, and then we'd make the walls fall down – somehow.'

'We'd go to jug,' Blackie said.

'Who's to prove? and anyway we wouldn't have pinched anything.' He added without the smallest flicker of glee, 'There wouldn't be anything to pinch after we'd finished.'

'I've never heard of going to prison for breaking things,' Summers said.

'There wouldn't be time,' Blackie said. 'I've seen housebreakers at work.'

'There are twelve of us,' T. said. 'We'd organize.'

'None of us know how . . .'

'I know,' T. said. He looked across at Blackie. 'Have you got a better plan?'

'Today,' Mike said tactlessly, 'we're pinching free rides . . .'

'Free rides,' T. said. 'Kid stuff. You can stand down, Blackie, if you'd rather . . .'

'The gang's got to vote.'

'Put it up then.'

11

Blackie said uneasily, 'It's proposed that tomorrow and Monday we destroy Old Misery's house.'

'Here, here,' said a fat boy called Joe.

'Who's in favour?'

T. said, 'It's carried.'

'How do we start?' Summers asked.

'He'll tell you,' Blackie said. It was the end of his leadership. He went away to the back of the car-park and began to kick a stone, dribbling it this way and that. There was only one old Morris in the park, for few cars were left there except lorries: without an attendant there was no safety. He took a flying kick at the car and scraped a little paint off the rear mudguard. Beyond, paying no more attention to him than to a stranger, the gang had gathered round T.; Blackie was dimly aware of the fickleness of favour. He thought of going home, of never re-turning, of letting them all discover the hollowness of T.'s lead-ership, but suppose after all what T. proposed was possible – nothing like it had ever been done before. The fame of the Wormsley Common car-park gang would surely reach around London. There would be headlines in the papers. Even the grown-up gangs who ran the betting at the all-in wrestling and the barrow-boys would hear with respect of how Old Misery's house had been destroyed. Driven by the pure, simple and al-truistic ambition of fame for the gang, Blackie came back to where T. stood in the shadow of Old Misery's wall.

T. was giving his orders with decision: it was as though this plan had been with him all his life, pondered through the seasons, now in his fifteenth year crystallized with the pain of puberty. 'You,' he said to Mike, 'bring some big nails, the big-gest you can find, and a hammer. Anybody who can, better bring a hammer and a screwdriver. We'll need plenty of them. Chisels too. We can't have too many chisels. Can anybody bring a saw?'

'I can,' Mike said.

'Not a child's saw,' T. said. 'A real saw.'

Blackie realized he had raised his hand like any ordinary member of the gang.

'Right, you bring one, Blackie. But now there's a difficulty.
We want a hacksaw.'

'What's a hacksaw?' someone asked.

'You can get 'em at Woolworth's,' Summers said.

The fat boy called Joe said gloomily, 'I knew it would end in
a collection.'

'I'll get one myself,' T. said. 'I don't want your money. But I
can't buy a sledge-hammer.'

Blackie said, 'They are working on No. 15. I know where
they'll leave their stuff for Bank Holiday.'

'Then that's all,' T. said. 'We meet here at nine sharp.'

'I've got to go to church,' Mike said.

'Come over the wall and whistle. We'll let you in.'

2

On Sunday morning all were punctual except Blackie, even
Mike. Mike had a stroke of luck. His mother felt ill, his father
was tired after Saturday night, and he was told to go to church
alone with many warnings of what would happen if he strayed.
Blackie had difficulty in smuggling out the saw, and then in
finding the sledge-hammer at the back of No. 15. He ap-
proached the house from a lane at the rear of the garden, for
fear of the policeman's beat along the main road. The tired
evergreens kept off a stormy sun: another wet Bank Holiday
was being prepared over the Atlantic, beginning in swirls of
dust under the trees. Blackie climbed the wall into Misery's
garden.

There was no sign of anybody anywhere. The lav stood like a
tomb in a neglected graveyard. The curtains were drawn. The
house slept. Blackie lumbered nearer with the saw and the
sledge-hammer. Perhaps after all nobody had turned up: the
plan had been a wild invention: they had woken wiser. But
when he came close to the back door he could hear a confusion
of sound hardly louder than a hive in swarm: a clickety-clack, a
bang bang, a scraping, a creaking, a sudden painful crack. He
thought: it's true, and whistled.

They opened the back door to him and he came in. He had at once the impression of organization, very different from the old happy-go-lucky ways under his leadership. For a while he wandered up and down stairs looking for T. Nobody addressed him: he had a sense of great urgency, and already he could begin to see the plan. The interior of the house was being carefully demolished without touching the walls. Summers with hammer and chisel was ripping out the skirting-boards in the ground floor dining-room: he had already smashed the panels of the door. In the same room Joe was heaving up the parquet blocks, exposing the soft wood floorboards over the cellar. Coils of wire came out of the damaged skirting and Mike sat happily on the floor clipping the wires.

On the curved stairs two of the gang were working hard with an inadequate child's saw on the banisters – when they saw Blackie's big saw they signalled for it wordlessly. When he next saw them a quarter of the banisters had been dropped into the hall. He found T. at last in the bathroom – he sat moodily in the least cared-for room in the house, listening to the sounds coming up from below.

'You've really done it,' Blackie said with awe. 'What's going to happen?'

'We've only just begun,' T. said. He looked at the sledge-hammer and gave his instructions. 'You stay here and break the bath and the wash-basin. Don't bother about the pipes. They come later.'

Mike appeared at the door. 'I've finished the wires, T.,' he said.

'Good. You've just got to go wandering round now. The kitchen's in the basement. Smash all the china and glass and bottles you can lay hold of. Don't turn on the taps – we don't want a flood – yet. Then go into all the rooms and turn out the drawers. If they are locked get one of the others to break them open. Tear up any papers you find and smash all the ornaments. Better take a carving knife with you from the kitchen. The bedroom's opposite here. Open the pillows and tear up the sheets. That's enough for the moment. And you, Blackie, when you've finished in here crack the plaster in the passage up with your sledge-hammer.'

'What are you going to do?' Blackie asked.

'I'm looking for something special,' T. said.

It was nearly lunch-time before Blackie had finished and went in search of T. Chaos had advanced. The kitchen was a shambles of broken glass and china. The dining-room was stripped of parquet, the skirting was up, the door had been taken off its hinges, and the destroyers had moved up a floor. Streaks of light came in through the closed shutters where they worked with the seriousness of creators – and destruction after all is a form of creation. A kind of imagination had seen this house as it had now become.

Mike said, 'I've got to go home for dinner.'

'Who else?' T. asked, but all the others on one excuse or another had brought provisions with them.

They squatted in the ruins of the room and swapped unwanted sandwiches. Half an hour for lunch and they were at work again. By the time Mike returned they were on the top floor, and by six the superficial damage was completed. The doors were all off, all the skirtings raised, the furniture pillaged and ripped and smashed – no one could have slept in the house except on a bed of broken plaster. T. gave his orders – eight o'clock next morning, and to escape notice they climbed singly over the garden wall, into the car-park. Only Blackie and T. were left: the light had nearly gone, and when they touched a switch, nothing worked – Mike had done his job thoroughly.

'Did you find anything special?' Blackie asked.

T. nodded. 'Come over here,' he said, 'and look.' Out of both pockets he drew bundles of pound notes. 'Old Misery's savings,' he said. 'Mike ripped out the mattress, but he missed them.'

'What are you going to do? Share them?'

'We aren't thieves,' T. said. 'Nobody's going to steal anything from this house. I kept these for you and me – a celebration.' He knelt down on the floor and counted them out – there were seventy in all. 'We'll burn them,' he said, 'one by one,' and taking it in turns they held a note upwards and lit the top corner, so that the flame burnt slowly towards their fingers. The grey ash floated above them and fell on their heads like age. 'I'd like to see Old Misery's face when we are through,' T. said.

'You hate him a lot?' Blackie asked.

'Of course I don't hate him,' T. said. 'There'd be no fun if I hated him.' The last burning note illuminated his brooding face. 'All this hate and love,' he said, 'it's soft, it's hooey. There's only things, Blackie,' and he looked round the room crowded with the unfamiliar shadows of half things, broken things, former things. 'I'll race you home, Blackie,' he said.

3

Next morning the serious destruction started. Two were missing – Mike and another boy whose parents were off to Southend and Brighton in spite of the slow warm drops that had begun to fall and the rumble of thunder in the estuary like the first guns of the old blitz. 'We've got to hurry,' T. said.

Summers was restive. 'Haven't we done enough?' he asked. 'I've been given a bob for slot machines. This is like work.'

'We've hardly started,' T. said. 'Why, there's all the floors left, and the stairs. We haven't taken out a single window. You voted like the others. We are going to *destroy* this house. There won't be anything left when we've finished.'

They began again on the first floor picking up the top floor-boards next the outer wall, leaving the joists exposed. Then they sawed through the joists and retreated into the hall, as what was left of the floor heeled and sank. They had learnt with practice, and the second floor collapsed more easily. By the evening an odd exhilaration seized them as they looked down the great hollow of the house. They ran risks and made mistakes: when they thought of the windows it was too late to reach them. 'Cor,' Joe said, and dropped a penny down into the dry rubble-filled well. It cracked and span amongst the broken glass.

'Why did we start this?' Summers asked with astonishment;

T. was already on the ground, digging at the rubble, clearing a space along the outer wall. 'Turn on the taps,' he said. 'It's too dark for anyone to see now, and in the morning it won't matter.' The water overtook them on the stairs and fell through the floorless rooms.

It was then they heard Mike's whistle at the back. 'Something's wrong,' Blackie said. They could hear his urgent breathing as they unlocked the door.

'The bogies?' Summers asked.

'Old Misery,' Mike said. 'He's on his way,' he said with pride.

'But why?' T. said. 'He told me . . .' He protested with the fury of the child he had never been, 'It isn't fair.'

'He was down at Southend,' Mike said, 'and he was on the train coming back. Said it was too cold and wet.' He paused and gazed at the water. 'My, you've had a storm here. Is the roof leaking?'

'How long will he be?'

'Five minutes. I gave Ma the slip and ran.'

'We better clear,' Summers said. 'We've done enough, anyway.'

'Oh no, we haven't. Anybody could do this – ' 'this' was the shattered hollowed house with nothing left but the walls. Yet walls could be preserved. Façades were valuable. They could build inside again more beautifully than before. This could again be a home. He said angrily, 'We've got to finish. Don't move. Let me think.'

'There's no time,' a boy said.

'There's got to be a way,' T. said. 'We couldn't have got this far . . .'

'We've done a lot,' Blackie said.

'No. No, we haven't. Somebody watch the front.'

'We can't do any more.'

'He may come in at the back.'

'Watch the back too.' T. began to plead. 'Just give me a minute and I'll fix it. I swear I'll fix it.' But his authority had gone with his ambiguity. He was only one of the gang. 'Please,' he said.

'Please,' Summers mimicked him, and then suddenly struck home with the fatal name. 'Run along home, Trevor.'

T. stood with his back to the rubble like a boxer knocked groggy against the ropes. He had no words as his dreams shook and slid. Then Blackie acted before the gang had time to laugh, pushing Summers backward. 'I'll watch the front, T.,' he said, and cautiously he opened the shutters of the hall. The grey wet common stretched ahead, and the lamps gleamed in the puddles. 'Someone's coming, T. No, it's not him. What's your plan, T.?'

'Tell Mike to go out to the lav and hide close beside it. When he hears me whistle he's got to count ten and start to shout.'

·'Shout what?'

'Oh, "Help", anything.'

'You hear, Mike,' Blackie said. He was the leader again. He took a quick look between the shutters. 'He's coming, T.'

'Quick, Mike. The lav. Stay here, Blackie, all of you, till I yell.'

'Where are you going, T.?'

'Don't worry. I'll see to this. I said I would, didn't I?'

Old Misery came limping off the common. He had mud on his shoes and he stopped to scrape them on the pavement's edge. He didn't want to soil his house, which stood jagged and dark between the bomb-sites, saved so narrowly, as he believed, from destruction. Even the fan-light had been left unbroken by the bomb's blast. Somewhere somebody whistled. Old Misery looked sharply round. He didn't trust whistles. A child was shouting: it seemed to come from his own garden. Then a boy ran into the road from the car-park. 'Mr Thomas,' he called, 'Mr Thomas.'

'What is it?'

'I'm terribly sorry, Mr Thomas. One of us got taken short, and we thought you wouldn't mind, and now he can't get out.'

'What do you mean, boy?'

'He's got stuck in your lav.'

'He'd no business . . . Haven't I seen you before?'

'You showed me your house.'

'So I did. So I did. That doesn't give you the right to . . .'

'Do hurry, Mr Thomas. He'll suffocate.'

'Nonsense. He can't suffocate. Wait till I put my bag in.'

'I'll carry your bag.'

'Oh no, you don't. I carry my own.'

'This way, Mr Thomas.'

'I can't get in the garden that way. I've got to go through the house.'

'But you *can* get in the garden this way, Mr Thomas. We often do.'

'You often do?' He followed the boy with a scandalized fascination. 'When? What right . . .?'

'Do you see . . .? the wall's low.'

'I'm not going to climb walls into my own garden. It's absurd.'

'This is how we do it. One foot here, one foot there, and over.' The boy's face peered down, an arm shot out, and Mr Thomas found his bag taken and deposited on the other side of the wall.

'Give me back my bag,' Mr Thomas said. From the loo a boy yelled and yelled. 'I'll call the police.'

'Your bag's all right, Mr Thomas. Look. One foot there. On your right. Now just above. To your left.' Mr Thomas climbed over his own garden wall. 'Here's your bag, Mr Thomas.'

'I'll have the wall built up,' Mr Thomas said, 'I'll not have you boys coming over here, using my loo.' He stumbled on the path, but the boy caught his elbow and supported him. 'Thank you, thank you, my boy,' he murmured automatically. Somebody shouted again through the dark. 'I'm coming, I'm coming,' Mr Thomas called. He said to the boy beside him, 'I'm not unreasonable. Been a boy myself. As long as things are done regular. I don't mind you playing round the place Saturday mornings. Sometimes I like company. Only it's got to be regular. One of you asks leave and I say Yes. Sometimes I'll say No. Won't feel like it. And you come in at the front door and out at the back. No garden walls.'

'Do get him out, Mr Thomas.'

'He won't come to any harm in my loo,' Mr Thomas said, stumbling slowly down the garden. 'Oh, my rheumatics,' he said. 'Always get 'em on Bank Holiday. I've got to be careful. There's loose stones here. Give me your hand. Do you know what my horoscope said yesterday? "Abstain from any dealings in first half of week. Danger of serious crash." That might be on this path,' Mr Thomas said. 'They speak in parables and double meanings.' He paused at the door of the loo. 'What's the matter in there?' he called. There was no reply.

'Perhaps he's fainted,' the boy said.

'Not in my loo. Here, you, come out,' Mr Thomas said, and giving a great jerk at the door he nearly fell on his back when it swung easily open. A hand first supported him and then pushed him hard. His head hit the opposite wall and he sat heavily down. His bag hit his feet. A hand whipped the key out of the lock and the door slammed. 'Let me out,' he called, and heard the key turn in the lock. 'A serious crash,' he thought, and felt dithery and confused and old.

A voice spoke to him softly through the star-shaped hole in the door. 'Don't worry, Mr Thomas,' it said, 'we won't hurt you, not if you stay quiet.'

Mr Thomas put his head between his hands and pondered. He had noticed that there was only one lorry in the car-park, and he felt certain that the driver would not come for it before the morning. Nobody could hear him from the road in front, and the lane at the back was seldom used. Anyone who passed there would be hurrying home and would not pause for what they would certainly take to be drunken cries. And if he did call 'Help', who, on a lonely Bank Holiday evening, would have the courage to investigate? Mr Thomas sat on the loo and pondered with the wisdom of age.

After a while it seemed to him that there were sounds in the silence – they were faint and came from the direction of his house. He stood up and peered through the ventilation-hole – between the cracks in one of the shutters he saw a light, not the light of a lamp, but the wavering light that a candle might give. Then he thought he heard the sound of hammering and scraping and chipping. He thought of burglars – perhaps they had employed the boy as a scout, but why should burglars engage in what sounded more and more like a stealthy form of carpentry? Mr Thomas let out an experimental yell, but nobody answered. The noise could not even have reached his enemies.

4

Mike had gone home to bed, but the rest stayed. The question of leadership no longer concerned the gang. With nails, chisels, screwdrivers, anything that was sharp and penetrating, they moved around the inner walls worrying at the mortar between the bricks. They started too high, and it was Blackie who hit on the damp course and realized the work could be halved if they weakened the joints immediately above. It was a long, tiring, unamusing job, but at last it was finished. The gutted house stood there balanced on a few inches of mortar between the damp course and the bricks.

There remained the most dangerous task of all, out in the open at the edge of the bomb-site. Summers was sent to watch the road for passers-by, and Mr Thomas, sitting on the loo, heard clearly now the sound of sawing. It no longer came from the house, and that a little reassured him. He felt less concerned. Perhaps the other noises too had no significance.

A voice spoke to him through the hole. 'Mr Thomas.'

'Let me out,' Mr Thomas said sternly.

'Here's a blanket,' the voice said, and a long grey sausage was worked through the hole and fell in swathes over Mr Thomas's head.

'There's nothing personal,' the voice said. 'We want you to be comfortable tonight.'

'Tonight,' Mr Thomas repeated incredulously.

'Catch,' the voice said. 'Penny buns – we've buttered them, and sausage-rolls. We don't want you to starve, Mr Thomas.'

Mr Thomas pleaded desperately. 'A joke's a joke, boy. Let me out and I won't say a thing. I've got rheumatics. I got to sleep comfortable.'

'You wouldn't be comfortable, not in your house, you wouldn't. Not now.'

'What do you mean, boy?' But the footsteps receded. There was only the silence of night: no sound of sawing. Mr Thomas tried one more yell, but he was daunted and rebuked by the silence – a long way off an owl hooted and made away again on its muffled flight through the soundless world.

At seven next morning the driver came to fetch his lorry. He climbed into the seat and tried to start the engine. He was vaguely aware of a voice shouting, but it didn't concern him. At last the engine responded and he backed the lorry until it touched the great wooden shore that supported Mr Thomas's house. That way he could drive right out and down the street without reversing. The lorry moved forward, was momentarily checked as though something were pulling it from behind, and then went on to the sound of a long rumbling crash. The driver was astonished to see bricks bouncing ahead of him, while stones hit the roof of his cab. He put on his brakes. When he climbed out the whole landscape had suddenly altered. There was no house beside the car-park, only a hill of rubble. He went round and examined the back of his lorry for damage, and found a rope tied there that was still twisted at the other end round part of a wooden strut.

The driver again became aware of somebody shouting. It came from the wooden erection which was the nearest thing to a house in that desolation of broken brick. The driver climbed the smashed wall and unlocked the door. Mr Thomas came out of the loo. He was wearing a grey blanket to which flakes of pastry adhered. He gave a sobbing cry. 'My house,' he said. 'Where's my house?'

'Search me,' the driver said. His eye lit on the remains of a bath and what had once been a dresser and he began to laugh. There wasn't anything left anywhere.

'How dare you laugh,' Mr Thomas said. 'It was my house. My house.'

'I'm sorry,' the driver said, making heroic efforts, but when he remembered the sudden check of his lorry, the crash of

22

bricks falling, he became convulsed again. One moment the
house had stood there with such dignity between the bomb-sites
like a man in a top hat, and then, bang, crash, there wasn't
anything left – not anything. He said, 'I'm sorry. I can't help it,
Mr Thomas. There's nothing personal, but you got to admit it's
funny.'

1954

SPECIAL DUTIES

WILLIAM FERRARO of Ferraro & Smith, lived in a great house in Montagu Square. One wing was occupied by his wife who believed herself to be an invalid and obeyed strictly the dictate that one should live every day as if it were one's last. For this reason her wing for the last ten years had invariably housed some Jesuit or Dominican priest with a taste for good wine and whisky and an emergency bell in his bedroom. Mr Ferraro looked after his salvation in more independent fashion. He retained the firm grasp on practical affairs that had enabled his grandfather, who had been a fellow exile with Mazzini, to found the great business of Ferraro & Smith in a foreign land. God has made man in his image, and it was not unreasonable for Mr Ferraro to return the compliment and to regard God as the director of some supreme business which yet depended for certain of its operations on Ferraro & Smith. The strength of a chain is in its weakest link, and Mr Ferraro did not forget his responsibility.

Before leaving for his office at 9.30 Mr Ferraro as a matter of courtesy would telephone to his wife in the other wing. 'Father Dewes speaking,' a voice would say.

'How is my wife?'

'She passed a good night.'

The conversation seldom varied. There had been a time when Father Dewes' predecessor made an attempt to bring Mr and Mrs Ferraro into a closer relationship, but he had desisted when he realized how hopeless his aim was, and how on the few occasions when Mr Ferraro dined with them in the other wing an inferior claret was served at table and no whisky was drunk before dinner.

Mr Ferraro, having telephoned from his bedroom where he took his breakfast, would walk, rather as God walked in the Garden, through his library lined with the correct classics and

24

his drawing-room, on the walls of which hung one of the most expensive art collections in private hands. Where one man would treasure a single Degas, Renoir, Cézanne, Mr Ferraro bought wholesale – he had six Renoirs, four Degas, five Cézannes. He never tired of their presence, they represented a substantial saving in death-duties.

On this particular Monday morning it was also May the first. The sense of spring had come punctually to London and the sparrows were noisy in the dust. Mr Ferraro too was punctual, but unlike the seasons he was as reliable as Greenwich time. With his confidential secretary – a man called Hopkinson – he went through the schedule for the day. It was not very onerous, for Mr Ferraro had the rare quality of being able to delegate responsibility. He did this the more readily because he was accustomed to make unexpected checks, and woe betide the employee who failed him. Even his doctor had to submit to a sudden counter-check from a rival consultant. 'I think,' he said to Hopkinson, 'this afternoon I will drop in to Christie's and see how Maverick is getting on.' (Maverick was employed as his agent in the purchase of pictures.) What better could be done on a fine May afternoon than check on Maverick? He added, 'Send in Miss Saunders,' and drew forward a personal file which even Hopkinson was not allowed to handle.

Miss Saunders moused in. She gave the impression of moving close to the ground. She was about thirty years old with indeterminate hair and eyes of a startling clear blue which gave her otherwise anonymous face a resemblance to a holy statue. She was described in the firm's books as 'assistant confidential secretary' and her duties were 'special' ones. Even her qualifications were special: she had been head girl at the Convent of Saint Latitudinaria, Woking, where she had won in three successive years the special prize for piety – a little triptych of Our Lady with a background of blue silk, bound in Florentine leather and supplied by Burns Oates & Washbourne. She also had a long record of unpaid service as a Child of Mary.

'Miss Saunders,' Mr Ferraro said, 'I find no account here of the indulgences to be gained in June.'

'I have it here, sir. I was late home last night as the plenary indulgence at St Etheldreda's entailed the Stations of the Cross.'

She laid a typed list on Mr Ferraro's desk: in the first column the date, in the second the church or place of pilgrimage where the indulgence was to be gained, and in the third column in red ink the number of days saved from the temporal punishments of Purgatory. Mr Ferraro read it carefully.

'I get the impression, Miss Saunders,' he said, 'that you are spending too much time on the lower brackets. Sixty days here, fifty days there. Are you sure you are not wasting your time on these. One indulgence of 300 days will compensate for many such. I noticed just now that your estimate for May is lower than your April figures, and your estimate for June is nearly down to the March level. Five plenary indulgences and 1,565 days – a very good April work. I don't want you to slacken off.'

'April is a very good month for indulgences, sir. There is Easter. In May we can depend only on the fact that it is Our Lady's month. June is not very fruitful, except at Corpus Christi. You will notice a little Polish church in Cambridgeshire ...'

'As long as you remember, Miss Saunders, that none of us is getting younger. I put a great deal of trust in you, Miss Saunders. If I were less occupied here, I could attend to some of these indulgences myself. You pay great attention, I hope, to the conditions.'

'Of course I do, Mr Ferraro.'

'You are always careful to be in a State of Grace?'

Miss Saunders lowered her eyes. 'That is not very difficult in my case, Mr Ferraro.'

'What is your programme today?'

'You have it there, Mr Ferraro.'

'Of course. St Praxted's, Canon Wood. That is rather a long way to go. You have to spend the whole afternoon on a mere sixty days' indulgence?'

'It was all I could find for today. Of course there are always the plenary indulgences at the Cathedral. But I know how you feel about not repeating during the same month.'

'My only point of superstition,' Mr Ferraro said. 'It has no basis, of course, in the teaching of the Church.'

'You wouldn't like an occasional repetition for a member of your family, Mr Ferraro, your wife ...?'

'We are taught, Miss Saunders, to pay first attention to our own souls. My wife should be looking after her own indulgences – she has an excellent Jesuit adviser – I employ you to look after mine.'

'You have no objection to Canon Wood?'

'If it is really the best you can do. So long as it does not involve overtime.'

'Oh no, Mr Ferraro. A decade of the Rosary, that's all.'

After an early lunch – a simple one in a City chop-house which concluded with some Stilton and a glass of excellent port – Mr Ferraro visited Christie's. Maverick was satisfactorily on the spot and Mr Ferraro did not bother to wait for the Bonnard and the Monet which his agent had advised him to buy. The day remained warm and sunny, but there were confused sounds from the direction of Trafalgar Square which reminded Mr Ferraro that it was Labour Day. There was something inappropriate to the sun and the early flowers under the park trees in these processions of men without ties carrying dreary banners covered with bad lettering. A desire came to Mr Ferraro to take a real holiday, and he nearly told his chauffeur to drive to Richmond Park. But he always preferred, if it were possible, to combine business with pleasure, and it occurred to him that if he drove out now to Canon Wood, Miss Saunders should be arriving about the same time, after her lunch interval, to start the afternoon's work.

Canon Wood was one of those new suburbs built around an old estate. The estate was a public park, the house, formerly famous as the home of a minor Minister who served under Lord North at the time of the American rebellion, was now a local museum, and a street had been built on the little windy hill-top once a hundred acre field: a Charrington coal agency, the window dressed with one large nugget in a metal basket, a Home & Colonial Stores, an Odeon cinema, a large Anglican church. Mr Ferraro told his driver to ask the way to the Roman Catholic church.

'There isn't one here,' the policeman said.

'St Praxted's?'

'There's no such place,' the policeman said.

Mr Ferraro, like a Biblical character, felt a loosening of the bowels.

'St Praxted's, Canon Wood.'

'Doesn't exist, sir,' the policeman said. Mr Ferraro drove slowly back towards the City. This was the first time he had checked on Miss Saunders – three prizes for piety had won his trust. Now on his homeward way he remembered that Hitler had been educated by the Jesuits, and yet hopelessly he hoped.

In his office he unlocked the drawer and took out the special file. Could he have mistaken Canonbury for Canon Wood? But he had not been mistaken, and suddenly a terrible doubt came to him how often in the last three years Miss Saunders had betrayed her trust. (It was after a severe attack of pneumonia three years ago that he had engaged her – the idea had come to him during the long insomnias of convalescence.) Was it possible that not one of these indulgences had been gained? He couldn't believe that. Surely a few of that vast total of 36,892 days must still be valid. But only Miss Saunders could tell him how many. And what had she been doing with her office time – those long hours of pilgrimage? She had once taken a whole week-end at Walsingham.

He rang for Mr Hopkinson, who could not help remarking on the whiteness of his employer's face. 'Are you feeling quite well, Mr Ferraro?'

'I have had a severe shock. Can you tell me where Miss Saunders lives?'

'She lives with an invalid mother near Westbourne Grove.'

'The exact address, please.'

Mr Ferraro drove into the dreary wastes of Bayswater: great family houses had been converted into private hotels or fortunately bombed into car parks. In the terraces behind dubious girls leant against the railings, and a street band blew harshly round a corner. Mr Ferraro found the house, but he could not bring himself to ring the bell. He sat crouched in his Daimler waiting for something to happen. Was it the intensity of his gaze that brought Miss Saunders to an upper window, a coincidence, or retribution? Mr Ferraro thought at first that it was the warmth of the day that had caused her to be so inefficiently clothed, as she slid the window a little wider open. But then an arm circled her waist, a young man's face looked down into the street, a hand pulled a curtain across with the familiarity of habit. It became obvious to Mr Ferraro that not even the conditions for an indulgence had been properly fulfilled.

If a friend could have seen Mr Ferraro that evening mounting the steps of Montagu Square, he would have been surprised at the way he had aged. It was almost as though he had assumed during the long afternoon those 36,892 days he had thought to have saved during the last three years from Purgatory. The curtains were drawn, the lights were on, and no doubt Father Dewes was pouring out the first of his evening whiskies in the other wing. Mr Ferraro did not ring the bell, but let himself quietly in. The thick carpet swallowed his footsteps like quicksand. He switched on no lights: only a red-shaded lamp in each room had been lit ready for his use and now guided his steps. The pictures in the drawing-room reminded him of death-duties: a great Degas bottom like an atomic explosion mushroomed above a bath: Mr Ferraro passed on into the library: the leather-bound classics reminded him of dead authors. He sat down in a chair and a slight pain in his chest reminded him of his double pneumonia. He was three years nearer death than when Miss Saunders was appointed first. After a long while Mr Ferraro knotted his fingers together in the shape some people use for prayer. With Mr Ferraro it was an indication of decision. The worst was over: time lengthened again ahead of him. He thought: 'Tomorrow I will set about getting a really reliable secretary.'

1954

THE BLUE FILM

'OTHER people enjoy themselves,' Mrs Carter said.

'Well,' her husband replied, 'we've seen . . .'

'The reclining Buddha, the emerald Buddha, the floating markets,' Mrs Carter said. 'We have dinner and then go home to bed.'

'Last night we went to Chez Eve . . .'

'If you weren't with *me*,' Mrs Carter said, 'you'd find . . . you know what I mean, Spots.'

It was true, Carter thought, eyeing his wife over the coffee-cups: her slave bangles chinked in time with her coffee-spoon: she had reached an age when the satisfied woman is at her most beautiful, but the lines of discontent had formed. When he looked at her neck he was reminded of how difficult it was to unstring a turkey. Is it my fault, he wondered, or hers – or was it the fault of her birth, some glandular deficiency, some in-herited characteristic? It was sad how when one was young, one so often mistook the signs of frigidity for a kind of distinction.

'You promised we'd smoke opium,' Mrs Carter said.

'Not here, darling. In Saigon. Here it's "not done" to smoke.'

'How conventional you are.'

'There'd be only the dirtiest of coolie places. You'd be con-spicuous. They'd stare at you.' He played his winning card. 'There'd be cockroaches.'

'I should be taken to plenty of Spots if I wasn't with a hus-band.'

He tried hopefully, 'The Japanese strip-teasers . . .' but she had heard all about them. 'Ugly women in bras,' she said. His irritation rose. He thought of the money he had spent to take his wife with him and to ease his conscience – he had been away too often without her, but there is no company more cheerless than that of a woman who is not desired. He tried to drink his coffee calmly: he wanted to bite the edge of the cup.

30

'You've spilt your coffee,' Mrs Carter said.

'I'm sorry.' He got up abruptly and said, 'All right. I'll fix something. Stay here.' He leant across the table. 'You'd better not be shocked,' he said. 'You've asked for it.'

'I don't think I'm usually the one who is shocked,' Mrs Carter said with a thin smile.

Carter left the hotel and walked up towards the New Road. A boy hung at his side and said, 'Young girl?'

'I've got a woman of my own,' Carter said gloomily.

'Boy?'

'No thanks.'

'French films?'

Carter paused. 'How much?'

They stood and haggled a while at the corner of the drab street. What with the taxi, the guide, the films, it was going to cost the best part of eight pounds, but it was worth it, Carter thought, if it closed her mouth for ever from demanding 'Spots'. He went back to fetch Mrs Carter.

They drove a long way and came to a halt by a bridge over a canal, a dingy lane overcast with indeterminate smells. The guide said, 'Follow me.'

Mrs Carter put a hand on Carter's arm. 'Is it safe?' she asked.

'How would I know?' he replied, stiffening under her hand.

They walked about fifty unlighted yards and halted by a bamboo fence. The guide knocked several times. When they were admitted it was to a tiny earth-floored yard and a wooden hut. Something – presumably human – was humped in the dark under a mosquito-net. The owner showed them into a tiny stuffy room with two chairs and a portrait of the King. The screen was about the size of a folio volume.

The first film was peculiarly unattractive and showed the rejuvenation of an elderly man at the hands of two blonde masseuses. From the style of the women's hairdressing the film must have been made in the late twenties. Carter and his wife sat in mutual embarrassment as the film whirled and clicked to a stop.

'Not a very good one,' Carter said, as though he were a connoisseur.

'So that's what they call a blue film,' Mrs Carter said. 'Ugly and not exciting.'

A second film started.

There was very little story in this. A young man – one couldn't see his face because of the period soft hat – picked up a girl in the street (her cloche hat extinguished her like a meat-cover) and accompanied her to her room. The actors were young: there was some charm and excitement in the picture. Carter thought, when the girl took off her hat, I know that face, and a memory which had been buried for more than a quarter of a century moved. A doll over a telephone, a pin-up girl of the period over the double bed. The girl undressed, folding her clothes very neatly: she leant over to adjust the bed, exposing herself to the camera's eye and to the young man: he kept his head turned from the camera. Afterwards, she helped him in turn to take off his clothes. It was only then he remembered – that particular playfulness confirmed by the birthmark on the man's shoulder.

Mrs Carter shifted on her chair. 'I wonder how they find the actors,' she said hoarsely.

'A prostitute,' he said. 'It's a bit raw, isn't it? Wouldn't you like to leave?' he urged her, waiting for the man to turn his head. The girl knelt on the bed and held the youth around the waist – she couldn't have been more than twenty. No, he made a calculation, twenty-one.

'We'll stay,' Mrs Carter said, 'we've paid.' She laid a dry hot hand on his knee.

'I'm sure we could find a better place than this.'

'No.'

The young man lay on his back and the girl for a moment left him. Briefly, as though by accident, he looked at the camera. Mrs Carter's hand shook on his knee. 'Good God,' she said, 'it's you.'

'It *was* me,' Carter said, 'thirty years ago.' The girl was climbing back on to the bed.

'It's revolting,' Mrs Carter replied.

'I don't remember it as revolting,' Carter replied.

'I suppose you went and gloated, both of you.'

'No, I never saw it.'

'Why did you do it? I can't look at you. It's shameful.'

'I asked you to come away.'

'Did they pay you?'

'They paid her. Fifty pounds. She needed the money badly.'

'And you had your fun for nothing?'

'Yes.'

'I'd never have married you if I'd known. Never.'

'That was a long time afterwards.'

'You still haven't said why. Haven't you any excuse?' She stopped. He knew she was watching, leaning forward, caught up herself in the heat of that climax more than a quarter of a century old.

Carter said, 'It was the only way I could help her. She'd never acted in one before. She wanted a friend.'

'A friend,' Mrs Carter said.

'I loved her.'

'You couldn't love a tart.'

'Oh yes, you can. Make no mistake about that.'

'You queued for her, I suppose.'

'You put it too crudely,' Carter said.

'What happened to her?'

'She disappeared. They always disappear.'

The girl leant over the young man's body and put out the light. It was the end of the film. 'I have new ones coming next week,' the Siamese said, bowing deeply. They followed their guide back down the dark lane to the taxi.

In the taxi Mrs Carter said, 'What was her name?'

'I don't remember.' A lie was easiest.

As they turned into the New Road she broke her bitter silence again. 'How could you have brought yourself . . .? It's so degrading. Suppose someone you knew – in business – recognized you.'

'People don't talk about seeing things like that. Anyway, I wasn't in business in those days.'

'Did it never worry you?'

'I don't believe I have thought of it once in thirty years.'

'How long did you know her?'

'Twelve months perhaps.'

'She must look pretty awful by now if she's alive. After all she was common even then.'

'I thought she looked lovely,' Carter said.

They went upstairs in silence. He went straight to the bathroom and locked the door. The mosquitoes gathered around the lamp and the great jar of water. As he undressed he caught glimpses of himself in the small mirror: thirty years had not been kind: he felt his thickness and his middle age. He thought: I hope to God she's dead. Please, God, he said, let her be dead. When I go back in there, the insults will start again.

But when he returned Mrs Carter was standing by the mirror. She had partly undressed. Her thin bare legs reminded him of a heron waiting for fish. She came and put her arms round him: a slave bangle joggled against his shoulder. She said, 'I'd forgotten how nice you looked.'

'I'm sorry. One changes.'

'I didn't mean that. I like you as you are.'

She was dry and hot and implacable in her desire. 'Go on,' she said, 'go on,' and then she screamed like an angry and hurt bird. Afterwards she said, 'It's years since that happened,' and continued to talk for what seemed a long half hour excitedly at his side. Carter lay in the dark silent, with a feeling of loneliness and guilt. It seemed to him that he had betrayed that night the only woman he loved.

1954

THE HINT OF AN EXPLANATION

A LONG train journey on a late December evening, in this new version of peace, is a dreary experience. I suppose that my fellow traveller and I could consider ourselves lucky to have a compartment to ourselves, even though the heating apparatus was not working, even though the lights went out entirely in the frequent Pennine tunnels and were too dim anyway for us to read our books without straining the eyes, and though there was no restaurant car to give at least a change of scene. It was when we were trying simultaneously to chew the same kind of dry bun bought at the same station buffet that my companion and I came together. Before that we had sat at opposite ends of the carriage, both muffled to the chin in overcoats, both bent low over type we could barely make out, but as I threw the remains of my cake under the seat our eyes met, and he laid his book down.

By the time we were half-way to Bedwell Junction we had found an enormous range of subjects for discussion; starting with buns and the weather, we had gone on to politics, the Government, foreign affairs, the atom bomb, and by an inevitable progression, God. We had not, however, become either shrill or acid. My companion, who now sat opposite me, leaning a little forward, so that our knees nearly touched, gave such an impression of serenity that it would have been impossible to quarrel with him, however much our views differed, and differ they did profoundly.

I had soon realized I was speaking to a Roman Catholic – to someone who believed – how do they put it? – in an omnipotent and omniscient Deity, while I am what is loosely called an agnostic. I have a certain intuition (which I do not trust, founded as it may well be on childish experiences and needs) that a God exists, and I am surprised occasionally into belief by the extraordinary coincidences that beset our path like the traps

35

set for leopards in the jungle, but intellectually I am revolted at the whole notion of such a God who can so abandon his creatures to the enormities of Free Will. I found myself expressing this view to my companion who listened quietly and with respect. He made no attempt to interrupt – he showed none of the impatience or the intellectual arrogance I have grown to expect from Catholics; when the lights of a wayside station flashed across his face which had escaped hitherto the rays of the one globe working in the compartment, I caught a glimpse suddenly of – what? I stopped speaking, so strong was the impression. I was carried back ten years, to the other side of the great useless conflict, to a small town, Gisors in Normandy. I was again, for a moment, walking on the ancient battlements and looking down across the grey roofs, until my eyes for some reason lit on one stony 'back' out of the many, where the face of a middle-aged man was pressed against a window pane (I suppose that face has ceased to exist now, just as perhaps the whole town with its medieval memories has been reduced to rubble). I remembered saying to myself with astonishment, 'that man is happy – completely happy.' I looked across the compartment at my fellow traveller, but his face was already again in shadow. I said weakly, 'When you think what God – if there is a God – allows. It's not merely the physical agonies, but think of the corruption, even of children . . .'

He said, 'Our view is so limited,' and I was disappointed at the conventionality of his reply. He must have been aware of my disappointment (it was as though our thoughts were huddled as closely as ourselves for warmth), for he went on, 'Of course there is no answer here. We catch hints . . .' and then the train roared into another tunnel and the lights again went out. It was the longest tunnel yet; we went rocking down it and the cold seemed to become more intense with the darkness, like an icy fog (when one sense – of sight – is robbed, the others grow more acute). When we emerged into the mere grey of night and the globe lit up once more, I could see that my companion was leaning back on his seat.

I repeated his last word as a question, 'Hints?'

'Oh, they mean very little in cold print – or cold speech,' he said, shivering in his overcoat. 'And they mean nothing at all to another human being than the man who catches them. They are not scientific evidence – or evidence at all for that matter. Events that don't, somehow, turn out as they were intended – by the human actors, I mean, or by the thing behind the human actors.'

'The thing?'

'The word Satan is so anthropomorphic.' I had to lean forward now: I wanted to hear what he had to say. I am – I really am, God knows – open to conviction. He said, 'One's words are so crude, but I sometimes feel pity for that thing. It is so continually finding the right weapon to use against its Enemy and the weapon breaks in its own breast. It sometimes seems to me so – powerless. You said something just now about the corruption of children. It reminded me of something in my own childhood. You are the first person – except for one – that I have thought of telling it to, perhaps because you are anonymous. It's not a very long story, and in a way it's relevant.'

I said, 'I'd like to hear it.'

'You mustn't expect too much meaning. But to me there seems to be a hint. That's all. A hint.'

He went slowly on turning his face to the pane, though he could have seen nothing in the whirling world outside except an occasional signal lamp, a light in a window, a small country station torn backwards by our rush, picking his words with precision. He said, 'When I was a child they taught me to serve at Mass. The church was a small one, for there were very few Catholics where I lived. It was a market town in East Anglia, surrounded by flat chalky fields and ditches – so many ditches. I don't suppose there were fifty Catholics all told, and for some reason there was a tradition of hostility to us. Perhaps it went back to the burning of a Protestant martyr in the sixteenth century – there was a stone marking the place near where the meat stalls stood on Wednesdays. I was only half aware of the enmity, though I knew that my school nickname of Popey Martin had something to do with my religion and I had heard that my father was very nearly excluded from the Constitutional Club when he first came to the town.

'Every Sunday I had to dress up in my surplice and serve Mass. I hated it – I have always hated dressing up in any way (which is funny when you come to think of it), and I never ceased to be afraid of losing my place in the service and doing something which would put me to ridicule. Our services were at a different hour from the Anglican, and as our small, far-from-select band trudged out of the hideous chapel the whole of the townsfolk seemed to be on the way past to the proper church – I always thought of it as the proper church. We had to pass the parade of their eyes, indifferent, supercilious, mocking; you can't imagine how seriously religion can be taken in a small town – if only for social reasons.

'There was one man in particular; he was one of the two bakers in the town, the one my family did not patronize. I don't think any of the Catholics patronized him because he was called a free-thinker – an odd title, for, poor man, no one's thoughts were less free than his. He was hemmed in by his hatred – his hatred of us. He was very ugly to look at, with one wall-eye and a head the shape of a turnip, with the hair gone on the crown, and he was unmarried. He had no interests, apparently, but his baking and his hatred, though now that I am older I begin to see other sides of his nature – it did contain, perhaps, a certain furtive love. One would come across him suddenly, sometimes, on a country walk, especially if one was alone and it was Sunday. It was as though he rose from the ditches and the chalk smear on his clothes reminded one of the flour on his working overalls. He would have a stick in his hand and stab at the hedges, and if his mood were very black he would call out after you strange abrupt words that were like a foreign tongue – I know the meaning of those words, of course, now. Once the police went to his house because of what a boy said he had seen, but nothing came of it except that the hate shackled him closer. His name was Blacker, and he terrified me.

'I think he had a particular hatred of my father – I don't know why. My father was manager of the Midland Bank, and it's possible that at some time Blacker may have had un-satisfactory dealings with the bank – my father was a very cautious man who suffered all his life from anxiety about money – his own and other people's. If I try to picture Blacker now I see him walking along a narrowing path between high windowless walls, and at the end of the path stands a small boy of ten – me. I don't know whether it's a symbolic picture or the memory of one of our encounters – our encounters somehow got more and more frequent. You talked just now about the corruption of children. That poor man was preparing to re-venge himself on everything he hated – my father, the Catholics, the God whom people persisted in crediting – by corrupting me. He had evolved a horrible and ingenious plan.

'I remember the first time I had a friendly word from him. I was passing his shop as rapidly as I could when I heard his voice call out with a kind of sly subservience as though he were an under-servant. "Master David," he called, "Master David," and I hurried on. But the next time I passed that way he was at his door (he must have seen me coming) with one of those curly cakes in his hand that we called Chelsea buns. I didn't want to take it, but he made me, and then I couldn't be other than polite when he asked me to come into his parlour behind the shop and see something very special.

'It was a small electric railway – a rare sight in those days, and he insisted on showing me how it worked. He made me turn the switches and stop and start it, and he told me that I could come in any morning and have a game with it. He used the word "game" as though it were something secret, and it's true that I never told my family of this invitation and of how, perhaps twice a week those holidays, the desire to control that little railway became overpowering, and looking up and down the street to see if I were observed, I would dive into the shop.'

Our larger, dirtier, adult train drove into a tunnel and the light went out. We sat in darkness and silence, with the noise of the train blocking our ears like wax. When we were through we didn't speak at once and I had to prick him into continuing.

'An elaborate seduction,' I said.

'Don't think his plans were as simple as that,' my companion said, 'or as crude. There was much more hate than love, poor man, in his make-up. Can you hate something you don't believe in? And yet he called himself a free-thinker. What an impossible paradox, to be free and to be so obsessed. Day by day all through those holidays his obsession must have grown, but he kept a grip; he bided his time. Perhaps that thing I spoke of gave him the strength and the wisdom. It was only a week from the end of the holidays that he spoke to me of what concerned him so deeply.

'I heard him behind me as I knelt on the floor, coupling two coaches. He said, "You won't be able to do this, Master David, when school starts." It wasn't a sentence that needed any comment from me any more than the one that followed, "You ought to have it for your own, you ought," but how skilfully and unemphatically he had sowed the longing, the idea of a possibility ... I was coming to his parlour every day now; you see I had to cram every opportunity in before the hated term started again, and I suppose I was becoming accustomed to Blacker, to that wall eye, that turnip head, that nauseating subservience. The Pope, you know, describes himself as "The servant of the servants of God", and Blacker – I sometimes think, that Blacker was "the servant of the servants of ..." well, let it be.

'The very next day, standing in the doorway watching me play, he began to talk to me about religion. He said, with what untruth even I recognized, how much he admired the Catholics; he wished he could believe like that, but how could a baker believe? He accented "a baker" as one might say a biologist, and the tiny train spun round the gauge O track. He said, "I can bake the things you eat just as well as any Catholic can," and disappeared into his shop. I hadn't the faintest idea what he meant. Presently he emerged again, holding in his hand a little wafer. "Here," he said, "eat that and tell me ..." When I put it in my mouth I could tell that it was made in the same way as our wafers for communion – he had got the shape a little

40

wrong, that was all, and I felt guilty and irrationally scared. "Tell me," he said, "what's the difference?"

' "Difference?" I asked.

' "Isn't that just the same as you eat in church?"

'I said smugly, "It hasn't been consecrated."

'He said, "Do you think if I put the two of them under a microscope, you could tell the difference?" But even at ten I had the answer to that question. "No," I said, "the – accidents don't change," stumbling a little on the word "accidents" which had suddenly conveyed to me the idea of death and wounds.

'Blacker said with sudden intensity, "How I'd like to get one of yours in my mouth – just to see . . ."'

'It may seem odd to you, but this was the first time that the idea of transubstantiation really lodged in my mind. I had learnt it all by rote; I had grown up with the idea. The Mass was as lifeless to me as the sentences in *De Bello Gallico*, communion a routine like drill in the school-yard, but here suddenly I was in the presence of a man who took it seriously, as seriously as the priest whom naturally one didn't count – it was his job. I felt more scared than ever.

'He said, "It's all nonsense, but I'd just like to have it in my mouth."'

' "You could if you were a Catholic," I said naïvely. He gazed at me with his one good eye like a Cyclops. He said, "You serve at Mass, don't you? It would be easy for you to get at one of those things. I tell you what I'd do – I'd swap this electric train set for one of your wafers – consecrated, mind. It's got to be consecrated."

' "I could get you one out of the box," I said. I think I still imagined that his interest was a baker's interest – to see how they were made.

' "Oh, no," he said. "I want to see what your God tastes like."

' "I couldn't do that."

' "Not for a whole electric train, just for yourself? You wouldn't have any trouble at home. I'd pack it up and put a label inside that your Dad could see – 'For my bank manager's little boy from a grateful client.' He'd be pleased as Punch with that."

'Now that we are grown men it seems a trivial temptation, doesn't it? But try to think back to your own childhood. There was a whole circuit of rails on the floor at our feet, straight rails and curved rails, and a little station with porters and passengers, a tunnel, a foot-bridge, a level crossing, two signals, buffers, of course – and above all, a turntable. The tears of longing came into my eyes when I looked at the turntable. It was my favourite piece – it looked so ugly and practical and true. I said weakly, "I wouldn't know how."

'How carefully he had been studying the ground. He must have slipped several times into Mass at the back of the church. It would have been no good, you understand, in a little town like that, presenting himself for communion. Everybody there knew him for what he was. He said to me, "When you've been given communion you could just put it under your tongue a moment. He serves you and the other boy first, and I saw you once go out behind the curtain straight afterwards. You'd forgotten one of those little bottles."

' "The cruet," I said.

' "Pepper and salt." He grinned at me jovially, and I – well, I looked at the little railway which I could no longer come and play with when term started. I said, "You'd just swallow it, wouldn't you?"

' "Oh, yes," he said, "I'd just swallow it."

'Somehow I didn't want to play with the train any more that day. I got up and made for the door, but he detained me, gripping my lapel. He said, "This will be a secret between you and me. Tomorrow's Sunday. You come along here in the afternoon. Put it in an envelope and post it in. Monday morning the train will be delivered bright and early."

' "Not tomorrow," I implored him.

' "I'm not interested in any other Sunday," he said. "It's your only chance." He shook me gently backwards and forwards. "It will always have to be a secret between you and me," he said. "Why, if anyone knew they'd take away the train and there'd be me to reckon with. I'd bleed you something awful. You know how I'm always about on Sunday walks. You can't avoid a man like me. I crop up. You wouldn't even be safe in your own house. I know ways to get into houses when people are asleep." He pulled me into the shop after him and opened a drawer. In the drawer was an odd-looking key and a cut-throat razor. He said, "That's a master key that opens all locks and that – that's what I bleed people with." Then he patted my cheek with his plump floury fingers and said, "Forget it. You and me are friends."

'That Sunday Mass stays in my head, every detail of it, as though it had happened only a week ago. From the moment of the Confession to the moment of Consecration it had a terrible importance; only one other Mass has ever been so important to me – perhaps not even one, for this was a solitary Mass which could never happen again. It seemed as final as the last Sacrament, when the priest bent down and put the wafer in my mouth where I knelt before the altar with my fellow server.

'I suppose I had made up my mind to commit this awful act – for, you know, to us it must always seem an awful act – from the moment when I saw Blacker watching from the back of the church. He had put on his best Sunday clothes, and as though he could never quite escape the smear of his profession, he had a dab of dried talcum on his cheek, which he had presumably applied after using that cut-throat of his. He was watching me closely all the time, and I think it was fear – fear of that terrible undefined thing called bleeding – as much as covetousness that drove me to carry out my instructions.

'My fellow server got briskly up and taking the communion plate preceded Father Carey to the altar rail where the other Communicants knelt. I had the Host lodged under my tongue: it felt like a blister. I got up and made for the curtain to get the cruet that I had purposely left in the sacristy. When I was there I looked quickly round for a hiding-place and saw an old copy of the *Universe* lying on a chair. I took the Host from my mouth and inserted it between two sheets – a little damp mess of pulp. Then I thought: perhaps Father Carey has put the

43

paper out for a particular purpose and he will find the Host before I have time to remove it, and the enormity of my act began to come home to me when I tried to imagine what punishment I should incur. Murder is sufficiently trivial to have its appropriate punishment, but for this act the mind boggled at the thought of any retribution at all. I tried to remove the Host, but it had stuck clammily between the pages and in desperation I tore out a piece of the newpaper and screwing the whole thing up, stuck it in my trouser pocket. When I came back through the curtain carrying the cruet my eyes met Blacker's. He gave me a grin of encouragement and unhappiness – yes, I am sure, unhappiness. Was it perhaps that the poor man was all the time seeking something incorruptible?

'I can remember little more of that day. I think my mind was shocked and stunned and I was caught up too in the family bustle of Sunday. Sunday in a provincial town is the day for relations. All the family are at home and unfamiliar cousins and uncles are apt to arrive packed in the back seats of other people's cars. I remember that some crowd of that kind descended on us and pushed Blacker temporarily out of the foreground of my mind. There was somebody called Aunt Lucy with a loud hollow laugh that filled the house with mechanical merriment like the sound of recorded laughter from inside a hall of mirrors, and I had no opportunity to go out alone even if I had wished to. When six o'clock came and Aunt Lucy and the cousins departed and peace returned, it was too late to go to Blacker's and at eight it was my own bed-time.

'I think I had half forgotten what I had in my pocket. As I emptied my pocket the little screw of newspaper brought quickly back the Mass, the priest bending over me, Blacker's grin. I laid the packet on the chair by my bed and tried to go to sleep, but I was haunted by the shadows on the wall where the curtains blew, the squeak of furniture, the rustle in the chimney, haunted by the presence of God there on the chair. The Host had always been to me – well, the Host. I knew theoretically, as I have said, what I had to believe, but suddenly, as someone whistled in the road outside, whistled secretively, knowingly, to me, I knew that this which I had beside my bed was something of infinite value – something a man would pay for with his whole peace of mind, something that was so hated one could love it as one loves an outcast or a bullied child. These are adult words and it was a child of ten who lay scared in bed, listening to the whistle from the road, Blacker's whistle, but I think he felt fairly clearly what I am describing now. That is what I meant when I said this Thing, whatever it is, that seizes every possible weapon against God, is always, everywhere, disappointed at the moment of success. It must have felt as certain of me as Blacker did. It must have felt certain, too, of Blacker. But I wonder, if one knew what happened later to that poor man, whether one would not find again that the weapon had been turned against its own breast.

'At last I couldn't bear that whistle any more and got out of bed. I opened the curtains a little way, and there right under my window, the moonlight on his face, was Blacker. If I had stretched my hand down, his fingers reaching up could almost have touched mine. He looked up at me, flashing the one good eye, with hunger – I realize now that near-success must have developed his obsession almost to the point of madness. Desperation had driven him to the house. He whispered up at me, "David, where is it?"

'I jerked my head back at the room. "Give it me," he said, "quick. You shall have the train in the morning."

'I shook my head. He said, "I've got the bleeder here, and the key. You'd better toss it down."

' "Go away," I said, but I could hardly speak with fear.

' "I'll bleed you first and then I'll have it just the same."

' "Oh no, you won't," I said. I went to the chair and picked it – Him – up. There was only one place where He was safe. I couldn't separate the Host from the paper, so I swallowed both. The newsprint stuck like a prune to the back of my throat, but I rinsed it down with water from the ewer. Then I went back to the window and looked down at Blacker. He began to wheedle me. "What have you done with it, David? What's the fuss? It's only a bit of bread," looking so longingly and pleadingly up at me that even as a child I wondered whether he could really think that, and yet desire it so much.

' "I swallowed it," I said.

' "Swallowed it?"

' "Yes," I said. "Go away." Then something happened which seems to me now more terrible than his desire to corrupt or my thoughtless act: he began to weep – the tears ran lopsidedly out of the one good eye and his shoulders shook. I only saw his face for a moment before he bent his head and strode off, the bald turnip head shaking, into the dark. When I think of it now, it's almost as if I had seen that Thing weeping for its inevitable defeat. It had tried to use me as a weapon and now I had broken in its hands and it wept its hopeless tears through one of Blacker's eyes.'

The black furnaces of Bedwell Junction gathered around the line. The points switched and we were tossed from one set of rails to another. A spray of sparks, a signal light changed to red, tall chimneys jetting into the grey night sky, the fumes of steam from stationary engines – half the cold journey was over and now remained the long wait for the slow cross-country train. I said, 'It's an interesting story. I think I should have given Blacker what he wanted. I wonder what he would have done with it.'

'I really believe,' my companion said, 'that he would first of all have put it under his microscope – before he did all the other things I expect he had planned.'

'And the hint?' I said. 'I don't quite see what you mean by that.'

'Oh, well,' he said vaguely, 'you know for me it was an odd beginning, that affair, when you come to think of it,' but I should never have known what he meant had not his coat, when he rose to take his bag from the rack, come open and disclosed the collar of a priest.

I said, 'I suppose you think you owe a lot to Blacker.'

'Yes,' he said. 'You see, I am a very happy man.'

1948

WHEN GREEK MEETS GREEK

1

WHEN the chemist had shut his shop for the night he went
through a door at the back of the hall that served both him and
the flats above, and then up two flights and a half of stairs
carrying an offering of a little box of pills. The box was
stamped with his name and address: Priskett, 14 New End
Street, Oxford. He was a middle-aged man with a thin
moustache and scared evasive eyes: he wore his long white coat
even when he was off duty as if it had the power of protecting
him like a King's uniform from his enemies. So long as he wore
it he was free from summary trial and execution.

On the top landing was a window: outside Oxford spread
through the spring evening: the peevish noise of innumerable
bicycles, the gasworks, the prison, and the grey spires, beyond
the bakers and confectioners, like paper frills. A door was
marked with a visiting-card Mr Nicholas Fennick, B.A.: the
chemist rang three short times.

The man who opened the door was sixty years old at least,
with snow-white hair and a pink babyish skin. He wore a mul-
berry velvet dinner jacket, and his glasses swung on the end of a
wide black ribbon. He said with a kind of boisterousness, 'Ah,
Priskett, step in, Priskett. I had just sported my oak for a
moment...'

'I brought you some more of my pills.'

'Invaluable, Priskett. If only you had taken a degree – the
Society of Apothecaries would have been enough – I would
have appointed you resident medical officer of St Ambrose's.'

'How's the college doing?'

'Give me your company for a moment in the common-room,
and you shall know all.'

Mr Fennick led the way down a little dark passage cluttered
with mackintoshes: Mr Priskett, feeling his way uneasily from
mackintosh to mackintosh, kicked in front of him a pair of

girl's shoes. 'One day,' Mr Fennick said, 'we must build . . .' and
he made a broad confident gesture with his glasses that seemed
to press back the walls of the common-room: a small round
table covered with a landlady's cloth, three or four shiny chairs
and a glass-fronted bookcase containing a copy of *Every Man
His Own Lawyer.* 'My niece Elisabeth,' Mr Fennick said, 'my
medical adviser.' A very young girl with a lean pretty face
nodded perfunctorily from behind a typewriter. 'I am going
to train Elisabeth,' Mr Fennick said, 'to act as bursar. The
strain of being both bursar and president of the college is upsetting my stomach. The pills . . . thank you.'

Mr Priskett said humbly, 'And what do you think of the
college, Miss Fennick?'

'My name's Cross,' the girl said. 'I think it's a good idea. I'm
surprised my uncle thought of it.'

'In a way it was – partly – my idea.'

'I'm more surprised still,' the girl said firmly.

Mr Priskett, folding his hands in front of his white coat as
though he were pleading before a tribunal, went on: 'You see, I
said to your uncle that with all these colleges being taken over
by the military and the tutors having nothing to do they ought
to start teaching by correspondence.'

'A glass of audit ale, Priskett?' Mr Fennick suggested. He
took a bottle of brown ale out of a cupboard and poured out
two gaseous glasses.

'Of course,' Mr Priskett pleaded, 'I hadn't thought of all this
– the common-room, I mean, and St Ambrose's.'

'My niece,' Mr Fennick said, 'knows very little of the set-up.'
He began to move restlessly around the room touching things
with his hand. He was rather like an aged bird of prey inspec-
ting the grim components of its nest.

The girl said briskly, 'As I see it, Uncle is running a swindle
called St Ambrose's College, Oxford.'

'Not a swindle, my dear. The advertisement was very carefully worded.' He knew it by heart: every phrase had been
carefully checked with his copy of *Every Man His Own Lawyer*
open on the table. He repeated it now in a voice full and husky

48

with bottled brown ale. 'War conditions prevent you going to Oxford. St Ambrose's – Tom Brown's old college – has made an important break with tradition. For the period of the war only it will be possible to receive tuition by post wherever you may be, whether defending the Empire on the cold rocks of Iceland or on the burning sands of Libya, in the main street of an American town or a cottage in Devonshire . . .'

'You've overdone it,' the girl said. 'You always do. That hasn't got a cultured ring. It won't catch anybody but suckers.'

'There are plenty of suckers,' Mr Fennick said.

'Go on.'

'Well, I'll skip that bit. "Degree-diplomas will be granted at the end of three terms instead of the usual three years." ' He explained, 'That gives a quick turnover. One can't wait for money these days. "Gain a real Oxford education at Tom Brown's old college. For full particulars of tuition fees, battels, etc., write to the Bursar." '

'And do you mean to say the University can't stop that?'

'Anybody,' Mr Fennick said with a kind of pride, 'can start a college anywhere. I've never said it was part of the University.'

'But battels – battels mean board and lodgings.'

'In this case,' Mr Fennick said, 'it's quite a nominal fee – to keep your name in perpetuity on the books of the old firm – I mean the college.'

'And the tuition . . .'

'Priskett here is the science tutor. I take history and classics. I thought that you, my dear, might tackle – economics?'

'I don't know anything about them.'

'The examinations, of course, have to be rather simple – within the capacity of the tutors. (There is an excellent public library here.) And another thing – the fees are returnable if the diploma-degree is not granted.'

'You mean . . .'

'Nobody will ever fail,' Mr Priskett brought breathlessly out with scared excitement.

'And you are really getting results?'

'I waited, my dear, until I could see the distinct possibility of at least six hundred a year for the three of us before I wired you. And today – beyond all my expectations – I have received a letter from Lord Driver. He is entering his son at St Ambrose's.'

'But how can he come here '

'In his absence, my dear, on his country's service. The Drivers have always been a military family. I looked them up in Debrett.'

'What do you think of it?' Mr Priskett asked with anxiety and triumph.

'I think it's rich. Have you arranged a boat-race?'

'There, Priskett,' Mr Fennick said proudly, raising his glass of audit ale, 'I told you she was a girl of the old stock.'

2

Directly he heard his landlady's feet upon the stairs the elderly man with the grey shaven head began to lay his wet tea-leaves round the base of the aspidistra. When she opened the door he was dabbing the tea-leaves in tenderly with his fingers. 'A lovely plant, my dear.'

But she wasn't going to be softened at once: he could tell that: she waved a letter at him. 'Listen,' she said, 'what's this Lord Driver business?'

'My name, my dear: a good Christian name like Lord George Sanger had.'

'Then why don't they put Mr Lord Driver on the letter?'

'Ignorance, just ignorance.'

'I don't want any hanky-panky from my house. It's always been honest.'

'Perhaps they didn't know if I was an esquire or just a plain mister, so they left it blank.'

'It's sent from St Ambrose's College, Oxford: people like that ought to know.'

'It comes, my dear, of having such a good address. W.1. And all the gentry live in Mewses.' He made a half-hearted snatch at the letter, but the landlady held it out of reach.

'What are the likes of you writing to Oxford College about?'

'My dear,' he said with strained dignity, 'I may have been a little unfortunate: it may even be that I have spent a few years in chokey, but I have the rights of a free man.'

'And a son in quod.'

'Not in quod, my dear. Borstal is quite another institution. It is – a kind of college.'

'Like St Ambrose's.'

'Perhaps not quite of the same rank.'

He was too much for her: he was usually in the end too much for her. Before his first stay at the Scrubs he had held a number of positions as manservant and even butler: the way he raised his eyebrows he had learned from Lord Charles Manville: he wore his clothes like an eccentric peer, and you might say that he had even learned the best way to pilfer from old Lord Bellen who had a penchant for silver spoons.

'And now, my dear, if you'd just let me have my letter?' He put his hand tentatively forward: he was as daunted by her as she was by him: they sparred endlessly and lost to each other; interminably the battle was never won – they were always afraid. This time it was his victory. She slammed the door. Suddenly, ferociously, when the door had closed, he made a little vulgar noise at the aspidistra. Then he put on his glasses and began to read.

His son had been accepted for St Ambrose's, Oxford. The great fact stared up at him above the sprawling decorative signature of the President. Never had he been more thankful for the coincidence of his name. 'It will be my great pleasure,' the President wrote, 'to pay personal attention to your son's career at St Ambrose's. In these days it is an honour to welcome a member of a great military family like yours.' Driver felt an odd mixture of amusement and of genuine pride. He'd put one over on them, but his breast swelled within his waistcoat at the idea that now he had a son at Oxford.

But there were two snags – minor snags when he considered how far he'd got already. It was apparently an old Oxford custom that fees should be paid in advance, and then there were the examinations. His son couldn't do them himself: Borstal would not allow it, and he wouldn't be out for another six months. Besides the whole beauty of the idea was that he should receive the gift of an Oxford degree as a kind of welcome home. Like a chess player who is always several moves ahead he was already seeing his way around these difficulties.

The fees he felt sure in his case were only a matter of bluff: a peer could always get credit, and if there was any trouble after the degree had been awarded, he could just tell them to sue and be damned. No Oxford college would like to admit that it had been imposed on by an old lag. But the examinations? A funny little knowing smile twitched the corners of his mouth: a memory of the Scrubs five years ago and the man they called Daddy, the Reverend Simon Milan. He was a short time prisoner – they were all short time prisoners at the Scrubs: no sentence of over three years was ever served there. He remembered the tall lean aristocratic parson with his iron-grey hair and his narrow face like a lawyer's which had gone somehow soft inside with too much love. A prison, when you came to think of it, contained as much knowledge as a University: there were doctors, financiers, clergy. He knew where he could find Mr Milan: he was employed in a boarding-house near Euston Square, and for a few drinks he would do most things – he would certainly make out some fine examination papers. 'I can just hear him now,' Driver reminded himself ecstatically, 'talking Latin to the warders.'

3

It was autumn in Oxford: people coughed in the long queues for sweets and cakes, and the mists from the river seeped into the cinemas past the commissionaires on the look-out for people without gas-masks. A few undergraduates picked their way through the evacuated swarm; they always looked in a hurry: so much had to be got through in so little time before the army claimed them. There were lots of pickings for racketeers, Elisabeth Cross thought, but not much of a chance for a girl to find a husband: the oldest Oxford racket had been elbowed out by the black markets in Woodbines, toffees, tomatoes.

There had been a few days last spring when she had treated St Ambrose's as a joke, but when she saw the money actually coming in, the whole thing seemed less amusing. Then for some weeks she was acutely unhappy – until she realized that of all the war-time rackets this was the most harmless. They were not reducing supplies like the Ministry of Food, or destroying confidence like the Ministry of Information: her uncle paid income tax, and they even to some extent educated people. The suckers, when they took their diploma-degrees, would know several things they hadn't known before.

But that didn't help a girl to find a husband.

She came moodily out of the matinée, carrying a bunch of papers she should have been correcting. There was only one 'student' who showed any intelligence at all, and that was Lord Driver's son. The papers were forwarded from 'somewhere in England' via London by his father; she had nearly found herself caught out several times on points of history, and her uncle she knew was straining his rusty Latin to the limit.

When she got home she knew that there was something in the air: Mr Priskett was sitting in his white coat on the edge of a chair and her uncle was finishing a stale bottle of beer. When something went wrong he never opened a new bottle: he believed in happy drinking. They watched her in silence. Mr Priskett's silence was gloomy, her uncle's preoccupied. Something had to be got round – it couldn't be the university authorities: they had stopped bothering him long ago – a lawyer's letter, an irascible interview, and their attempt to maintain 'a monopoly of local education' – as Mr Fennick put it – had ceased.

'Good evening,' Elisabeth said. Mr Priskett looked at Mr Fennick and Mr Fennick frowned.

'Has Mr Priskett run out of pills?'

Mr Priskett winced.

'I've been thinking,' Elisabeth said, 'that as we are now in the third term of the academic year, I should like a rise in salary.'

Mr Priskett drew in his breath sharply, keeping his eyes on Mr Fennick.

'I should like another three pounds a week.'

Mr Fennick rose from his table; he glared ferociously into the top of his dark ale, his frown beetled. The chemist scraped his chair a little backward. And then Mr Fennick spoke.

'We are such stuff as dreams are made on,' he said and hic-cupped slightly.

'Kidneys,' Elisabeth said.

'Rounded by a sleep. And these our cloud-capped towers ...'

'You are misquoting.'

'Vanished into air, into thin air.'

'You've been correcting the English papers.'

'Unless you allow me to think, to think rapidly and deeply, there won't be any more examination papers,' Mr Fennick said.

'Trouble?'

'I've always been a Republican at heart. I don't see why we want a hereditary peerage.'

'*À la lanterne*,' Elisabeth said.

'This man Lord Driver: why should a mere accident of birth ...?'

'He refuses to pay?'

'It isn't that. A man like that expects credit: it's right that he should have credit. But he's written to say that he's coming down tomorrow to see his boy's college. The old fat-headed sentimental fool,' Mr Fennick said.

'I knew you'd be in trouble sooner or later.'

'That's the sort of damn fool comfortless thing a girl would say.'

'It just needs brain.'

Mr Fennick picked up a brass ash-tray – and then put it down again carefully.

'It's quite simple as soon as you begin to think.'

'Think?'

Mr Priskett scraped a chair-leg.

'I'll meet him at the station with a taxi, and take him to – say Balliol. Lead him straight through into the inner quad, and there you'll be, just looking as if you'd come out of the Master's lodging.'

'He'll know it's Balliol.'

'He won't. Anybody who knew Oxford couldn't be stupid enough to send his son to St Ambrose's.'

'Of course it's true. These military families are a bit crass.'

'You'll be in an enormous hurry. Convocation or something. Whip him round the Hall, the Chapel, the Library, and hand him back to me outside the Master's. I'll take him out to lunch and see him into his train. It's simple.'

Mr Fennick said broodingly, 'Sometimes I think you're a terrible girl, terrible. Is there nothing you wouldn't think up?'

'I believe,' Elisabeth said, 'that if you're going to play your own game in a world like this, you've got to play it properly. Of course,' she said, 'if you are going to play a different game, you go to a nunnery or to the wall and like it. But I've only got one game to play.'

4

It really went off very smoothly. Driver found Elisabeth at the barrier: she didn't find him because she was expecting something different. Something about him worried her; it wasn't his clothes or the monocle he never seemed to use – it was something subtler than that. It was almost as though he were afraid of her, he was so ready to fall in with her plans. 'I don't want to be any trouble, my dear, any trouble at all. I know how busy the President must be.' When she explained that they would be lunching together in town, he even seemed relieved. 'It's just the bricks of the dear old place,' he said. 'You mustn't mind my being a sentimentalist, my dear.'

'Were you at Oxford?'

'No, no. The Drivers, I'm afraid, have neglected the things of the mind.'

'Well, I suppose a soldier needs brains?'

He took a sharp look at her, and then answered in quite a

different sort of voice, 'We believed so in the Lancers.' Then he strolled beside her to the taxi, twirling his monocle, and all the way up from the station he was silent, taking little quiet sideways peeks at her, appraising, approving.

'So this is St Ambrose's,' he said in a hearty voice just before the porter's lodge and she pushed him quickly by, through the first quad, towards the Master's house, where on the doorstep with a B.A. gown over his arm stood Mr Fennick permanently posed like a piece of garden statuary. 'My uncle, the President,' Elisabeth said.

'A charming girl, your niece,' Driver said as soon as they were alone together. He had really only meant to make conversation, but as soon as he had spoken the old two crooked minds began to move in harmony.

'She's very home-loving,' Mr Fennick said. 'Our famous elms,' he went on, waving his hand skywards. 'St Ambrose's rooks.'

'Crooks?' Driver exclaimed.

'Rooks. In the elms. One of our great modern poets wrote about them. "St Ambrose elms, oh St Ambrose elms", and about "St Ambrose rooks calling in wind and rain".'

'Pretty. Very pretty.'

'Nicely turned, I think.'

'I meant your niece.'

'Ah, yes. This way to the Hall. Up these steps. So often trodden, you know, by Tom Brown.'

'Who was Tom Brown?'

'The great Tom Brown – one of Rugby's famous sons.' He added thoughtfully, 'She'll make a fine wife – and mother.'

'Young men are beginning to realize that the flighty ones are not what they want for a lifetime.'

They stopped by mutual consent on the top step: they nosed towards each other like two old blind sharks who each believes that what stirs the water close to him is tasty meat.

'Whoever wins her,' Mr Fennick said, 'can feel proud. She'll make a fine hostess ...'

'I and my son,' Driver said, 'have talked seriously about

marriage. He takes rather an old-fashioned view. He'll make a good husband . . .'

They walked into the hall, and Mr Fennick led the way round the portraits. 'Our founder,' he said, pointing at a full-bottomed wig. He chose it deliberately: he felt it smacked a little of himself. Before Swinburne's portrait he hesitated: then pride in St Ambrose's conquered caution. 'The great poet Swinburne,' he said. 'We sent him down.'

'Expelled him?'

'Yes. Bad morals.'

'I'm glad you are strict about those.'

'Ah, your son is in safe hands at St Amb's.'

'It makes me very happy,' Driver said. He began to scrutinize the portrait of a nineteenth-century divine. 'Fine brushwork,' he said. 'Now religion – I believe in religion. Basis of the family.' He said with a burst of confidence. 'You know our young people ought to meet.'

Mr Fennick gleamed happily. 'I agree.'

'If he passes . . .'

'Oh, he'll certainly pass,' Mr Fennick said.

'He'll be on leave in a week or two. Why shouldn't he take his degree in person?'

'Well, there'd be difficulties.'

'Isn't it the custom?'

'Not for postal graduates. The Vice-Chancellor likes to make a small distinction . . . but Lord Driver, in the case of so distinguished an alumnus, I suggest that I should be deputed to present the degree to your son in London.'

'I'd like him to see his college.'

'And so he shall in happier days. So much of the college is shut now. I would like him to visit it for the first time when its glory is restored. Allow me and my niece to call on you.'

'We are living very quietly.'

'Not serious financial trouble, I hope?'

'Oh, no, no.'

'I'm so glad. And now let us rejoin the dear girl.'

It always seemed to be more convenient to meet at railway stations. The coincidence didn't strike Mr Fennick who had fortified himself for the journey with a good deal of audit ale, but it struck Elisabeth. The college lately had not been fulfilling expectations, and that was partly due to the laziness of Mr Fennick: from his conversation lately it almost seemed as though he had begun to regard the college as only a step to something else – what she couldn't quite make out. He was always talking about Lord Driver and his son Frederick and the responsibilities of the peerage. His Republican tendencies had quite lapsed. 'That dear boy,' was the way he referred to Frederick, and he marked him 100% for Classics. 'It's not often Latin and Greek go with military genius,' he said. 'A remarkable boy.'

'He's not so hot on economics,' Elisabeth said.

'We mustn't demand too much book-learning from a soldier.'

At Paddington Lord Driver waved anxiously to them through the crowd; he wore a very new suit – one shudders to think how many coupons had been gambled away for the occasion. A little behind him was a very young man with a sullen mouth and a scar on his cheek. Mr Fennick bustled forward; he wore a black raincoat over his shoulder like a cape and carrying his hat in his hand he disclosed his white hair venerably among the porters.

'My son – Frederick,' Lord Driver said. The boy sullenly took off his hat and put it on again quickly: they wore their hair in the army very short.

'St Ambrose's welcomes her new graduate,' Mr Fennick said. Frederick grunted.

The presentation of the degree was made in a private room at Mount Royal. Lord Driver explained that his house had been bombed – a time bomb, he added, a rather necessary explanation since there had been no raids recently. Mr Fennick was satisfied if Lord Driver was. He had brought up a B.A. gown, a mortar-board and a Bible in his suitcase, and he made quite an imposing little ceremony between the book-table, the sofa and the radiator, reading out a Latin oration and tapping Frederick lightly on the head with the Bible. The degree-diploma had been expensively printed in two colours by an Anglo-Catholic firm. Elisabeth was the only uneasy person there. Could the world, she wondered, really contain two such suckers? What was this painful feeling growing up in her that perhaps it contained four?

After a little light lunch with bottled brown beer – 'almost as good, if I may say so, as our audit ale,' Mr Fennick beamed – the President and Lord Driver made elaborate moves to drive the two young people together. 'We've got to talk a little business,' Mr Fennick said, and Lord Driver hinted, 'You've not been to the movies for a year, Frederick.' They were driven out together into bombed shabby Oxford Street while the old men rang cheerfully down for whisky.

'What's the idea?' Elisabeth said.

He was good-looking; she liked his scar and his sullenness; there was almost too much intelligence and purpose in his eyes. Once he took off his hat and scratched his head: Elisabeth again noticed his short hair. He certainly didn't look a military type. And his suit, like his father's, looked new and ready-made. Hadn't he had any clothes to wear when he came on leave?

'I suppose,' she said, 'they are planning a wedding.'

His eyes lit gleefully up. 'I wouldn't mind,' he said.

'You'd have to get leave from your C.O., wouldn't you?'

'C.O.?' he asked in astonishment, flinching a little like a boy who has been caught out, who hasn't been prepared beforehand with that question. She watched him carefully, remembering all the things that had seemed to her odd since the beginning.

'So you haven't been to the movies for a year,' she said.

'I've been on service.'

'Not even an Ensa show?'

'Oh, I don't count those.'

'It must be awfully like being in prison.'

He grinned weakly, walking faster all the time, so that she

might easily have been pursuing him through the Hyde Park gates.

'Come clean,' she said. 'Your father's not Lord Driver.'

'Oh yes, he is.'

'Any more than my uncle's President of a College.'

'What?' He began to laugh – it was an agreeable laugh, a laugh you couldn't trust but a laugh which made you laugh back and agree that in a crazy world like this all sorts of things didn't matter a hang. 'I'm just out of Borstal,' he said. 'What's yours?'

'Oh, I haven't been in prison yet.'

He said, 'You'll never believe me, but all that ceremony – it looked phoney to me. Of course Dad swallowed it.'

'And my uncle swallowed you . . . I couldn't quite.'

'Well, the wedding's off. In a way I'm sorry.'

'I'm still free.'

'Well,' he said, 'we might discuss it,' and there in the pale Autumn sunlight of the Park they did discuss it – from all sorts of angles. There were bigger frauds all round them: officials of the Ministries passed carrying little portfolios; controllers of this and that purred by in motor-cars, and men with the big blank faces of advertisement hoardings strode purposefully in khaki with scarlet tabs down Park Lane from the Dorchester. Their fraud was a small one by the world's standard, and a harmless one: the boy from Borstal and the girl from nowhere at all – from the draper's counter and the semi-detached villa. 'He's got a few hundred stowed away, I'm sure of that,' said Fred. 'He'd make a settlement if he thought he could get the President's niece.'

'I wouldn't be surprised if Uncle had five hundred. He'd put it all down for Lord Driver's son.'

'We'd take over this college business. With a bit of capital we could really make it go. It's just chicken-feed now.'

They fell in love for no reason at all, in the park, on a bench to save twopences, planning their fraud on the old frauds they knew they could outdo. Then they went back and Elisabeth declared herself before she'd got properly inside the door. 'Frederick and I want to get married.' She almost felt sorry for the old fools as their faces lit up, suddenly, simultaneously, because everything had been so easy, and then darkened with caution as they squinted at each other. 'This is very surprising,' Lord Driver said, and the President said, 'My goodness, young people work fast.'

All night the two old men planned their settlements, and the two young ones sat happily back in a corner, watching them fence, with the secret knowledge that the world is always open to the young.

1941

MEN AT WORK

RICHARD SKATE had taken a couple of hours away from the Ministry to see whether his house was still standing after the previous night's raid. He was a thin, pale, hungry-looking man of early middle age. All his life had been spent in keeping his nose above water, lecturing at night-schools and acting as temporary English master at some of the smaller public schools and in the process he had acquired a small house, a wife and one child – a rather precocious girl with a talent for painting who despised him. They lived in the country, his house was cut off from him by the immeasurable distance of bombed London – he visited it hurriedly twice a week, and his whole world was now the Ministry, the high heartless building with complicated lifts and long passages like those of a liner and lavatories where the water never ran hot and the nail-brushes were chained like Bibles. Central heating gave it a stuffy smell of mid-Atlantic except in the passages where the windows were always open for fear of blast and the cold winds whistled in. One expected to see people wrapped in rugs lying in deckchairs and the messengers carried round minutes like soup. Skate slept downstairs in the basement on a camp-bed, emerging at about ten o'clock for breakfast, and these imprisoned weeks were beginning to give him the appearance of a pit-pony – a purblind air as of something that lived underground. The Establishments branch of the Ministry of Information thought it wise to send a minute to the staff advising them to spend an hour or two a day in the open air, and some members did indeed reach the King's Arms at the corner. But Skate didn't drink.

And yet in spite of everything he was happy. Showing his pass at the outer gate, nodding to the Home Guard who was a specialist in early Icelandic customs, he was happy. For his nose was now well above water: he had a permanent job, he was a Civil Servant. His ambition had been to be a playwright (one

Sunday performance in St John's Wood had enabled him to register as a dramatist in the Central Register), and now that the London theatres were most of them closed, he was no longer taunted by the sight of other men's success.

He opened the door of his dark room. It had been built of plywood in a passage, for as the huge staff of the Ministry accumulated like a kind of fungoid life – old divisions sprouting daily new sections which then broke away and became divisions and spawned in turn – the five hundred rooms of the great university block became inadequate: corners of passages were turned into rooms, and corridors disappeared overnight.

'All well?' his assistant asked: the large-breasted young woman who mothered him, bringing him cups of coffee when he looked peaky and guarding the telephone.

'Oh, yes, thanks. It's still there. A pane of glass gone, that's all.'

'A Mr Savage rang up.'

'Oh, did he? What did he want?'

'He said he'd joined the Air Force and wanted to show you his uniform.'

'Old Savage,' Skate said. 'He always was a bit wild.'

The telephone rang, and Miss Manners grasped it like an enemy.

'Yes,' she said, 'yes, R.S. is back. It's H.G.,' she explained to Skate. All the junior staff called people by initials: it was a sort of social compromise, between a Christian name and a Mr. It made telephone conversations as obscure as a cable in code.

'Hello, Graves. Yes, it's still standing. Will you be at the Book Committee? I simply haven't got any agenda. Can't you invent something?' He said to Miss Manners, 'Graves wants to know who'll be at the Committee.'

Miss Manners recited quickly down the phone, 'R.K., D.H., F.L., and B.L. says he'll be late. All right, I'll tell R.S. Goodbye.' She said to Skate, 'H.G. asks why you don't just put Report on Progress down on the agenda.'

'He will have his little joke,' Skate said miserably. 'As if there could be any progress.'

'You want your tea,' Miss Manners said. She unlocked a
drawer and took out Skate's teaspoon. No teaspoons had been
supplied in the Ministry after the initial loss of 6,000 in the
opening months of the war, and indeed it was becoming more
and more necessary to lock everything portable up. Even the
blankets disappeared from the A.R.P. shelters. Like the wreck
of a German plane the place seemed to be the prey of the relic-
hunters, so that one could foresee the day when only the heavy
Portland stone would remain, stripped bare, scorched by incendiaries and pitted with bullet-holes where the Home Guard un-
loaded their rifles.

'Oh dear, oh dear,' Skate said, 'I must get this agenda done.'
His worry was only skin deep: it was all a game played in a
corner under the gigantic shadow. Propaganda was a means of
passing the time: work was not done for its usefulness but for
its own sake – simply as an occupation. He wrote wearily down
'The Problem of India' on the agenda.

Leaving his room Skate stood aside for an odd little procession of old men in robes, led by a mace-bearer. They passed
– one of them sneezing – towards the Chancellor's Hall, like
humble ghosts still carrying out the ritual of another age. They
had once been kings in this palace, the gigantic building had
been built to house them, and now the civil servants passed up
and down through their procession as though it had no more
consistency than smoke. Long before he reached the room
where the Book Committee sat he heard a familiar voice saying,
'What we want is a really colossal campaign . . .' It was King, of
course, putting his shoulder to the war-effort: these outbreaks
occurred periodically like desire. King had been an advertising
man, and the need to sell something would regularly overcome
him. Memories of Ovaltine and Halitosis and the Mustard
Club sought an outlet all the time, until suddenly, overwhelm-
ingly, he would begin to sell the war. The Treasury and the
Stationery Office always saw to it that his great schemes came to
nothing: only once, because somebody was on holiday, a King
campaign really got under way. It was when the meat ration
went down to a shilling; the hoardings all over London carried a

curt King message. 'DON'T GROUSE ABOUT MUTTON. WHAT'S WRONG WITH YOUR GREENS?' A ribald Labour member asked a question in Parliament, the posters were withdrawn at a cost of twenty thousand pounds, the Permanent Secretary resigned, the Prime Minister stood by the Minister who stood by his staff ('I consider we are one of the fighting services'), and King, after being asked to resign, was instead put in charge of the Books Division of the Ministry at a higher salary. Here it was felt he could do no harm.

Skate slid in and handed round copies of the agenda unobtrusively like a maid laying napkins. He didn't bother to listen to King: something about a series of pamphlets to be distributed free to six million people really explaining what we were fighting for. 'Tell 'em what freedom means,' King said. 'Democracy. Don't use long words.'

Hill said, 'I don't think the Stationery Office ...' Hill's thin voice was always the voice of reason. He was said to be the author of the official explanation and defence of the Ministry's existence: 'A negative action may have positive results.'

On Skate's agenda was written:

1. Arising from the Minutes.
2. Pamphlet in Welsh on German labour conditions.
3. Facilities for Wilkinson to visit the A.T.S.
4. Objections to proposed Bone pamphlet.
5 Suggestion for a leaflet from Meat Marketing Board.
6. The Problem of India.

The list, Skate thought, looked quite impressive.

'Of course,' King went on, 'the details need working out. We've got to get the right authors. Priestley and people like him. I feel there won't be any difficulty about money if we can present a really clear case. Would you look into it, Skate, and report back?'

Skate agreed. He didn't know what it was all about, but that didn't matter. A few minutes would be passed to and fro, and King's blood would cool in the process. To send a minute to anybody else in the great building and to receive a reply took at

least twenty-four hours; on an urgent matter an exchange of
three minutes might be got through in a week. Time outside the
Ministry went at quite a different pace. Skate remembered how
the minutes on who should write a 'suggested' pamphlet about
the French war-effort were still circulating indecisively while
Germany broke the line, passed the Somme, occupied Paris and
received the delegates at Compiègne.

The committee as usual lasted an hour – it was always, to
Skate, an agreeable meeting with men from other divisions, the
Religions Division, the Empire Division and so on. Sometimes
they co-opted another man they thought was nice. It gave an
opportunity for all sorts of interesting discussions – on books
and authors and artists and plays and films. The agenda didn't
really matter: it was quite easy to invent one at the last moment.

Today everybody was in a good temper; there hadn't been
any bad news for a week, and as the policy of the latest Permanent Secretary was that the Ministry should not do anything
to attract attention, there was no reason to fear a purge in the
immediate future. The decision, too, eased everybody's work.
And there was quite a breath of the larger life in the matter of
Wilkinson. Wilkinson was a very popular novelist who wanted
to sound a clarion-note to women, and he had asked permission
to make a special study of the A.T.S. Now the military authorities refused permission – nobody knew why. Speculation continued for ten minutes. Skate said he thought Wilkinson was a
bad writer and King disagreed – that led to a general literary
discussion. Lewis from the Empire Division, who had fought in
Gallipoli during the last war, dozed uneasily.

He woke up when they got on to the Bone pamphlet. Bone
had been asked to write a pamphlet about the British Empire: it
was to be distributed, fifty thousand copies of it, free at public
meetings. But now that it was in type, all sorts of tactless
phrases were discovered by the experts. India objected to a
reference to Canadian dairy herds, and Australia objected to a
phrase about Botany Bay. The Canadian authority was certain
that mention of Wolfe would antagonize the French-
Canadians, and the New Zealand authority felt that undue

emphasis had been laid on the Australian fruit-farms. Meanwhile the public meetings had all been held, so that there was no means of distributing the pamphlet. Somebody suggested that it might be sent to America for the New York World Fair, but the American Division then demanded certain cuts in the references to the War of Independence, and by the time those had been made the World Fair had closed. Now Bone had written objecting to his own pamphlet which he said was unrecognizable.

'We could get somebody else to sign it,' Skate suggested – but that meant paying another fee, and the Treasury, Hill said, would never sanction that.

'Look here, Skate,' King said, 'you're a literary man. You write to Bone and sort of smooth things over.'

Lowndes came in hurriedly, smelling a little of wine. He said, 'Sorry to be late. Had to lunch a man on business. Seen the news?'

'No.'

'Daylight raids again. Fifty Nazi planes shot down. They are turning on the heat. Fifteen of ours lost.'

'We must really get Bone's pamphlet out,' Hill said.

Skate suddenly, to his surprise, said savagely, 'That'll show them,' and then sat down in humble collapse as though he had been caught out in treachery.

'Well,' Hill said, 'we mustn't get rattled, Skate. Remember what the Minister said: It's our duty just to carry on our work whatever happens.'

'Yes, I didn't mean anything.'

Without reaching a decision on the Bone pamphlet they passed on to the Meat Marketing Leaflet. Nobody was interested in this, so the matter was left in Skate's hands to report back. 'You talk to 'em, Skate,' King said. 'Good idea. You know about these things. Might ask Priestley,' he vaguely added, and then frowned thoughtfully at that old-timer on the minutes, 'The Problem of India'. 'Need we really discuss it this week?' he said. 'There's nobody here who knows about India. Let's get in Lawrence next week.'

'Good chap, Lawrence,' Lowndes said. 'Wrote a naughty novel once called *Parson's Pleasure.*'

'We'll co-opt him,' King said.

The Book Committee was over for another week, and since the room would be empty now until morning, Skate opened the big windows against the night's blast. Far up in the pale enormous sky little white lines, like the phosphorescent spoor of snails, showed where men were going home after work.

1940

ALAS, POOR MALING

POOR inoffensive ineffectual Maling! I don't want you to smile at Maling and his borborygmi, as the doctors always smiled when he consulted them, as they must have smiled even after the sad climax of September 3rd, 1940, when his borborygmi held up for twenty-four fatal hours the amalgamation of the Simcox and Hythe Newsprint Companies. Simcox's interests had always been dearer to Maling than life: hard-driven, conscientious, happy in his work, he wanted no position higher than their secretary, and those twenty-four hours happened – for reasons it is unwise to go into here, for they involve intricacies in British income-tax law – to be fatal to the company's existence. After that day he dropped altogether out of sight, and I shall always believe he crept away to die of a broken heart in some provincial printing works. Alas, poor Maling!

It was the doctors who called his complaint borborygmi: in England we usually call it just 'tummy rumbles'. I believe it's quite a harmless kind of indigestion, but in Maling's case it took a rather odd form. His stomach, he used to complain, blinking sadly downwards through his semi-circular reading glasses, had 'an ear'. It used to pick up notes in an extraordinary way and give them out again after meals. I shall never forget one embarrassing tea at the Piccadilly Hotel in honour of a party of provincial printers: it was the year before the war, and Maling had been attending the Symphony Concerts at Queen's Hall (he never went again). In the distance a dance orchestra had been playing 'The Lambeth Walk' (how tired one got of that tune in 1938 with its waggery and false bonhomie and its 'ois'). Suddenly in the happy silence between dances, as the printers sat back from a ruin of toasted tea-cakes, there emerged – faint as though from a distant part of the hotel, sad and plangent – the opening bars of a Brahms Concerto. A Scottish printer, who

69

had an ear for good music, exclaimed with dour relish, 'My goodness, how that mon can play.' Then the music stopped abruptly, and an odd suspicion made me look at Maling. He was red as beetroot. Nobody noticed because the dance orchestra began again to the Scotsman's disgust with 'Boomps-a-Daisy', and I think I was the only one who detected a curious faint undertone of 'The Lambeth Walk' apparently coming from the chair where Maling sat.

It was after ten, when the printers had piled into taxis and driven away to Euston, that Maling told me about his stomach. 'It's quite unaccountable,' he said, 'like a parrot. It seems to pick up things at random.' He added with tears in his voice, 'I can't enjoy food any more. I never know what's going to happen afterwards. This afternoon wasn't the worst. Sometimes it's quite loud.' He brooded forlornly. 'When I was a boy I liked listening to German bands . . .'

'Haven't you seen a doctor?'

'They don't understand. They say it's just indigestion and nothing to worry about. Nothing to worry about! But then when I've been seeing a doctor it's always lain quiet.' I noticed that he spoke of his stomach as if it were a detested animal. He gazed bleakly at his knuckles and said, 'Now I've become afraid of any new noise. I never know. It doesn't take any notice of some, but others seem . . . well, to fascinate it. At a first hearing. Last year when they took up Piccadilly it was the road drills. I used to get them all over again after dinner.'

I said rather stupidly, 'I suppose you've tried the usual salts,' and I remember – it was my last sight of him – his expression of despair as though he had ceased to expect comprehension from any living soul.

It was my last sight of him because the war pitched me out of the printing trade into all sorts of odd occupations, and it was only at second-hand that I heard the account of the strange board meeting which broke poor Maling's heart.

What the papers called the blitz-and-pieces krieg against Britain had been going on for about a week: in London we were just settling down to air-raid alarms at the rate of five or six a

70

day, but the 3rd of September, the anniversary of the war, had so far been relatively peaceful. There was a general feeling, however, that Hitler might celebrate the anniversary with a big attack. It was therefore in an atmosphere of some tension that Simcox and Hythe had their joint meeting.

It took place in the traditional grubby little room above the Simcox offices in Fetter Lane: the round table dating from the original Joshua Simcox, the steel engraving of a printing works dated 1875, and an irrelevant copy of a Bible which had always been the only book in the big glass bookcase except for a volume of type faces. Old Sir Joshua Simcox was in the chair: you can picture his snow-white hair and the pale pork-like Nonconformist features. Wesby Hythe was there, and half a dozen other directors with narrow canny faces and neat black coats: they all looked a little strained. If the new income-tax regulations were to be evaded, they had to work quickly. As for Maling he crouched over his pad, nervously ready to advise anybody on anything.

There was one interruption during the reading of the minutes. Wesby Hythe, who was an invalid, complained that a typewriter in the next room was getting on his nerves. Maling blushed and went out: I think he must have swallowed a tablet because the typewriter stopped. Hythe was impatient. 'Hurry up,' he said, 'hurry up. We haven't all night.' But that was exactly what they had.

After the minutes had been read Sir Joshua began explaining elaborately in a Yorkshire accent that their motives were entirely patriotic: they hadn't any intention of evading tax: they just wanted to contribute to the war effort, drive, economy . . . He said, 'The proof of the pudden' . . .' and at that moment the air-raid sirens started. As I have said a mass attack was expected: it wasn't the time for delay: a dead man couldn't evade income tax. The directors gathered up their papers and bolted for the basement.

All except Maling. You see, he knew the truth. I think it had been the reference to pudding which had roused the sleeping animal. Of course he should have confessed, but think for a moment: would you have had the courage, after watching those elderly men with white slips to their waistcoats pelt with a horrifying lack of dignity to safety? I know I should have done exactly what Maling did, have followed Sir Joshua down to the basement in the desperate hope that for once the stomach would do the right thing and make amends. But it didn't. The joint boards of Simcox and Hythe stayed in the basement for twelve hours, and Maling stayed with them, saying nothing. You see, for some unaccountable reason of taste, poor Maling's stomach had picked up the note of the Warning only too effectively, but it had somehow never taken to the All Clear.

1940

THE CASE FOR THE DEFENCE

It was the strangest murder trial I ever attended. They named it the Peckham murder in the headlines, though Northwood Street, where the old woman was found battered to death, was not strictly speaking in Peckham. This was not one of those cases of circumstantial evidence in which you feel the jurymen's anxiety – because mistakes *have* been made – like domes of silence muting the court. No, this murderer was all but found with the body; no one present when the Crown counsel outlined his case believed that the man in the dock stood any chance at all.

He was a heavy stout man with bulging bloodshot eyes. All his muscles seemed to be in his thighs. Yes, an ugly customer, one you wouldn't forget in a hurry – and that was an important point because the Crown proposed to call four witnesses who hadn't forgotten him, who had seen him hurrying away from the little red villa in Northwood Street. The clock had just struck two in the morning.

Mrs Salmon in 15 Northwood Street had been unable to sleep; she heard a door click shut and thought it was her own gate. So she went to the window and saw Adams (that was his name) on the steps of Mrs Parker's house. He had just come out and he was wearing gloves. He had a hammer in his hand and she saw him drop it into the laurel bushes by the front gate. But before he moved away, he had looked up – at her window. The fatal instinct that tells a man when he is watched exposed him in the light of a street-lamp to her gaze – his eyes suffused with horrifying and brutal fear, like an animal's when you raise a whip. I talked afterwards to Mrs Salmon, who naturally after the astonishing verdict went in fear herself. As I imagine did all the witnesses – Henry MacDougall, who had been driving home from Benfleet late and nearly ran Adams down at the corner of Northwood Street. Adams was walking in the middle of the road looking dazed. And old Mr Wheeler, who lived next door to Mrs Parker, at No. 12, and was wakened by a noise – like a chair falling – through the thin-as-paper villa wall, and got up and looked out of the window, just as Mrs Salmon had done, saw Adams's back and, as he turned, those bulging eyes. In Laurel Avenue he had been seen by yet another witness – his luck was badly out; he might as well have committed the crime in broad daylight.

'I understand,' counsel said, 'that the defence proposes to plead mistaken identity. Adams's wife will tell you that he was with her at two in the morning on February 14, but after you have heard the witnesses for the Crown and examined carefully the features of the prisoner, I do not think you will be prepared to admit the possibility of a mistake.'

It was all over, you would have said, but the hanging.

After the formal evidence had been given by the policeman who had found the body and the surgeon who examined it, Mrs Salmon was called. She was the ideal witness, with her slight Scotch accent and her expression of honesty, care and kindness.

The counsel for the Crown brought the story gently out. She spoke very firmly. There was no malice in her, and no sense of importance at standing there in the Central Criminal Court with a judge in scarlet hanging on her words and the reporters writing them down. Yes, she said, and then she had gone downstairs and rung up the police station.

'And do you see the man here in court?'

She looked straight at the big man in the dock, who stared hard at her with his pekingese eyes without emotion.

'Yes,' she said, 'there he is.'

'You are quite certain?'

She said simply, 'I couldn't be mistaken, sir.'

It was all as easy as that.

'Thank you, Mrs Salmon.'

Counsel for the defence rose to cross-examine. If you had reported as many murder trials as I have, you would have known beforehand what line he would take. And I was right, up to a point.

'Now, Mrs Salmon, you must remember that a man's life may depend on your evidence.'

'I do remember it, sir.'

'Is your eyesight good?'

'I have never had to wear spectacles, sir.'

'You are a woman of fifty-five?'

'Fifty-six, sir.'

'And the man you saw was on the other side of the road?'

'Yes, sir.'

'And it was two o'clock in the morning. You must have re-markable eyes, Mrs Salmon?'

'No, sir. There was moonlight, and when the man looked up, he had the lamplight on his face.'

'And you have no doubt whatever that the man you saw is the prisoner?'

I couldn't make out what he was at. He couldn't have ex-pected any other answer than the one he got.

'None whatever, sir. It isn't a face one forgets.'

Counsel took a look round the court for a moment. Then he said, 'Do you mind, Mrs Salmon, examining again the people in court? No, not the prisoner. Stand up, please, Mr Adams,' and there at the back of the court with thick stout body and mus-cular legs and a pair of bulging eyes, was the exact image of the man in the dock. He was even dressed the same – tight blue suit and striped tie.

'Now think very carefully, Mrs Salmon. Can you still swear that the man you saw drop the hammer in Mrs Parker's garden was the prisoner – and not this man, who is his twin brother?'

Of course she couldn't. She looked from one to the other and didn't say a word.

There the big brute sat in the dock with his legs crossed, and there he stood too at the back of the court and they both stared at Mrs Salmon. She shook her head.

What we saw then was the end of the case. There wasn't a witness prepared to swear that it was the prisoner he'd seen. And the brother? He had his alibi, too; he was with his wife.

And so the man was acquitted for lack of evidence. But

75

whether – if he did the murder and not his brother – he was punished or not, I don't know. That extraordinary day had an extraordinary end. I followed Mrs Salmon out of court and we got wedged in the crowd who were waiting, of course, for the twins. The police tried to drive the crowd away, but all they could do was keep the road-way clear for traffic. I learned later that they tried to get the twins to leave by a back way, but they wouldn't. One of them – no one knew which – said, 'I've been acquitted, haven't I?' and they walked bang out of the front entrance. Then it happened. I don't know how, though I was only six feet away. The crowd moved and somehow one of the twins got pushed on to the road right in front of a bus.

He gave a squeal like a rabbit and that was all; he was dead, his skull smashed just as Mrs Parker's had been. Divine vengeance? I wish I knew. There was the other Adams getting on his feet from beside the body and looking straight over at Mrs Salmon. He was crying, but whether he was the murderer or the innocent man nobody will ever be able to tell. But if you were Mrs Salmon, could you sleep at night?

1939

A LITTLE PLACE
OFF THE EDGWARE ROAD

CRAVEN came up past the Achilles statue in the thin summer rain. It was only just after lighting-up time, but already the cars were lined up all the way to the Marble Arch, and the sharp acquisitive faces peered out ready for a good time with anything possible which came along. Craven went bitterly by with the collar of his mackintosh tight round his throat: it was one of his bad days.

All the way up the Park he was reminded of passion, but you needed money for love. All that a poor man could get was lust. Love needed a good suit, a car, a flat somewhere, or a good hotel. It needed to be wrapped in cellophane. He was aware all the time of the stringy tie beneath the mackintosh, and the frayed sleeves: he carried his body about with him like something he hated. (There were moments of happiness in the British Museum reading-room, but the body called him back.) He bore, as his only sentiment, the memory of ugly deeds committed on park chairs. People talked as if the body died too soon – that wasn't the trouble, to Craven, at all. The body kept alive – and through the glittering tinselly rain, on his way to a rostrum, he passed a little man in a black suit carrying a banner, 'The Body shall rise again.' He remembered a dream from which three times he had woken trembling: he had been alone in the huge dark cavernous burying ground of all the world. Every grave was connected to another under the ground: the globe was honeycombed for the sake of the dead, and on each occasion of dreaming he had discovered anew the horrifying fact that the body doesn't decay. There are no worms and dissolution. Under the ground the world was littered with masses of dead flesh ready to rise again with their warts and boils and eruptions. He had lain in bed and remembered – as 'tidings of great joy' – that the body after all was corrupt.

He came up into the Edgware Road walking fast – the Guardsmen were out in couples, great languid elongated beasts – the bodies like worms in their tight trousers. He hated them, and hated his hatred because he knew what it was, envy. He was aware that every one of them had a better body than himself: indigestion creased his stomach: he felt sure that his breath was foul – but who could he ask? Sometimes he secretly touched himself here and there with scent: it was one of his ugliest secrets. Why should he be asked to believe in the resurrection of this body he wanted to forget? Sometimes he prayed at night (a hint of religious belief was lodged in his breast like a worm in a nut) that *his* body at any rate should never rise again.

He knew all the side streets round the Edgware Road only too well: when a mood was on, he simply walked until he tired, squinting at his own image in the windows of Salmon & Gluckstein and the A.B.C.s. So he noticed at once the posters outside the disused theatre in Culpar Road. They were not unusual, for sometimes Barclays Bank Dramatic Society would hire the place for an evening – or an obscure film would be trade-shown there. The theatre had been built in 1920 by an optimist who thought the cheapness of the site would more than counter-balance its disadvantage of lying a mile outside the conventional theatre zone. But no play had ever succeeded, and it was soon left to gather rat-holes and spider-webs. The covering of the seats was never renewed, and all that ever happened to the place was the temporary false life of an amateur play or a trade show.

Craven stopped and read – there were still optimists it appeared, even in 1939, for nobody but the blindest optimist could hope to make money out of the place as 'The Home of the Silent Film'. The first season of 'primitives' was announced (a high-brow phrase): there would never be a second. Well, the seats were cheap, and it was perhaps worth a shilling to him, now that he was tired, to get in somewhere out of the rain. Craven bought a ticket and went in to the darkness of the stalls.

In the dead darkness a piano tinkled something monotonous

recalling Mendelssohn: he sat down in a gangway seat, and could immediately feel the emptiness all round him. No, there would never be another season. On the screen a large woman in a kind of toga wrung her hands, then wobbled with curious jerky movements towards a couch. There she sat and stared out like a sheep-dog distractedly through her loose and black and stringy hair. Sometimes she seemed to dissolve altogether into dots and flashes and wiggly lines. A sub-title said, 'Pompilia betrayed by her beloved Augustus seeks an end to her troubles.'

Craven began at last to see – a dim waste of stalls. There were not twenty people in the place – a few couples whispering with their heads touching, and a number of lonely men like himself, wearing the same uniform of the cheap mackintosh. They lay about at intervals like corpses – and again Craven's obsession returned: the tooth-ache of horror. He thought miserably – I am going mad: other people don't feel like this. Even a disused theatre reminded him of those interminable caverns where the bodies were waiting for resurrection.

'A slave to his passion Augustus calls for yet more wine.'

A gross middle-aged Teutonic actor lay on an elbow with his arm round a large woman in a shift. The Spring Song tinkled ineptly on, and the screen flickered like indigestion. Somebody felt his way through the darkness, scrabbling past Craven's knees – a small man: Craven experienced the unpleasant feeling of a large beard brushing his mouth. Then there was a long sigh as the newcomer found the next chair, and on the screen events had moved with such rapidity that Pompilia had already stabbed herself – or so Craven supposed – and lay still and buxom among her weeping slaves.

A low breathless voice sighed out close to Craven's ear, 'What's happened? Is she asleep?'

'No. Dead.'

'Murdered?' the voice asked with a keen interest.

'I don't think so. Stabbed herself.'

Nobody said 'Hush': nobody was enough interested to object to a voice. They drooped among the empty chairs in attitudes of weary inattention.

79

The film wasn't nearly over yet: there were children somehow to be considered: was it all going on to a second generation? But the small bearded man in the next seat seemed to be interested only in Pompilia's death. The fact that he had come in at that moment apparently fascinated him. Craven heard the word 'co-incidence' twice, and he went on talking to himself about it in low out-of-breath tones. 'Absurd when you come to think of it,' and then 'no blood at all'. Craven didn't listen: he sat with his hands clasped between his knees, facing the fact as he had faced it so often before, that he was in danger of going mad. He had to pull himself up, take a holiday, see a doctor (God knew what infection moved in his veins). He became aware that his bearded neighbour had addressed him directly. 'What?' he asked impatiently, 'what did you say?'

'There would be more blood than you can imagine.'

'What are you talking about?'

When the man spoke to him, he sprayed him with damp breath. There was a little bubble in his speech like an impediment. He said, 'When you murder a man . . .'

'This was a woman,' Craven said impatiently.

'That wouldn't make any difference.'

'And it's got nothing to do with murder anyway.'

'That doesn't signify.' They seemed to have got into an absurd and meaningless wrangle in the dark.

'I know, you see,' the little bearded man said in a tone of enormous conceit.

'Know what?'

'About such things,' he said with guarded ambiguity.

Craven turned and tried to see him clearly. Was he mad? Was this a warning of what he might become – babbling incomprehensibly to strangers in cinemas? He thought, By God, no, trying to see: I'll be sane yet. I *will* be sane. He could make out nothing but a small black hump of body. The man was talking to himself again. He said, 'Talk. Such talk. They'll say it was all for fifty pounds. But that's a lie. Reasons and reasons. They always take the first reason. Never look behind. Thirty years of reasons. Such simpletons,' he added again in that tone of breathlessness and unbounded conceit. So this was madness. So long as he could realize that, he must be sane himself – relatively speaking. Not so sane perhaps as the seekers in the park or the Guardsmen in the Edgware Road, but saner than this. It was like a message of encouragement as the piano tinkled on.

Then again the little man turned and sprayed him. 'Killed herself, you say? But who's to know that? It's not a mere question of what hand holds the knife.' He laid a hand suddenly and confidingly on Craven's: it was damp and sticky: Craven said with horror as a possible meaning came to him, 'What are you talking about?'

'I know,' the little man said. 'A man in my position gets to know almost everything.'

'What is your position?' Craven asked, feeling the sticky hand on his, trying to make up his mind whether he was being hysterical or not – after all, there were a dozen explanations – it might be treacle.

'A pretty desperate one *you'd* say.' Sometimes the voice almost died in the throat altogether. Something incomprehensible had happened on the screen – take your eyes from these early pictures for a moment and the plot had proceeded on at such a pace ... Only the actors moved slowly and jerkily. A young woman in a night-dress seemed to be weeping in the arms of a Roman centurion: Craven hadn't seen either of them before. '*I am not afraid of death, Lucius – in your arms.*'

The little man began to titter – knowingly. He was talking to himself again. It would have been easy to ignore him altogether if it had not been for those sticky hands which he now removed: he seemed to be fumbling at the seat in front of him. His head had a habit of lolling sideways – like an idiot child's. He said distinctly and irrelevantly: 'Bayswater Tragedy.'

'What was that?' Craven said. He had seen those words on a poster before he entered the park.

'What?'

81

'About the tragedy.'

'To think they call Cullen Mews Bayswater.' Suddenly the little man began to cough – turning his face towards Craven and coughing right at him: it was like vindictiveness. The voice said, 'Let me see. My umbrella.' He was getting up.

'You didn't have an umbrella.'

'My umbrella,' he repeated. 'My – ' and seemed to lose the word altogether. He went scrabbling out past Craven's knees.

Craven let him go, but before he had reached the billowy dusty curtains of the Exit the screen went blank and bright – the film had broken, and somebody immediately turned up one dirt-choked chandelier above the circle. It shone down just enough for Craven to see the smear on his hands. This wasn't hysteria: this was a fact. He wasn't mad: he had sat next to a madman who in some mews – what was the name, Colon, Collin ... Craven jumped up and made his own way out: the black curtain flapped in his mouth. But he was too late: the man had gone and there were three turnings to choose from. He chose instead a telephone-box and dialled with a sense odd for him of sanity and decision 999.

It didn't take two minutes to get the right department. They were interested and very kind. Yes, there had been a murder in a mews – Cullen Mews. A man's neck had been cut from ear to ear with a bread knife – a horrid crime. He began to tell them how he had sat next the murderer in a cinema: it couldn't be anyone else: there was blood on his hands – and he remembered with repulsion as he spoke the damp beard. There must have been a terrible lot of blood. But the voice from the Yard interrupted him. 'Oh no,' it was saying, 'we have the murderer – no doubt of it at all. It's the body that's disappeared.'

Craven put down the receiver. He said to himself aloud, 'Why should this happen to *me*? Why to *me*?' He was back in the horror of his dream – the squalid darkening street outside was only one of the innumerable tunnels connecting grave to grave where the imperishable bodies lay. He said, 'It was a dream, a dream,' and leaning forward he saw in the mirror above the telephone his own face sprinkled by tiny drops of blood like dew from a scent-spray. He began to scream, 'I won't go mad. I won't go mad. I'm sane. I won't go mad.' Presently a little crowd began to collect, and soon a policeman came.

1939

ACROSS THE BRIDGE

'THEY say he's worth a million,' Lucia said. He sat there in the little hot damp Mexican square, a dog at his feet, with an air of immense and forlorn patience. The dog attracted your attention at once; for it was very nearly an English setter, only something had gone wrong with the tail and the feathering. Palms wilted over his head, it was all shade and stuffiness round the band-stand, radios talked loudly in Spanish from the little wooden sheds where they changed your pesos into dollars at a loss. I could tell he didn't understand a word from the way he read his newspaper – as I did myself picking out the words which were like English ones. 'He's been here a month,' Lucia said, 'they turned him out of Guatemala and Honduras.'

You couldn't keep any secrets for five hours in this border town. Lucia had only been twenty-four hours in the place, but she knew all about Mr Joseph Calloway. The only reason I didn't know about him (and I'd been in the place two weeks) was because I couldn't talk the language any more than Mr Calloway could. There wasn't another soul in the place who didn't know the story – the whole story of Halling Investment Trust and the proceedings for extradition. Any man doing dusty business in any of the wooden booths in the town is better fitted by long observation to tell Mr Calloway's tale than I am, except that I was in – literally – at the finish. They all watched the drama proceed with immense interest, sympathy and respect. For, after all, he had a million.

Every once in a while through the long steamy day, a boy came and cleaned Mr Calloway's shoes: he hadn't the right words to resist them – they pretended not to know his English. He must have had his shoes cleaned the day Lucia and I watched him at least half a dozen times. At midday he took a stroll across the square to the Antonio Bar and had a bottle of beer, the setter sticking to heel as if they were out for a country

84

walk in England (he had, you may remember, one of the biggest estates in Norfolk). After his bottle of beer, he would walk down between the money-changers' huts to the Rio Grande and look across the bridge into the United States: people came and went constantly in cars. Then back to the square till lunchtime. He was staying in the best hotel, but you don't get good hotels in this border town: nobody stays in them more than a night. The good hotels were on the other side of the bridge: you could see their electric signs twenty storeys high from the little square at night, like lighthouses marking the United States.

You may ask what I'd been doing in so drab a spot for a fortnight. There was no interest in the place for anyone; it was just damp and dust and poverty, a kind of shabby replica of the town across the river. Both had squares in the same spots; both had the same number of cinemas. One was cleaner than the other, that was all, and more expensive, much more expensive. I'd stayed across there a couple of nights waiting for a man a tourist bureau said was driving down from Detroit to Yucatan and would sell a place in his car for some fantastically small figure – twenty dollars, I think it was. I don't know if he existed or was invented by the optimistic half-caste in the agency; anyway, he never turned up and so I waited, not much caring, on the cheap side of the river. It didn't much matter; I was living. One day I meant to give up the man from Detroit and go home or go south, but it was easier not to decide anything in a hurry. Lucia was just waiting for a car the other way, but she didn't have to wait so long. We waited together and watched Mr Calloway waiting – for God knows what.

I don't know how to treat this story – it was a tragedy for Mr Calloway, it was poetic retribution, I suppose, in the eyes of the shareholders whom he'd ruined with his bogus transactions, and to Lucia and me, at this stage, it was comedy – except when he kicked the dog. I'm not a sentimentalist about dogs, I prefer people to be cruel to animals rather than to human beings, but I couldn't help being revolted at the way he'd kick that animal – with a hint of cold-blooded venom, not in anger but as if he were getting even for some trick it had played him a long while ago. That generally happened when he returned from the bridge: it was the only sign of anything resembling emotion he showed. Otherwise he looked a small, set, gentle creature with silver hair and a silver moustache and gold-rimmed glasses, and one gold tooth like a flaw in character.

Lucia hadn't been accurate when she said he'd been turned out of Guatemala and Honduras; he'd left voluntarily when the extradition proceedings seemed likely to go through and moved north. Mexico is still not a very centralized state, and it is possible to get round governors as you can't get round cabinet ministers or judges. And so he waited there on the border for the next move. That earlier part of the story was, I suppose, dramatic, but I didn't watch it and I can't invent what I haven't seen – the long waiting in ante-rooms, the bribes taken and refused, and growing fear of arrest, and then the flight – in gold-rimmed glasses – covering his tracks as well as he could, but this wasn't finance and he was an amateur at escape. And so he'd washed up here, under my eyes and Lucia's eyes, sitting all day under the bandstand, nothing to read but a Mexican paper, nothing to do but look across the river at the United States, quite unaware, I suppose, that everyone knew everything about him, once a day kicking his dog. Perhaps in its semi-setter way it reminded him too much of the Norfolk estate – though that, too, I suppose, was the reason he kept it.

And the next act again was pure comedy. I hesitate to think what this man worth a million was costing his country as they edged him out from this land and that. Perhaps somebody was getting tired of the business, and careless; anyway, they sent across two detectives with an old photograph. He'd grown his silvery moustache since that had been taken, and he'd aged a lot, and they couldn't catch sight of him. They hadn't been across the bridge two hours when everybody knew that there were two foreign detectives in town looking for Mr Calloway – everybody knew, that is to say, except Mr Calloway, who couldn't talk Spanish. There were plenty of people who could have told him in English, but they didn't. It wasn't cruelty, it was a sort of awe and respect: like a bull, he was on show, sitting there mournfully in the plaza with his dog, a magnificent spectacle for which we all had ring-side seats.

I ran into one of the policemen in the Bar Antonio. He was disgusted; he had had some idea that when he crossed the bridge life was going to be different, so much more colour and sun, and – I suspect – love, and all he found were wide mud streets where the nocturnal rain lay in pools, and mangy dogs, smells and cockroaches in his bedroom, and the nearest to love, the open door of the Academia Comercial, where pretty mestizo girls sat all morning learning to typewrite. Tip-tap-tip-tap-tip – perhaps they had a dream too – jobs on the other side of the bridge, where life was going to be so much more luxurious, refined and amusing.

We got into conversation; he seemed surprised that I knew who they both were and what they wanted. He said, 'We've got information this man Calloway's in town.'

'He's knocking around somewhere,' I said.

'Could you point him out?'

'Oh, I don't know him by sight,' I said.

He drank his beer and thought a while. 'I'll go out and sit in the plaza. He's sure to pass sometime.'

I finished my beer and went quickly off and found Lucia. I said, 'Hurry, we're going to see an arrest.' We didn't care a thing about Mr Calloway, he was just an elderly man who kicked his dog and swindled the poor, and deserved anything he got. So we made for the plaza; we knew Calloway would be there, but it had never occurred to either of us that the detectives wouldn't recognize him. There was quite a surge of people round the place; all the fruit-sellers and boot-blacks in town seemed to have arrived together; we had to force our way through, and there in the little green stuffy centre of the place, sitting on adjoining seats, were the two plain-clothes men and Mr Calloway. I've never known the place so silent; everybody was on tiptoe, and the plain-clothes men were staring at the crowd for Mr Calloway, and Mr Calloway sat on his usual seat staring out over the money-changing booths at the United States.

'It can't go on. It just can't,' Lucia said. But it did. It got more fantastic still. Somebody ought to write a play about it. We sat as close as we dared. We were afraid all the time we were going to laugh. The semi-setter scratched for fleas and Mr Calloway watched the U.S.A. The two detectives watched the crowd, and the crowd watched the show with solemn satisfaction. Then one of the detectives got up and went over to Mr Calloway. That's the end, I thought. But it wasn't, it was the beginning. For some reason they had eliminated him from their list of suspects. I shall never know why. The man said:

'You speak English?'

'I *am* English,' Mr Calloway said.

Even that didn't tear it, and the strangest thing of all was the way Mr Calloway came alive. I don't think anybody had spoken to him like that for weeks. The Mexicans were too respectful – he was a man with a million – and it had never occurred to Lucia and me to treat him casually like a human being; even in our eyes he had been magnified by the colossal theft and the world-wide pursuit.

He said, 'This is rather a dreadful place, don't you think?'

'It is,' the policeman said.

'I can't think what brings anybody across the bridge.'

'Duty,' the policeman said gloomily. 'I suppose you are passing through.'

'Yes,' Mr Calloway said.

'I'd have expected over here there'd have been – you know what I mean – life. You read things about Mexico.'

'Oh, life,' Mr Calloway said. He spoke firmly and precisely, as if to a committee of shareholders. 'That begins on the other side.'

'You don't appreciate your own country until you leave it.'

'That's very true,' Mr Calloway said. 'Very true.'

At first it was difficult not to laugh, and then after a while there didn't seem to be much to laugh at: an old man imagining all the fine things going on beyond the international bridge. I think he thought of the town opposite as a combination of London and Norfolk – theatres and cocktail bars, a little shooting and a walk round the field at evening with the dog – that miserable imitation of a setter – poking the ditches. He'd never been across, he couldn't know it was just the same thing over again – even the same layout; only the streets were paved and the hotels had ten more storeys, and life was more expensive, and everything was a little bit cleaner. There wasn't anything Mr Calloway would have called living – no galleries, no bookshops, just *Film Fun* and the local paper, and *Click* and *Focus* and the tabloids.

'Well,' said Mr Calloway, 'I think I'll take a stroll before lunch. You need an appetite to swallow the food here. I generally go down and look at the bridge about now. Care to come, too?'

The detective shook his head. 'No,' he said, 'I'm on duty. I'm looking for a fellow.' And that, of course, gave *him* away. As far as Mr Calloway could understand, there was only one 'fellow' in the world anyone was looking for – his brain had eliminated friends who were seeking their friends, husbands who might be waiting for their wives, all objectives of any search but just the one. The power of elimination was what had made him a financier – he could forget the people behind the shares.

That was the last we saw of him for a while. We didn't see him going into the Botica Paris to get his aspirin, or walking back from the bridge with his dog. He simply disappeared, and when he disappeared, people began to talk and the detectives heard the talk. They looked silly enough, and they got busy after the very man they'd been sitting next to in the garden. Then they, too, disappeared. They, as well as Mr Calloway, had gone to the state capital to see the Governor and the Chief of Police, and it must have been an amusing sight there, too, as they bumped into Mr Calloway and sat with him in the waiting-rooms. I suspect Mr Calloway was generally shown in first, for everyone knew he was worth a million. Only in Europe is it possible for a man to be a criminal as well as a rich man.

Anyway, after about a week the whole pack of them returned by the same train. Mr Calloway travelled Pullman, and the two policemen travelled in the day coach. It was evident that they hadn't got their extradition order.

Lucia had left by that time. The car came and went across the bridge. I stood in Mexico and watched her get out at the United States Customs. She wasn't anything in particular, but she looked beautiful at a distance as she gave me a wave out of the United States and got back into the car. And I suddenly felt sympathy for Mr Calloway, as if there were something over there which you couldn't find here, and turning round I saw him back on his old beat, with the dog at his heels.

I said, 'Good afternoon', as if it had been all along our habit to greet each other. He looked tired and ill and dusty, and I felt sorry for him – to think of the kind of victory he'd been winning, with so much expenditure of cash and care – the prize this dirty and dreary town, the booths of the money-changers, the awful little beauty parlours with their wicker chairs and sofas looking like the reception rooms of brothels, that hot and stuffy garden by the bandstand.

He replied gloomily, 'Good afternoon', and the dog started to sniff at some ordure and he turned and kicked it with fury, with depression, with despair.

And at that moment a taxi with the two policemen in it passed us on its way to the bridge. They must have seen that kick; perhaps they were cleverer than I had given them credit for, perhaps they were just sentimental about animals, and thought they'd do a good deed, and the rest happened by accident. But the fact remains – those two pillars of the law set about the stealing of Mr Calloway's dog.

He watched them go by. Then he said, 'Why don't you go across?'

'It's cheaper here,' I said.

'I mean just for an evening. Have a meal at that place we can see at night in the sky. Go to the theatre.'

90

'There isn't one.'

He said angrily, sucking his gold tooth, 'Well, anyway, get away from here.' He stared down the hill and up the other side. He couldn't see that the street climbing up from the bridge contained only the same money-changers' booths as this one.

I said, 'Why don't *you* go?'

He said evasively, 'Oh – business.'

I said, 'It's only a question of money. You don't *have* to pass by the bridge.'

He said with faint interest, 'I don't talk Spanish.'

'There isn't a soul here,' I said, 'who doesn't talk English.'

He looked at me with surprise. 'Is that so?' he said. 'Is that so?'

It's as I have said; he'd never tried to talk to anyone, and they respected him too much to talk to him – he was worth a million. I don't know whether I'm glad or sorry that I told him that. If I hadn't, he might be there now, sitting by the bandstand having his shoes cleaned – alive and suffering.

Three days later his dog disappeared. I found him looking for it calling softly and shamefacedly between the palms of the garden. He looked embarrassed. He said in a low angry voice, 'I *hate* that dog. The beastly mongrel,' and called 'Rover, Rover' in a voice which didn't carry five yards. He said, 'I bred setters once. I'd have shot a dog like that.' It reminded him, I *was* right, of Norfolk, and he lived in the memory, and he hated it for its imperfection. He was a man without a family and without friends, and his only enemy was that dog. You couldn't call the law an enemy; you have to be intimate with an enemy.

Late that afternoon someone told him they'd seen the dog walking across the bridge. It wasn't true, of course, but we didn't know that then – they paid a Mexican five pesos to smuggle it across. So all that afternoon and the next Mr Calloway sat in the garden having his shoes cleaned over and over again, and thinking how a dog could just walk across like that, and a human being, an immortal soul, was bound here in the awful routine of the little walk and the unspeakable meals and the aspirin at the botica. That dog was seeing things he couldn't see – that hateful dog. It made him mad – I think literally mad. You must remember the man had been going on for months. He had a million and he was living on two pounds a week, with nothing to spend his money on. He sat there and brooded on the hideous injustice of it. I think he'd have crossed over one day in any case, but the dog was the last straw.

Next day when he wasn't to be seen, I guessed he'd gone across and I went too. The American town is as small as the Mexican. I knew I couldn't miss him if he was there, and I was still curious. A little sorry for him, but not too much.

I caught sight of him first in the only drug-store, having a coca-cola, and then once outside a cinema looking at the posters; he had dressed with extreme neatness, as if for a party, but there was no party. On my third time round, I came on the detectives – they were having coca-colas in the drug-store, and they must have missed Mr Calloway by inches. I went in and sat down at the bar.

'Hello,' I said, 'you still about.' I suddenly felt anxious for Mr Calloway. I didn't want them to meet.

One of them said, 'Where's Calloway?'

'Oh,' I said, 'he's hanging on.'

'But not his dog,' he said and laughed. The other looked a little shocked, he didn't like anyone to *talk* cynically about a dog. Then they got up – they had a car outside.

'Have another?' I said.

'No thanks. We've got to keep going.'

The men bent close and confided to me, 'Calloway's on this side.'

'No!' I said.

'And his dog.'

'He's looking for it,' the other said.

'I'm damned if he is,' I said, and again one of them looked a little shocked, as if I'd insulted the dog.

I don't think Mr Calloway was looking for his dog, but his dog certainly found him. There was a sudden hilarious yapping from the car and out plunged the semi-setter and gambolled furiously down the street. One of the detectives – the sentimental one – was into the car before we got to the door and was off after the dog. Near the bottom of the long road to the bridge was Mr Calloway – I do believe he'd come down to look at the Mexican side when he found there was nothing but the drug-store and the cinemas and the paper shops on the American. He saw the dog coming and yelled at it to go home – 'home, home, home,' as if they were in Norfolk – it took no notice at all, pelting towards him. Then he saw the police car coming, and ran. After that, everything happened too quickly, but I think the order of events was this – the dog started across the road right in front of the car, and Mr Calloway yelled, at the dog or the car, I don't know which. Anyway, the detective swerved – he said later, weakly, at the inquiry, that he couldn't run over a dog, and down went Mr Calloway, in a mess of broken glass and gold rims and silver hair, and blood. The dog was on to him before any of us could reach him licking and whimpering and licking. I saw Mr Calloway put up his hand, and down it went across the dog's neck and the whimper rose to a stupid bark of triumph, but Mr Calloway was dead – shock and a weak heart.

'Poor old geezer,' the detective said, 'I bet he really loved that dog,' and it's true that the attitude in which he lay looked more like a caress than a blow. I thought it was meant to be a blow, but the detective may have been right. It all seemed to me a little too touching to be true as the old crook lay there with his arm over the dog's neck, dead with his million between the money-changers' huts, but it's as well to be humble in the face of human nature. He had come across the river for something, and it may, after all, have been the dog he was looking for. It sat there, baying its stupid and mongrel triumph across his body, like a piece of sentimental statuary: the nearest he could get to the fields, the ditches, the horizon of his home. It was comic and it was pitiable, but it wasn't less comic because the man was dead. Death doesn't change comedy to tragedy, and if that last gesture was one of affection, I suppose it was only one more indication of a human being's capacity for self-deception, our baseless optimism that is so much more appalling than our despair.

1938

A DRIVE IN THE COUNTRY

As every other night she listened to her father going round the house, locking the doors and windows. He was head clerk at Bergson's Export Agency, and lying in bed she would think with dislike that his home was like his office, run on the same lines, its safety preserved with the same meticulous care, so that he could present a faithful steward's account to the managing-director. Regularly every Sunday he presented the account, accompanied by his wife and two daughters, in the little neo-Gothic church in Park Road. They always had the same pew, they were always five minutes early, and her father sang loudly with no sense of tune, holding an outsize prayer book on the level of his eyes. 'Singing songs of exultation' – he was presenting the week's account (one household duly safeguarded) – 'marching to the Promised Land.' When they came out of church, she looked carefully away from the corner by the 'Bricklayers' Arms' where Fred always stood, a little lit because the Arms had been open for half an hour, with his air of unbalanced exultation.

She listened: the back door closed, she could hear the catch of the kitchen window click, and the restless pad of his feet going back to try the front door. It wasn't only the outside doors he locked: he locked the empty rooms, the bathroom, the lavatory. He was locking something out, but obviously it was something capable of penetrating his first defences. He raised his second line all the way up to bed.

She laid her ear against the thin wall of the jerry-built villa and could hear the faint voices from the neighbouring room; as she listened they came clearer as though she were turning the knob of a wireless set. Her mother said ... 'margarine in the cooking ...' and her father said '... much easier in fifteen years'. Then the bed creaked and there were dim sounds of tenderness and comfort between the two middle-aged strangers

95

in the next room. In fifteen years, she thought unhappily, the house will be his; he had paid twenty-five pounds down and the rest he was paying month by month as rent. 'Of course,' he was in the habit of saying after a good meal, 'I've improved the property,' and he expected at least one of them to follow him into his study. 'I've wired this room for power,' he padded back past the little downstairs lavatory, 'this radiator,' the final stroke of satisfaction, 'the garden', and if it was a fine evening he would fling the french window of the dining-room open on the little carpet of grass as carefully kept as a college lawn. 'A pile of bricks,' he'd say, 'that's all it was.' Five years of Saturday afternoons and fine Sundays had gone into the patch of turf, the surrounding flower-bed, the one apple-tree which regularly produced one crimson tasteless apple more each year.

'Yes,' he said, 'I've improved the property,' looking round for a nail to drive in, a weed to be uprooted. 'If we had to sell now, we should get back more than I've paid from the society.' It was more than a sense of property, it was a sense of honesty. Some people who bought their houses through the society let them go to rack and ruin and then cleared out.

She stood with her ear against the wall, a small, furious, immature figure. There was no more to be heard from the other room, but in her inner ear she still heard the chorus of a property owner, the tap-tap of a hammer, the scrape of a spade, the whistle of radiator steam, a key turning, a bolt pushed home, the little trivial sounds of men building barricades. She stood planning her treachery.

It was a quarter past ten; she had an hour in which to leave the house, but it did not take so long. There was really nothing to fear. They had played their usual rubber of three-handed bridge while her sister altered a dress for the local 'hop' next night; after the rubber she had boiled a kettle and brought in a pot of tea; then she had filled the hot-water bottles and put them in the beds while her father locked up. He had no idea whatever that she was an enemy.

She put on a scarf and a heavy coat because it was still cold at night; the spring was late that year, as her father commented, watching for the buds on the apple-tree. She didn't pack a suit-case; that would have reminded her too much of week-ends at the sea, a family expedition to Ostend from all of which one returned; she wanted to match the odd reckless quality of Fred's mind. This time she wasn't going to return. She went softly downstairs into the little crowded hall, unlocked the door. All was quiet upstairs, and she closed the door behind her.

She was touched by a faint feeling of guilt because she couldn't lock it from the outside. But her guilt vanished by the time she reached the end of the crazy paved path and turned to the left down the road which after five years was still half made, past the gaps between the villas where the wounded fields re-mained grimly alive in the form of thin grass and heaps of clay and dandelions.

She walked fast, passing a long line of little garages like the graves in a Latin cemetery where the coffin lies below the fading photograph of its occupant. The cold night air touched her with exhilaration. She was ready for anything, as she turned by the Belisha beacon into the shuttered shopping street; she was like a recruit in the first months of a war. The choice made she could surrender her will to the strange, the exhilarating, the gigantic event.

Fred, as he had promised, was at the corner where the road turned down towards the church; she could taste the spirit on his lips as they kissed, and she was satisfied that no one else could have so adequately matched the occasion; his face was bright and reckless in the lamp-light, he was as exciting and strange to her as the adventure. He took her arm and ran her into a blind unlighted alley, then left her for a moment until two headlamps beamed softly at her out of the cavern. She cried with astonishment, 'You've got a car?' and felt the jerk of his nervous hand urging her towards it. 'Yes,' he said, 'do you like it?' grinding into second gear, changing clumsily into top as they came out between the shuttered windows.

She said, 'It's lovely. Let's drive a long way.'

'We will,' he said, watching the speedometer needle go quivering to fifty-five.

'Does it mean you've got a job?'

'There are no jobs,' he said, 'they don't exist any more than the Dodo. Did you see that bird?' he asked sharply, turning his headlights full on as they passed the turning to the housing estate and quite suddenly came out into the country between a café ('Draw in here'), a boot-shop ('Buy the shoes worn by your favourite film star'), and an undertaker's with a large white angel lit by a neon light.

'I didn't see any bird.'

'Not flying at the windscreen?'

'No.'

'I nearly hit it,' he said. 'It would have made a mess. Bad as those fellows who run someone down and don't stop. Should *we* stop?' he asked, turning out his switchboard light so that they couldn't see the needle vibrate to sixty.

'Whatever you say,' she said, sitting deep in a reckless dream.

'You going to love me tonight?'

'Of course I am.'

'Never going back there?'

'No,' she said, abjuring the tap of hammer, the click of latch, the pad of slippered feet making the rounds.

'Want to know where we are going?'

'No.' A little flat cardboard copse ran forward into the green light and darkly by. A rabbit turned its scut and vanished into a hedge. He said, 'Have you any money?'

'Half a crown.'

'Do you love me?' For a long time she expended on his lips all she had patiently had to keep in reserve, looking the other way on Sunday mornings, saying nothing when his name came up at meals with disapproval. She expended herself against dry unresponsive lips as the car leapt ahead and his foot trod down on the accelerator. He said, 'It's the hell of a life.'

She echoed him, 'The hell of a life.'

He said, 'There's a bottle in my pocket. Have a drink.'

'I don't want one.'

'Give me one then. It has a screw top,' and with one hand on her and one on the wheel he tipped his head, so that she could pour a little whisky into his mouth out of the quarter bottle. 'Do you mind?' he said.

'Of course I don't mind.'

'You can't save,' he said, 'on ten shillings a week pocket-money. I lay it out the best I can. It needs a hell of a lot of thought. To give variety. Half a crown on Weights. Three and six on whisky. A shilling on the pictures. That leaves three shillings for beer. I take my fun once a week and get it over.'

The whisky had dribbled on to his tie and the smell filled the small coupé. It pleased her. It was *his* smell. He said, 'They grudge it me. They think I ought to get a job. When you're that age you don't realize there aren't any jobs for some of us – any more for ever.'

'I know,' she said. 'They are old.'

'How's your sister?' he asked abruptly; the bright glare swept the road ahead of them clean of small scurrying birds and animals.

'She's going to the hop tomorrow. I wonder where we shall be.'

He wouldn't be drawn; he had his own idea and kept it to himself.

'I'm loving this.'

He said, 'There's a club out this way. At a road-house. Mick made me a member. Do you know Mick?'

'No.'

'Mick's all right. If they know you, they'll serve you drinks till midnight. We'll look in there. Say hullo to Mick. And then in the morning – we'll decide that later when we've had a few drinks.'

'Have you the money?' A small village, a village fast asleep already behind closed doors and windows, sailed down the hill towards them as if it was being carried smoothly by a landslide into the scarred plain from which they'd come. A low grey Norman church, an inn without a sign, a clock striking eleven. He said, 'Look in the back. There's a suitcase there.'

'It's locked.'

'I forgot the key,' he said.

'What's in it?'

'A few things,' he said vaguely. 'We could pop them for drinks.'

'What about a bed?'

'There's the car. You are not scared, are you?'

'No,' she said. 'I'm not scared. This is – ' but she hadn't words for the damp cold wind, the darkness, the strangeness, the smell of whisky and the rushing car. 'It moves,' she said. 'We must have gone a long way already. This is real country,' seeing an owl sweep low on furry wings over a ploughed field.

'You've got to go farther than this for real country,' he said. 'You won't find it yet on *this* road. We'll be at the road-house soon.'

She discovered in herself a nostalgia for their dark windy solitary progress. She said, 'Need we go to the club? Can't we go farther into the country?'

He looked sideways at her; he had always been open to *any* suggestion: like some meteorological instrument, he was made for the winds to blow through. 'Of course,' he said, 'anything you like.' He didn't give the club a second thought; they swept past it a moment later, a long lit Tudor bungalow, a crash of voices, a bathing-pool filled for some reason with hay. It was immediately behind them, a patch of light whipping round a corner out of sight.

He said, 'I suppose this is country now. They none of them get farther than the club. We're quite alone now. We could lie in these fields till doomsday as far as *they* are concerned, though I suppose a ploughman ... if they do plough here.' He raised his foot from the accelerator and let the car's speed gradually diminish. Somebody had left a wooden gate open into a field and he turned the car in; they jolted a long way down the field beside the hedge and came to a standstill. He turned out the headlamps and they sat in the tiny glow of the switchboard light. 'Peaceful,' he said uneasily; and they heard a screech owl hunting overhead and a small rustle in the hedge where something went into hiding. They belonged to the city; they hadn't a name for anything round them; the tiny buds breaking in the bushes were nameless. He nodded at a group of dark trees at the hedge ends. 'Oaks?'

'Elms?' she asked, and their mouths went together in a mutual ignorance. The touch excited her; she was ready for the most reckless act; but from his mouth, the dry spiritous lips, she gained a sense that he was less excited than he had hoped to be.

She said, to reassure herself, 'It's good to be here – miles away from anyone we know.'

'I dare say Mick's there. Down the road.'

'Does he know?'

'Nobody knows.'

She said, 'That's how I wanted it. How did you get this car?'

He grinned at her with unbalanced amusement. 'I saved from the ten shillings.'

'No but how? Did someone lend it you?'

'Yes,' he said. He suddenly pushed the door open and said, 'Let's take a walk.'

'We've never walked in the country before.' She took his arm, and she could feel the tense nerves responding to her touch. It was what she liked; she couldn't tell what he would do next. She said, 'My father calls you crazy. I like you crazy. What's all this stuff?' kicking at the ground.

'Clover,' he said, 'isn't it? I don't know.' It was like being in a foreign city where you can't understand the names on shops, the traffic signs: nothing to catch hold of, to hold you down to this and that, adrift together in a dark vacuum. 'Shouldn't you turn on the headlamps?' she said. 'It won't be so easy finding our way back. There's not much moon.' Already they seemed to have gone a long way from the car; she couldn't see it clearly any longer.

'We'll find our way,' he said. 'Somehow. Don't worry.' At the hedge end they came to the trees. He pulled a twig down and felt the sticky buds. 'What is it? Beech?'

'I don't know.'

He said, 'If it had been warmer, we could have slept out here.

You'd think we might have had that much luck, tonight of all nights. But it's cold and it's going to rain.'

'Let's come in the summer,' but he didn't answer. Some other wind had blown, she could tell it, and already he had lost interest in her. There was something hard in his pocket; it hurt her side; she put her hand in. The metal chamber had absorbed all the cold there had been in the windy ride. She whispered fearfully, 'Why are you carrying that?' She had always before drawn a line round his recklessness. When her father had said he was crazy she had secretly and possessively smiled because she thought she knew the extent of his craziness. Now, while she waited for him to answer her, she could feel his craziness go on and on, out of her reach, out of her sight; she couldn't see where it ended; it had no end, she couldn't possess it any more than she could possess a darkness or a desert.

'Don't be scared,' he said. 'I didn't mean you to find that tonight.' He suddenly became more tender than he had ever been; he put his hand on her breast; it came from his fingers, a great soft meaningless flood of tenderness. He said, 'Don't you see? Life's hell. There's nothing we can do.' He spoke very gently, but she had never been more aware of his recklessness: he was open to every wind, but the wind now seemed to have set from the east: it blew like sleet through his words. 'I haven't a penny,' he said. 'We can't live on nothing. It's no good hoping that I'll get a job.' He repeated, 'There aren't any more jobs any more. And every year, you know, there's less chance, because there are more people younger than I am.'

'But why,' she said, 'have we come – ?'

He became softly and tenderly lucid. 'We do love each other. don't we? We can't live without each other. It's no good hanging around, is it, waiting for our luck to change. We don't even get a fine night,' he said, feeling for rain with his hand. 'We can have a good time tonight – in the car – and then in the morning –'

'No, no,' she said. She tried to get away from him. 'I couldn't. It's horrible. I never said –'

'You wouldn't know anything,' he said gently and inexorably.

Her words, she could realize now, had never made any real impression; he was swayed by them but no more than he was swayed by anything: now that the wind had set, it was like throwing scraps of paper towards the sky to speak at all, or to argue. He said, 'Of course we neither of us believe in God, but there may be a chance, and it's company, going together like that.' He added with pleasure, 'It's a gamble,' and she remembered more occasions than she could count when their last coppers had gone ringing down in fruit machines.

He pulled her closer and said with complete assurance, 'We love each other. It's the only way, you know. You can trust me.' He was like a skilled logician; he knew all the stages of the argument. She despaired of catching him out on any point but the premise: we love each other. *That* she doubted for the first time, faced by the mercilessness of his egotism. He repeated, 'It will be company.'

She said, 'There must be some way . . .'

'Why *must*?'

'Otherwise, people would be doing it all the time – everywhere!'

'They are,' he said triumphantly, as if it were more important for him to find his argument flawless than to find – well, a way, a way to go on living. 'You've only got to read the papers,' he said. He whispered gently, endearingly, as if he thought the very sound of the words tender enough to dispel all fear. 'They call it a suicide pact. It's happening all the time.'

'I couldn't. I haven't the nerve.'

'You needn't do anything,' he said. 'I'll do it all.'

His calmness horrified her. 'You mean – you'd kill me?'

He said, 'I love you enough for that, I promise it won't hurt you.' He might have been persuading her to play some trivial and uncongenial game. 'We shall be together always.' He added rationally, 'Of course, if there *is* an always,' and suddenly she saw his love as a mere flicker of gas flame playing on the marshy depth of his irresponsibility, but now she realized that it was without any limit at all; it closed over the head. She pleaded, 'There are things we can sell. That suitcase.'

She knew that he was watching her with amusement, that he had rehearsed all her arguments and had an answer; he was only pretending to take her seriously. 'We might get fifteen shillings,' he said. 'We could live a day on that – but we shouldn't have much fun.'

'The things inside it?'

'Ah, that's another gamble. They might be worth thirty shillings. Three days, that would give us – with economy.'

'We might get a job.'

'I've been trying for a good many years now.'

'Isn't there the dole?'

'I'm not an insured worker. I'm one of the ruling class.'

'Your people, they'd give us something.'

'But we've got our pride, haven't we?' he said with remorseless conceit.

'The man who lent you the car?'

He said, 'You remember Cortez, the fellow who burnt his boats? I've burned mine. I've *got* to kill myself. You see, I stole that car. We'd be stopped in the next town. It's too late even to go back.' He laughed; he had reached the climax of his argument and there was nothing more to dispute about. She could tell that he was perfectly satisfied and perfectly happy. It infuriated her. '*You've* got to, maybe. But I haven't. Why should I kill myself? What right have you – ?' She dragged herself away from him and felt against her back the rough massive trunk of the living tree.

'Oh,' he said in an irritated tone, 'of course if you like to go on without me.' She had admired his conceit; he had always carried his unemployment with a manner. Now you could no longer call it conceit: it was a complete lack of any values. 'You can go home,' he said, 'though I don't quite know how – I can't drive you back because I'm staying here. You'll be able to go to the hop tomorrow night. And there's a whist-drive, isn't there, in the church hall? My dear, I wish you joy of home.'

There was a savagery in his manner. He took security, peace, order in his teeth and worried them so that she couldn't help feeling a little pity for what they had joined in despising: a hammer tapped at her heart, driving in a nail here and a nail

104

there. She tried to think of a bitter retort, for after all there was something to be said for the negative virtues of doing no injury, of simply going on, as her father was going on for another fifteen years. But the next moment she felt no anger. They had trapped each other. He had always wanted this: the dark field, the weapon in his pocket, the escape and the gamble; but she less honestly had wanted a little of both worlds: irresponsibility and a safe love, danger and a secure heart.

He said, 'I'm going now. Are you coming?'

'No,' she said. He hesitated; the recklessness for a moment wavered; a sense of something lost and bewildered came to her through the dark. She wanted to say: Don't be a fool. Leave the car where it is. Walk back with me, and we'll get a lift home, but she knew any thought of hers had occurred to him and been answered already: ten shillings a week, no job, getting older. Endurance was a virtue of one's fathers.

He suddenly began to walk fast down the hedge; he couldn't see where he was going; he stumbled on a root and she heard him swear. 'Damnation' – the little commonplace sound in the darkness overwhelmed her with pain and horror. She cried out, 'Fred. Fred. Don't do it,' and began to run in the opposite direction. She couldn't stop him and she wanted to be out of hearing. A twig broke under her foot like a shot, and the owl screamed across the ploughed field beyond the hedge. It was like a rehearsal with sound effects. But when the real shot came, it was quite different: a thud like a gloved hand striking a door and no cry at all. She didn't notice it at first and afterwards she thought that she had never been conscious of the exact moment when her lover ceased to exist.

She bruised herself against the car, running blindly; a blue-spotted Woolworth handkerchief lay on the seat in the light of the switchboard bulb. She nearly took it, but no, she thought, no one must know that I have been here. She turned out the light and picked her way as quietly as she could across the clover. She could begin to be sorry when she was safe. She wanted to close a door behind her, thrust a bolt down, hear the catch grip.

It wasn't ten minutes walk down the deserted lane to the

road-house. Tipsy voices spoke a foreign language, though it was the language Fred had spoken. She could hear the clink of coins in fruit machines, the hiss of soda; she listened to these sounds like an enemy, planning her escape. They frightened her like something mindless: there was no appeal one could make to that egotism. It was simply a Want to be satisfied; it gaped at her like a mouth. A man was trying to wind up his car; the self-starter wouldn't work. He said, 'I'm a Bolshie. Of course I'm a Bolshie. I believe – '

A thin girl with red hair sat on the step and watched him. 'You're all wrong,' she said.

'I'm a Liberal Conservative.'

'You *can't* be a liberal Conservative.'

'Do you love me?'

'I love Joe.'

'You *can't* love Joe.'

'Let's go home, Mike.'

The man tried to wind up the car again, and she came up to them as if she'd come out of the club and said, 'Give me a lift?'

'Course. Delighted. Get in.'

'Won't the car go?'

'No.'

'Have you flooded – ?'

'That's an idea.' He lifted the bonnet and she pressed the self-starter. It began to rain slowly and heavily and drenchingly, the kind of rain you always expect to fall on graves, and her thoughts went down the lane towards the field, the hedge, the trees – oak, beech, elm? She imagined the rain on his face, the pool collecting in each eye-socket and streaming down on either side the nose. But she could feel nothing but gladness because she had escaped from him.

'Where are you going?' she said.

'Devizes.'

'I thought you might be going to London.'

'Where do *you* want to go to?'

'Golding's Park.'

'Let's go to Golding's Park.'

The red-haired girl said, 'I am going in, Mike. It's raining.'

'Aren't you coming?'

'I'm going to find Joe.'

'All right.' He smashed his way out of the little car-park, bending his mudguard on a wooden post, scraping the paint of another car.

'That's the wrong way,' she said.

'We'll turn.' He backed the car into a ditch and out again. 'Was a good party,' he said. The rain came down harder; it blinded the windscreen and the electric wiper wouldn't work, but her companion didn't care. He drove straight on at forty miles an hour; it was an old car, it wouldn't do any more; the rain leaked through the hood. He said, 'Twis' that knob. Have a tune,' and when she turned it and the dance music came through, he said, 'That's Harry Roy. Know him anywhere,' driving into the thick wet night carrying the hot music with them. Presently he said, 'A friend of mine, one of the best, you'd know him, Peter Weatherall. You know him.'

'No.'

'You must know Peter. Haven't seen him about lately. Goes off on the drink for weeks. They sent out an SOS for Peter once in the middle of the dance music. "Missing from Home". We were in the car. We had a laugh about that.'

She said, 'Is that what people do – when people are missing?'

'Know this tune,' he said. 'This isn't Harry Roy. This is Alf Cohen.'

She said suddenly, 'You're Mike, aren't you? Wouldn't *you* lend – '

He sobered up. 'Stony broke,' he said. 'Comrades in misfortune. Try Peter. Why do you want to go to Golding's Park?'

'My home.'

'You mean you live there?'

'Yes.' She said, 'Be careful. There's a speed limit here.' He was perfectly obedient. He raised his foot and let the car crawl at fifteen miles an hour. The lamp standards marched unsteadily to meet them and lit his face: he was quite old, forty if a day, ten years older than Fred. He wore a striped tie and she could see his sleeve was frayed. He had more than ten shillings a week, but perhaps not so very much more. His hair was going thin.

'You can drop me here,' she said. He stopped the car and she got out and the rain went on. He followed her on to the road. 'Let me come in?' he asked. She shook her head; the rain wetted them through; behind her was the pillar-box, the Belisha beacon, the road through the housing estate. 'Hell of a life,' he said politely, holding her hand, while the rain drummed on the hood of the cheap car and ran down his face, across his collar and the school tie. But she felt no pity, no attraction, only a faint horror and repulsion. A kind of dim recklessness gleamed in his wet eye, as the hot music of Alf Cohen's band streamed from the car, a faded irresponsibility. 'Le's go back,' he said, 'le's go somewhere. Le's go for a ride in the country. Le's go to Maidenhead,' holding her hand limply.

She pulled it away, he didn't resist, and walked down the half-made road to No. 64. The crazy paving in the front garden seemed to hold her feet firmly up. She opened the door and heard through the dark and the rain a car grind into second gear and drone away – certainly not towards Maidenhead or Devizes or the country. Another wind must have blown.

Her father called down from the first landing: 'Who's there?'

'It's me,' she said. She explained, 'I had a feeling you'd left the door unbolted.'

'And had I?'

'No,' she said gently, 'it's bolted all right,' driving the bolt softly and firmly home. She waited till his door closed. She touched the radiator to warm her fingers – he had put it in himself, he had improved the property; in fifteen years, she thought, it will be ours. She was quite free from pain, listening to the rain on the roof; he had been over the whole roof that winter inch by inch, there was nowhere for the rain to enter. It was kept outside, drumming on the shabby hood, pitting the clover field. She stood by the door, feeling only the faint repulsion she always had for things weak and crippled, thinking, 'It isn't tragic at all,' and looking down with an emotion like tenderness at the flimsy bolt from a sixpenny store any man could have broken, but which a Man had put in, the head clerk of Bergson's.

1937

THE INNOCENT

IT was a mistake to take Lola there. I knew it the moment we alighted from the train at the small country station. On an autumn evening one remembers more of childhood than at any other time of year, and her bright veneered face, the small bag which hardly pretended to contain our things for the night, simply didn't go with the old grain warehouses across the small canal, the few lights up the hill, the posters of an ancient film. But she said, 'Let's go into the country,' and Bishop's Hendron was, of course, the first name which came into my head. Nobody would know me there now, and it hadn't occurred to me that it would be I who remembered.

Even the old porter touched a chord. I said, 'There'll be a four-wheeler at the entrance,' and there was, though at first I didn't notice it, seeing the two taxis and thinking, 'The old place is coming on.' It was very dark, and the thin autumn mist, the smell of wet leaves and canal water were deeply familiar.

Lola said, 'But why did you choose this place? It's grim.' It was no use explaining to her why it wasn't grim to me, that that sand heap by the canal had always been there (when I was three I remember thinking it was what other people meant by the seaside). I took the bag (I've said it was light; it was simply a forged passport of respectability) and said we'd walk. We came up over the little humpbacked bridge and passed the alms-houses. When I was five I saw a middle-aged man run into one to commit suicide; he carried a knife and all the neighbours pursued him up the stairs. She said, 'I never thought the country was like *this*.' They were ugly alms-houses, little grey stone boxes, but I knew them as I knew nothing else. It was like listening to music, all that walk.

But I had to say something to Lola. It wasn't her fault that she didn't belong here. We passed the school, the church, and came round into the old wide High Street and the sense of the

110

first twelve years of life. If I hadn't come, I shouldn't have known that sense would be so strong, because those years hadn't been particularly happy or particularly miserable; they had been ordinary years, but now with the smell of wood fires, of the cold striking up from the dark damp paving stones, I thought I knew what it was that held me. It was the smell of innocence.

I said to Lola, 'It's a good inn, and there'll be nothing here, you'll see, to keep us up. We'll have dinner and drinks and go to bed.' But the worst of it was that I couldn't help wishing that I were alone. I hadn't been back all these years; I hadn't realized how well I remembered the place. Things I'd quite forgotten, like that sand heap, were coming back with an effect of pathos and nostalgia. I could have been very happy that night in a melancholy autumnal way, wandering about the little town, picking up clues to that time of life when, however miserable we are, we have expectations. It wouldn't be the same if I came back again, for then there would be the memories of Lola, and Lola meant just nothing at all. We had happened to pick each other up at a bar the day before and liked each other. Lola was all right, there was no one I would rather spend the night with, but she didn't fit in with *these* memories. We ought to have gone to Maidenhead. That's country too.

The inn was not quite where I remembered it. There was the Town Hall, but they had built a new cinema with a Moorish dome and a café, and there was a garage which hadn't existed in my time. I had forgotten too the turning to the left up a steep villaed hill.

'I don't believe that road was there in my day,' I said.

'Your day?' Lola asked.

'Didn't I tell you? I was born here.'

'You must get a kick out of bringing me here,' Lola said. 'I suppose you used to think of nights like this when you were a boy.'

'Yes,' I said, because it wasn't her fault. She was all right. I liked her scent. She used a good shade of lipstick. It was costing me a lot, a fiver for Lola and then all the bills and fares and drinks, but I'd have thought it money well spent anywhere else in the world.

I lingered at the bottom of that road. Something was stirring in the mind, but I don't think I should have remembered what, if a crowd of children hadn't come down the hill at that moment into the frosty lamplight, their voices sharp and shrill, their breath fuming as they passed under the lamps. They all carried linen bags, and some of the bags were embroidered with initials. They were in their best clothes and a little self-conscious. The small girls kept to themselves in a kind of compact beleaguered group, and one thought of hair ribbons and shining shoes and the sedate tinkle of a piano. It all came back to me: they had been to a dancing lesson, just as I used to go, to a small square house with a drive of rhododendrons half-way up the hill. More than ever I wished that Lola were not with me, less than ever did she fit, as I thought 'something's missing from the picture', and a sense of pain glowed dully at the bottom of my brain.

We had several drinks at the bar, but there was half an hour before they would agree to serve dinner. I said to Lola, 'You don't want to drag round this town. If you don't mind, I'll just slip out for ten minutes and look at a place I used to know.' She didn't mind. There was a local man, perhaps a schoolmaster, at the bar simply longing to stand her a drink. I could see how he envied me, coming down with her like this from town just for a night.

I walked up the hill. The first houses were all new. I resented them. They hid such things as fields and gates I might have remembered. It was like a map which had got wet in the pocket and pieces had stuck together; when you opened it there were whole patches hidden. But half-way up, there the house really was, the drive; perhaps the same old lady was giving lessons. Children exaggerate age. She may not in those days have been more than thirty-five. I could hear the piano. She was following the same routine. Children under eight, 6–7 p.m. Children eight to thirteen, 7–8. I opened the gate and went in a little way. I was trying to remember.

I don't know what brought it back. I think it was simply the autumn, the cold, the wet frosting leaves, rather than the piano, which had played different tunes in those days. I remembered the small girl as well as one remembers anyone without a photograph to refer to. She was a year older than I was: she must have been just on the point of eight. I loved her with an intensity I have never felt since, I believe, for anyone. At least I have never made the mistake of laughing at children's love. It has a terrible inevitability of separation because there *can* be no satisfaction. Of course one invents tales of houses on fire, of war and forlorn charges which prove one's courage in her eyes, but never of marriage. One knows without being told that that can't happen, but the knowledge doesn't mean that one suffers less. I remembered all the games of blind-man's buff at birthday parties when I vainly hoped to catch her, so that I might have the excuse to touch and hold her, but I never caught her; she always kept out of my way.

But once a week for two winters I had my chance: I danced with her. That made it worse (it was cutting off our only contact) when she told me during one of the last lessons of the winter that next year she would join the older class. She liked me too, I knew it, but we had no way of expressing it. I used to go to her birthday parties and she would come to mine, but we never even ran home together after the dancing class. It would have seemed odd; I don't think it occurred to us. I had to join my own boisterous teasing male companions, and she the besieged, the hustled, the shrilly indignant sex on the way down the hill.

I shivered there in the mist and turned my coat collar up. The piano was playing a dance from an old C. B. Cochran revue. It seemed a long journey to have taken to find only Lola at the end of it. There *is* something about innocence one is never quite resigned to lose. Now when I am unhappy about a girl, I can simply go and buy another one. Then the best I could think of was to write some passionate message and slip it into a hole (it was extraordinary how I began to remember everything) in the woodwork of the gate. I had once told her about the hole, and sooner or later I was sure she would put in her fingers and find the message. I wondered what the message could have been. One wasn't able to express much, I thought, in those days; but because the expression was inadequate, it didn't mean that the pain was shallower than what one sometimes suffered now. I remembered how for days I had felt in the hole and always found the message there. Then the dancing lessons stopped. Probably by the next winter I had forgotten.

As I went out of the gate I looked to see if the hole existed. It was there. I put in my finger, and, in its safe shelter from the seasons and the years, the scrap of paper rested yet. I pulled it out and opened it. Then I struck a match, a tiny glow of heat in the mist and dark. It was a shock to see by its diminutive flame a picture of crude obscenity. There could be no mistake; there were my initials below the childish inaccurate sketch of a man and woman. But it woke fewer memories than the fume of breath, the linen bags, a damp leaf, or the pile of sand. I didn't recognize it; it might have been drawn by a dirty-minded stranger on a lavatory wall. All I could remember was the purity, the intensity, the pain of that passion.

I felt at first as if I had been betrayed. 'After all,' I told myself, 'Lola's not so much out of place here.' But later that night, when Lola turned away from me and fell asleep, I began to realize the deep innocence of that drawing. I had believed I was drawing something with a meaning and beautiful; it was only now after thirty years of life that the picture seemed obscene.

1937

THE BASEMENT ROOM

1

WHEN the front door had shut the two of them out and the butler Baines had turned back into the dark and heavy hall, Philip began to live. He stood in front of the nursery door, listening until he heard the engine of the taxi die out along the street. His parents were safely gone for a fortnight's holiday; he was 'between nurses', one dismissed and the other not arrived; he was alone in the great Belgravia house with Baines and Mrs Baines.

He could go anywhere, even through the green baize door to the pantry or down the stairs to the basement living-room. He felt a happy stranger in his home because he could go into any room and all the rooms were empty.

You could only guess who had once occupied them: the rack of pipes in the smoking-room beside the elephant tusks, the carved wood tobacco jar; in the bedroom the pink hangings and the pale perfumes and three-quarter finished jars of cream which Mrs Baines had not yet cleared away for her own use; the high glaze on the never-opened piano in the drawing-room, the china clock, the silly little tables and the silver. But here Mrs Baines was already busy, pulling down the curtains, covering the chairs in dust-sheets.

'Be off out of here, Master Philip,' and she looked at him with her peevish eyes, while she moved round, getting everything in order, meticulous and loveless and doing her duty.

Philip Lane went downstairs and pushed at the baize door; he looked into the pantry, but Baines was not there, then he set foot for the first time on the stairs to the basement. Again he had the sense: this is life. All his seven nursery years vibrated with the strange, the new experience. His crowded brain was like a city which feels the earth tremble at a distant earthquake shock. He was apprehensive, but he was happier than he had ever been. Everything was more important than before.

Baines was reading a newspaper in his shirt-sleeves. He said, 'Come in, Phil, and make yourself at home. Wait a moment and I'll do the honours,' and going to a white cleaned cupboard he brought out a bottle of ginger-beer and half a Dundee cake. 'Half past eleven in the morning,' Baines said. 'It's opening time, my boy,' and he cut the cake and poured out the ginger-beer. He was more genial than Philip had ever known him, more at his ease, a man in his own home.

'Shall I call Mrs Baines?' Philip asked, and he was glad when Baines said no. She was busy. She liked to be busy, so why interfere with her pleasure?

'A spot of drink at half past eleven,' Baines said, pouring himself out a glass of ginger-beer, 'gives an appetite for chop and does no man any harm.'

'A chop?' Philip asked.

'Old Coasters,' Baines said, 'they call all food chop.'

'But it's not a chop?'

'Well, it might be, you know, if cooked with palm oil. And then some paw-paw to follow.'

Philip looked out of the basement window at the dry stone yard, the ash-can and the legs going up and down beyond the railings.

'Was it hot there?'

'Ah, you never felt such heat. Not a nice heat, mind, like you get in the park on a day like this. Wet,' Baines said, 'corruption.' He cut himself a slice of cake. 'Smelling of rot,' Baines said, rolling his eyes round the small basement room, from clean cupboard to clean cupboard, the sense of bareness, of nowhere to hide a man's secrets. With an air of regret for something lost he took a long draught of ginger-beer.

'Why did father live out there?'

'It was his job,' Baines said, 'same as this is mine now. And it was mine then too. It was a man's job. You wouldn't believe it now, but I've had forty niggers under me, doing what I told them to.'

'Why did you leave?'

'I married Mrs Baines.'

116

Philip took the slice of Dundee cake in his hand and munched it round the room. He felt very old, independent and judicial; he was aware that Baines was talking to him as man to man. He never called him Master Philip as Mrs Baines did, who was servile when she was not authoritative.

Baines had seen the world; he had seen beyond the railings. He sat there over his ginger pop with the resigned dignity of an exile; Baines didn't complain; he had chosen his fate, and if his fate was Mrs Baines he had only himself to blame.

But today – the house was almost empty and Mrs Baines was upstairs and there was nothing to do – he allowed himself a little acidity.

'I'd go back tomorrow if I had the chance.'

'Did you ever shoot a nigger?'

'I never had any call to shoot,' Baines said. 'Of course I carried a gun. But you didn't need to treat them bad. That just made them stupid. Why,' Baines said, bowing his thin grey hair with embarrassment over the ginger pop, 'I loved some of those damned niggers. I couldn't help loving them. There they'd be laughing, holding hands; they liked to touch each other; it made them feel fine to know the other fellow was around. It didn't mean anything we could understand; two of them would go about all day without loosing hold, grown men; but it wasn't love; it didn't mean anything we could understand.'

'Eating between meals,' Mrs Baines said. 'What would your mother say, Master Philip?'

She came down the steep stairs to the basement, her hands full of pots of cream and salve, tubes of grease and paste. 'You oughtn't to encourage him, Baines,' she said, sitting down in a wicker armchair and screwing up her small ill-humoured eyes at the Coty lipstick, Pond's cream, the Leichner rouge and Cyclax powder and Elizabeth Arden astringent.

She threw them one by one into the wastepaper basket. She saved only the cold cream. 'Tell the boy stories,' she said. 'Go along to the nursery, Master Philip, while I get lunch.'

Philip climbed the stairs to the baize door. He heard Mrs Baines's voice like the voice in a nightmare when the small Price light has guttered in the saucer and the curtains move; it was sharp and shrill and full of malice, louder than people ought to speak, exposed.

'Sick to death of your ways, Baines, spoiling the boy. Time you did some work about the house,' but he couldn't hear what Baines said in reply. He pushed open the baize door, came up like a small earth animal in his grey flannel shorts into a wash of sunlight on a parquet floor, the gleam of mirrors dusted and polished and beautified by Mrs Baines.

Something broke downstairs, and Philip sadly mounted the stairs to the nursery. He pitied Baines; it occurred to him how happily they could live together in the empty house if Mrs Baines were called away. He didn't want to play with his Meccano sets; he wouldn't take out his train or his soldiers; he sat at the table with his chin on his hands: this is life; and suddenly he felt responsible for Baines, as if he were the master of the house and Baines an ageing servant who deserved to be cared for. There was not much one could do; he decided at least to be good.

He was not surprised when Mrs Baines was agreeable at lunch; he was used to her changes. Now it was 'another helping of meat, Master Philip', or 'Master Philip, a little more of this nice pudding'. It was a pudding he liked, Queen's pudding with a perfect meringue, but he wouldn't eat a second helping lest she might count that a victory. She was the kind of woman who thought that any injustice could be counterbalanced by something good to eat.

She was sour, but she liked making sweet things; one never had to complain of a lack of jam or plums; she ate well herself and added soft sugar to the meringue and the strawberry jam. The half-light through the basement window set the motes moving above her pale hair like dust as she sifted the sugar, and Baines crouched over his plate saying nothing.

Again Philip felt responsibility. Baines had looked forward to this, and Baines was disappointed: everything was being spoilt. The sensation of disappointment was one which Philip could share; he could understand better than anyone this grief, something hoped for not happening, something promised not fulfilled, something exciting which turned dull. 'Baines,' he said, 'will you take me for a walk this afternoon?'

'No,' Mrs Baines said, 'no. That he won't. Not with all the silver to clean.'

'There's a fortnight to do it in', Baines said.

'Work first, pleasure afterwards.'

Mrs Baines helped herself to some more meringue.

Baines put down his spoon and fork and pushed his plate away. 'Blast,' he said.

'Temper,' Mrs Baines said, 'temper. Don't you go breaking any more things, Baines, and I won't have you swearing in front of the boy. Master Philip, if you've finished you can get down.'

She skinned the rest of the meringue off the pudding.

'I want to go for a walk,' Philip said.

'You'll go and have a rest.'

'I want to go for a walk.'

'Master Philip,' Mrs Baines said. She got up from the table, leaving her meringue unfinished, and came towards him, thin, menacing, dusty in the basement room. 'Master Philip, you just do as you're told.' She took him by the arm and squeezed it; she watched him with a joyless passionate glitter and above her head the feet of typists trudged back to the Victoria offices after the lunch interval.

'Why shouldn't I go for a walk?'

But he weakened; he was scared and ashamed of being scared. This was life; a strange passion he couldn't understand moving in the basement room. He saw a small pile of broken glass swept into a corner by the wastepaper basket. He looked at Baines for help and only intercepted hate; the sad hopeless hate of something behind bars.

'Why shouldn't I?' he repeated.

'Master Philip,' Mrs Baines said, 'you've got to do as you're told. You mustn't think just because your father's away there's nobody here to – '

'You wouldn't dare,' Philip cried, and was startled by Baines's low interjection:

'There's nothing she wouldn't dare.'

'I hate you,' Philip said to Mrs Baines. He pulled away from her and ran to the door, but she was there before him; she was old, but she was quick.

'Master Philip,' she said, 'you'll say you're sorry.' She stood in front of the door quivering with excitement. 'What would your father do if he heard you say that?'

She put a hand out to seize him, dry and white with constant soda, the nails cut to the quick, but he backed away and put the table between them, and suddenly to his surprise she smiled; she became again as servile as she had been arrogant. 'Get along with you, Master Philip,' she said with glee, 'I see I'm going to have my hands full till your father and mother come back.'

She left the door unguarded and when he passed her she slapped him playfully. 'I've got too much to do today to trouble about you. I haven't covered half the chairs,' and suddenly even the upper part of the house became unbearable to him as he thought of Mrs Baines moving around shrouding the sofas, laying out the dust-sheets.

So he wouldn't go upstairs to get his cap but walked straight out across the shining hall into the street, and again, as he looked this way and looked that way, it was life he was in the middle of.

2

The pink sugar cakes in the window on a paper doily, the ham, the slab of mauve sausage, the wasps driving like small torpedoes across the pane caught Philip's attention. His feet were tired by pavements; he had been afraid to cross the road, had simply walked first in one direction, then in the other. He was nearly home now; the square was at the end of the street; this was a shabby outpost of Pimlico, and he smudged the pane with his nose looking for sweets, and saw between the cake and ham a different Baines. He hardly recognized the bulbous eyes, the bald forehead. This was a happy, bold and buccaneering

120

Baines, even though it was, when you looked closer, a desperate
Baines.

Philip had never seen the girl, but he remembered Baines had
a niece. She was thin and drawn, and she wore a white mackintosh; she meant nothing to Philip; she belonged to a world
about which he knew nothing at all. He couldn't make up
stories about her, as he could make them up about withered Sir
Hubert Reed, the Permanent Secretary, about Mrs Wince-
Dudley who came up once a year from Penstanley in Suffolk
with a green umbrella and an enormous black handbag, as he
could make them up about the upper servants in all the houses
where he went to tea and games. She just didn't belong. He
thought of mermaids and Undine, but she didn't belong there
either, nor to the adventures of Emil, nor to the Bastables. She
sat there looking at an iced pink cake in the detachment and
mystery of the completely disinherited, looking at the half-used
pots of powder which Baines had set out on the marble-topped
table between them.

Baines was urging, hoping, entreating, commanding, and the
girl looked at the tea and the china pots and cried. Baines passed
his handkerchief across the table, but she wouldn't wipe her
eyes; she screwed it in her palm and let the tears run down,
wouldn't do anything, wouldn't speak, would only put up a
silent resistance to what she dreaded and wanted and refused to
listen to at any price. The two brains battled over the tea-cups
loving each other, and there came to Philip outside, beyond the
ham and wasps and dusty Pimlico pane, a confused indication
of the struggle.

He was inquisitive and he didn't understand and he wanted to
know. He went and stood in the doorway to see better, he was
less sheltered than he had ever been; other people's lives for the
first time touched and pressed and moulded. He would never
escape that scene. In a week he had forgotten it, but it con-
ditioned his career, the long austerity of his life; when he
was dying, rich and alone, it was said that he asked: 'Who is
she?'

Baines had won; he was cocky and the girl was happy. She wiped her face, she opened a pot of powder, and their fingers touched across the table. It occurred to Philip that it might be amusing to imitate Mrs Baines's voice and to call 'Baines' to him from the door.

His voice shrivelled them; you couldn't describe it in any other way, it made them smaller, they weren't together any more. Baines was the first to recover and trace the voice, but that didn't make things as they were. The sawdust was spilled out of the afternoon; nothing you did could mend it, and Philip was scared. 'I didn't mean . . .' He wanted to say that he loved Baines, that he had only wanted to laugh at Mrs Baines. But he had discovered you couldn't laugh at Mrs Baines. She wasn't Sir Hubert Reed, who used steel nibs and carried a pen-wiper in his pocket; she wasn't Mrs Wince-Dudley; she was darkness when the night-light went out in a draught; she was the frozen blocks of earth he had seen one winter in a graveyard when someone said, 'They need an electric drill'; she was the flowers gone bad and smelling in the little closet room at Penstanley. There was nothing to laugh about. You had to endure her when she was there and forget about her quickly when she was away, suppress the thought of her, ram it down deep.

Baines said, 'It's only Phil,' beckoned him in and gave him the pink iced cake the girl hadn't eaten, but the afternoon was broken, the cake was like dry bread in the throat. The girl left them at once: she even forgot to take the powder. Like a blunt icicle in her white mackintosh she stood in the doorway with her back to them, then melted into the afternoon.

'Who is she?' Philip asked. 'Is she your niece?'

'Oh, yes,' Baines said, 'that's who she is; she's my niece,' and poured the last drops of water on to the coarse black leaves in the teapot.

'May as well have another cup,' Baines said.

'The cup that cheers,' he said hopelessly, watching the bitter black fluid drain out of the spout.

'Have a glass of ginger pop, Phil?'

'I'm sorry. I'm sorry, Baines.'

'It's not your fault, Phil. Why, I could really believe it wasn't you at all, but her. She creeps in everywhere.' He fished two leaves out of his cup and laid them on the back of his hand, a thin soft flake and a hard stalk. He beat them with his hand: 'Today,' and the stalk detached itself, 'tomorrow, Wednesday, Thursday, Friday, Saturday, Sunday,' but the flake wouldn't come, stayed where it was, drying under his blows, with a resistance you wouldn't believe it to possess. 'The tough one wins,' Baines said.

He got up and paid the bill and out they went into the street. Baines said, 'I don't ask you to say what isn't true. But you needn't actually *tell* Mrs Baines you met us here.'

'Of course not,' Philip said, and catching something of Sir Hubert Reed's manner, 'I understand, Baines.' But he didn't understand a thing; he was caught up in other people's darkness.

'It was stupid,' Baines said. 'So near home, but I hadn't time to think, you see. I'd got to see her.'

'I haven't time to spare,' Baines said. 'I'm not young. I've got to see that she's all right.'

'Of course you have, Baines.'

'Mrs Baines will get it out of you if she can.'

'You can trust me, Baines,' Philip said in a dry important Reed voice; and then, 'Look out. She's at the window watching.' And there indeed she was, looking up at them, between the lace curtains, from the basement room, speculating. 'Need we go in, Baines?' Philip asked, cold lying heavy on his stomach like too much pudding; he clutched Baines's arm.

'Careful,' Baines said softly, 'careful.'

'But need we go in, Baines? It's early. Take me for a walk in the park.'

'Better not.'

'But I'm frightened, Baines.'

'You haven't any cause,' Baines said. 'Nothing's going to hurt you. You just run along upstairs to the nursery. I'll go down by the area and talk to Mrs Baines.' But he stood hesitating at the top of the stone steps pretending not to see her, where she watched between the curtains. 'In at the front door, Phil, and up the stairs.'

Philip didn't linger in the hall; he ran, slithering on the parquet Mrs Baines had polished, to the stairs. Through the drawing-room doorway on the first floor he saw the draped chairs; even the china clock on the mantel was covered like a canary's cage. As he passed, it chimed the hour, muffled and secret under the duster. On the nursery table he found his supper laid out: a glass of milk and a piece of bread and butter, a sweet biscuit, and a little cold Queen's pudding without the meringue. He had no appetite; he strained his ears for Mrs Baines's coming, for the sound of voices, but the basement held its secrets; the green baize door shut off that world. He drank the milk and ate the biscuit, but he didn't touch the rest, and presently he could hear the soft precise footfalls of Mrs Baines on the stairs: she was a good servant, she walked softly; she was a determined woman, she walked precisely.

But she wasn't angry when she came in; she was ingratiating as she opened the night nursery door – 'Did you have a good walk, Master Philip?' – pulled down the blinds, laid out his pyjamas, came back to clear his supper. 'I'm glad Baines found you. Your mother wouldn't have liked your being out alone.' She examined the tray. 'Not much appetite, have you, Master Philip? Why don't you try a little of this nice pudding? I'll bring you up some more jam for it.'

'No, no, thank you, Mrs Baines,' Philip said.

'You ought to eat more,' Mrs Baines said. She sniffed round the room like a dog. 'You didn't take any pots out of the wastepaper basket in the kitchen, did you, Master Philip?'

'No,' Philip said.

'Of course you wouldn't. I just wanted to make sure.' She patted his shoulder and her fingers flashed to his lapel; she picked off a tiny crumb of pink sugar. 'Oh, Master Philip,' she said, 'that's why you haven't any appetite. You've been buying sweet cakes. That's not what your pocket money's for.'

'But I didn't,' Philip said, 'I didn't.'

She tasted the sugar with the tip of her tongue.

'Don't tell lies to me, Master Philip. I won't stand for it any more than your father would.'

'I didn't, I didn't,' Philip said. 'They gave it me. I mean Baines,' but she had pounced on the word 'they'. She had got what she wanted; there was no doubt about that, even when you didn't know what it was she wanted. Philip was angry and miserable and disappointed because he hadn't kept Baines's secret. Baines oughtn't to have trusted him; grown-up people should keep their own secrets, and yet here was Mrs Baines immediately entrusting him with another.

'Let me tickle your palm and see if you can keep a secret.' But he put his hand behind him; he wouldn't be touched. 'It's a secret between us, Master Philip, that I know all about them. I suppose she was having tea with him,' she speculated.

'Why shouldn't she?' he asked, the responsibility for Baines weighing on his spirit, the idea that he had got to keep her secret when he hadn't kept Baines's making him miserable with the unfairness of life. 'She was nice.'

'She was nice, was she?' Mrs Baines said in a bitter voice he wasn't used to.

'And she's his niece.'

'So that's what he said,' Mrs Baines struck softly back at him like the clock under the duster. She tried to be jocular. 'The old scoundrel. Don't you tell him I know, Master Philip.' She stood very still between the table and the door, thinking very hard, planning something. 'Promise you won't tell. I'll give you that Meccano set, Master Philip . . .'

He turned his back on her; he wouldn't promise, but he wouldn't tell. He would have nothing to do with their secrets, the responsibilities they were determined to lay on him. He was only anxious to forget. He had received already a larger dose of life than he had bargained for, and he was scared. 'A 2A Meccano set, Master Philip.' He never opened his Meccano set again, never built anything, never created anything, died the old dilettante, sixty years later with nothing to show rather than preserve the memory of Mrs Baines's malicious voice saying good night, her soft determined footfalls on the stairs to the basement, going down, going down.

3

The sun poured in between the curtains and Baines was beating a tattoo on the water-can. 'Glory, glory,' Baines said. He sat down on the end of the bed and said, 'I beg to announce that Mrs Baines has been called away. Her mother's dying. She won't be back till tomorrow.'

'Why did you wake me up so early?' Philip complained. He watched Baines with uneasiness; he wasn't going to be drawn in; he'd learnt his lesson. It wasn't right for a man of Baines's age to be so merry. It made a grown person human in the same way that you were human. For if a grown-up could behave so childishly, you were liable to find yourself in their world. It was enough that it came at you in dreams: the witch at the corner, the man with a knife. So 'It's very early,' he whined, even though he loved Baines, even though he couldn't help being glad that Baines was happy. He was divided by the fear and the attraction of life.

'I want to make this a long day,' Baines said. 'This is the best time.' He pulled the curtains back. 'It's a bit misty. The cat's been out all night. There she is, sniffing round the area. They haven't taken in any milk at 59. Emma's shaking out the mats at 63.' He said, 'This was what I used to think about on the Coast: somebody shaking mats and the cat coming home. I can see it today,' Baines said, 'just as if I was still in Africa. Most days you don't notice what you've got. It's a good life if you don't weaken.' He put a penny on the washstand. 'When you've dressed, Phil, run and get a *Mail* from the barrow at the corner. I'll be cooking the sausages.'

'Sausages?'

'Sausages,' Baines said. 'We're going to celebrate today.' He celebrated at breakfast, restless, cracking jokes, unaccountably merry and nervous. It was going to be a long, long day, he kept on coming back to that: for years he had waited for a long day, he had sweated in the damp Coast heat, changed shirts, gone down with fever, lain between the blankets and sweated, all in the hope of this long day, that cat sniffing round the area, a bit of mist, the mats beaten at 63. He propped the *Mail* in front of the coffee-pot and read pieces aloud. He said, 'Cora Down's been married for the fourth time.' He was amused, but it wasn't his idea of a long day. His long day was the Park, watching the riders in the Row, seeing Sir Arthur Stillwater pass beyond the rails ('He dined with us once in Bo; up from Freetown; he was governor there'), lunch at the Corner House for Philip's sake (he'd have preferred himself a glass of stout and some oysters at the York bar), the Zoo, the long bus ride home in the last summer light: the leaves in the Green Park were beginning to turn and the motors nuzzled out of Berkeley Street with the low sun gently glowing on their windscreens. Baines envied no one, not Cora Down, or Sir Arthur Stillwater, or Lord Sandale, who came out on to the steps of the Army and Navy and then went back again – he hadn't anything to do and might as well look at another paper. 'I said don't let me see you touch that black again.' Baines had led a man's life; everyone on top of the bus pricked his ears when he told Philip all about it.

'Would you have shot him?' Philip asked, and Baines put his head back and tilted his dark respectable manservant's hat to a better angle as the bus swerved round the Artillery Memorial.

'I wouldn't have thought twice about it. I'd have shot to kill,' he boasted, and the bowed figure went by, the steel helmet, the heavy cloak, the down-turned rifle and the folded hands.

'Have you got the revolver?'

'Of course I've got it,' Baines said. 'Don't I need it with all the burglaries there've been?' This was the Baines whom Philip loved: not Baines singing and carefree, but Baines responsible, Baines behind barriers, living his man's life.

All the buses streamed out from Victoria like a convoy of aeroplanes to bring Baines home with honour. 'Forty blacks under me,' and there waiting near the area steps was the proper reward, love at lighting-up time.

'It's your niece,' Philip said, recognizing the white mack-intosh, but not the happy sleepy face. She frightened him like an unlucky number; he nearly told Baines what Mrs Baines had said; but he didn't want to bother, he wanted to leave things alone.

'Why, so it is,' Baines said. 'I shouldn't wonder if she was going to have a bit of supper with us.' But he said, they'd play a game, pretend they didn't know her, slip down the area steps, 'and here,' Baines said, 'we are,' lay the table, put out the cold sausages, a bottle of beer, a bottle of ginger pop, a flagon of harvest burgundy. 'Everyone his own drink,' Baines said. 'Run upstairs, Phil, and see if there's been a post.'

Philip didn't like the empty house at dusk before the lights went on. He hurried. He wanted to be back with Baines. The hall lay there in quiet and shadow prepared to show him something he didn't want to see. Some letters rustled down and someone knocked. 'Open in the name of the Republic.' The tumbrils rolled, the head bobbed in the bloody basket. Knock, knock, and the postman's footsteps going away. Philip gathered the letters. The slit in the door was like the grating in a jeweller's window. He remembered the policeman he had seen peer through. He had said to his nurse, 'What's he doing?' and when she said, 'He's seeing if everything's all right,' his brain immedi-ately filled with images of all that might be wrong. He ran to the baize door and the stairs. The girl was already there and Baines was kissing her. She leant breathless against the dresser.

'Here's Emmy, Phil.'

'There's a letter for you, Baines.'

'Emmy,' Baines said, 'it's from her.' But he wouldn't open it. 'You bet she's coming back.'

'We'll have supper, anyway,' Emmy said. 'She can't harm that.'

'You don't know her,' Baines said. 'Nothing's safe. Damn it,' he said, 'I was a man once,' and he opened the letter.

'Can I start?' Philip asked, but Baines didn't hear; he pre-sented in his stillness an example of the importance grown-up people attached to the written word: you had to write your thanks, not wait and speak them, as if letters couldn't lie. But Philip knew better than that, sprawling his thanks across a page to Aunt Alice who had given him a teddy bear he was too old for. Letters could lie all right, but they made the lie permanent. They lay as evidence against you: they made you meaner than the spoken word.

'She's not coming back till tomorrow night,' Baines said. He opened the bottles, he pulled up the chairs, he kissed Emmy again against the dresser.

'You oughtn't to,' Emmy said, 'with the boy here.'

'He's got to learn,' Baines said, 'like the rest of us,' and he helped Philip to three sausages. He only took one himself; he said he wasn't hungry, but when Emmy said she wasn't hungry either he stood over her and made her eat. He was timid and rough with her and made her drink the harvest burgundy because he said she needed building up; he wouldn't take no for an answer, but when he touched her his hands were light and clumsy too, as if he was afraid to damage something delicate and didn't know how to handle anything so light.

'This is better than milk and biscuits, eh?'

'Yes,' Philip said, but he was scared, scared for Baines as much as for himself. He couldn't help wondering at every bite, at every draught of the ginger pop, what Mrs Baines would say if she ever learnt of this meal; he couldn't imagine it, there was a depth of bitterness and rage in Mrs Baines you couldn't sound. He said, 'She won't be coming back tonight?' but you could tell by the way they immediately understood him that she wasn't really away at all; she was there in the basement with them, driving them to longer drinks and louder talk, biding her time for the right cutting word. Baines wasn't really happy; he was only watching happiness from close to instead of from far away.

'No,' he said, 'she'll not be back till late tomorrow.' He couldn't keep his eyes off happiness. He'd played around as much as other men; he kept on reverting to the Coast as if to excuse himself for his innocence. He wouldn't have been so innocent if he'd lived his life in London, so innocent when it came to tenderness. 'If it was you, Emmy,' he said, looking at the white dresser, the scrubbed chairs, 'this'd be like a home.' Already the room was not quite so harsh; there was a little dust in corners, the silver needed a final polish, the morning's paper lay untidily on a chair. 'You'd better go to bed, Phil; it's been a long day.'

They didn't leave him to find his own way up through the dark shrouded house; they went with him, turning on lights, touching each other's fingers on the switches. Floor after floor they drove the night back. They spoke softly among the covered chairs. They watched him undress, they didn't make him wash or clean his teeth, they saw him into bed and lit his night-light and left his door ajar. He could hear their voices on the stairs, friendly like the guests he heard at dinner-parties when they moved down the hall, saying good night. They belonged; wherever they were they made a home. He heard a door open and a clock strike, he heard their voices for a long while, so that he felt they were not far away and he was safe. The voices didn't dwindle, they simply went out, and he could be sure that they were still somewhere not far from him, silent together in one of the many empty rooms, growing sleepy together as he grew sleepy after the long day.

He just had time to sigh faintly with satisfaction, because this too perhaps had been life, before he slept and the inevitable terrors of sleep came round him: a man with a tricolour hat beat at the door on His Majesty's service, a bleeding head lay on the kitchen table in a basket, and the Siberian wolves crept closer. He was bound hand and foot and couldn't move; they leapt round him breathing heavily; he opened his eyes and Mrs Baines was there, her grey untidy hair in threads over his face, her black hat askew. A loose hairpin fell on the pillow and one musty thread brushed his mouth. 'Where are they?' she whispered. 'Where are they?'

4

Philip watched her in terror. Mrs Baines was out of breath as if she had been searching all the empty rooms, looking under loose covers.

With her untidy grey hair and her black dress buttoned to her throat, her gloves of black cotton, she was so like the witches of his dreams that he didn't dare to speak. There was a stale smell in her breath.

'She's here,' Mrs Baines said, 'you can't deny she's here.' Her face was simultaneously marked with cruelty and misery; she wanted to 'do things' to people, but she suffered all the time. It would have done her good to scream, but she daren't do that: it would warn them. She came ingratiatingly back to the bed where Philip lay rigid on his back and whispered, 'I haven't forgotten the Meccano set. You shall have it tomorrow, Master Philip. We've got secrets together, haven't we? Just tell me where they are.'

He couldn't speak. Fear held him as firmly as any nightmare. She said, 'Tell Mrs Baines, Master Philip. You love your Mrs Baines, don't you?' That was too much; he couldn't speak, but he could move his mouth in terrified denial, wince away from her dusty image.

She whispered, coming closer to him, 'Such deceit. I'll tell your father. I'll settle with you myself when I've found them. You'll smart; I'll see you smart.' Then immediately she was still listening. A board had creaked on the floor below, and a moment later, while she stooped listening above his bed, there came the whispers of two people who were happy and sleepy together after a long day. The night-light stood beside the mirror and Mrs Baines could see there her own reflection, misery and cruelty wavering in the glass, age and dust and nothing to hope for. She sobbed without tears, a dry, breathless sound, but her cruelty was a kind of pride which kept her going; it was her best quality, she would have been merely pitiable without it. She went out of the door on tiptoe, feeling her way across the landing, going so softly down the stairs that no one behind a shut door could hear her. Then there was complete silence again; Philip could move; he raised his knees; he sat up in bed; he wanted to die. It wasn't fair, the walls were down again between his world and theirs, but this time it was something worse than merriment that the grown people made him share; a passion moved in the house he recognized but could not understand.

It wasn't fair, but he owed Baines everything: the Zoo, the ginger pop, the bus ride home. Even the supper called to his loyalty. But he was frightened; he was touching something he touched in dreams; the bleeding head, the wolves, the knock, knock, knock. Life fell on him with savagery, and you couldn't blame him if he never faced it again in sixty years. He got out of bed. Carefully from habit he put on his bedroom slippers and tiptoed to the door: it wasn't quite dark on the landing below because the curtains had been taken down for the cleaners and the light from the street washed in through the tall windows. Mrs Baines had her hand on the glass door-knob; she was very carefully turning it; he screamed: 'Baines, Baines.'

Mrs Baines turned and saw him cowering in his pyjamas by the banisters; he was helpless, more helpless even than Baines, and cruelty grew at the sight of him and drove her up the stairs. The nightmare was on him again and he couldn't move; he hadn't any more courage left, he couldn't even scream.

But the first cry brought Baines out of the best spare bedroom and he moved quicker than Mrs Baines. She hadn't reached the top of the stairs before he'd caught her round the waist. She drove her black cotton gloves at his face and he bit her hand. He hadn't time to think, he fought her like a stranger, but she fought back with knowledgeable hate. She was going to teach them all and it didn't really matter whom she began with; they had all deceived her; but the old image in the glass was by her side, telling her she must be dignified, she wasn't young enough to yield her dignity; she could beat his face, but she mustn't bite; she could push, but she mustn't kick.

Age and dust and nothing to hope for were her handicaps. She went over the banisters in a flurry of black clothes and fell into the hall; she lay before the front door like a sack of coals which should have gone down the area into the basement. Philip saw; Emmy saw; she sat down suddenly in the doorway of the best spare bedroom with her eyes open as if she were too tired to stand any longer. Baines went slowly down into the hall.

It wasn't hard for Philip to escape; they'd forgotten him completely. He went down the back, the servants' stairs, because Mrs Baines was in the hall. He didn't understand what she was doing lying there; like the pictures in a book no one had read to him, the things he didn't understand terrified him. The whole house had been turned over to the grown-up world; he wasn't safe in the night nursery; their passions had flooded in. The only thing he could do was to get away, by the back stairs, and up through the area, and never come back. He didn't think of the cold, of the need for food and sleep; for an hour it would seem quite possible to escape from people for ever.

He was wearing pyjamas and bedroom slippers when he came up into the square, but there was no one to see him. It was that hour of the evening in a residential district when everyone is at the theatre or at home. He climbed over the iron railings into the little garden: the plane-trees spread their large pale palms between him and the sky. It might have been an illimitable forest into which he had escaped. He crouched behind a trunk and the wolves retreated; it seemed to him between the little iron seat and the tree-trunk that no one would ever find him again. A kind of embittered happiness and self-pity made him cry; he was lost; there wouldn't be any more secrets to keep; he surrendered responsibility once and for all. Let grown-up people keep to their world and he would keep to his, safe in the small garden between the plane-trees.

Presently the door of 48 opened and Baines looked this way and that; then he signalled with his hand and Emmy came; it was as if they were only just in time for a train, they hadn't a chance of saying good-bye. She went quickly by like a face at a window swept past the platform, pale and unhappy and not wanting to go. Baines went in again and shut the door; the light was lit in the basement, and a policeman walked round the square, looking into the areas. You could tell how many families were at home by the lights behind the first-floor curtains.

Philip explored the garden: it didn't take long: a twenty-yard square of bushes and plane-trees, two iron seats and a gravel path, a padlocked gate at either end, a scuffle of old leaves. But he couldn't stay: something stirred in the bushes and two illuminated eyes peered out at him like a Serbian wolf, and he thought how terrible it would be if Mrs Baines found him there. He'd have no time to climb the railings; she'd seize him from behind.

He left the square at the unfashionable end and was immediately among the fish-and-chip shops, the little stationers selling *Bagatelle*, among the accommodation addresses and the dingy hotels with open doors. There were few people about because the pubs were open, but a blowsy woman carrying a parcel called out to him across the street and the commissionaire outside a cinema would have stopped him if he hadn't crossed the road. He went deeper: you could go farther and lose yourself more completely here than among the plane-trees. On the fringe of the square he was in danger of being stopped and taken back: it was obvious where he belonged; but as he went deeper he lost the marks of his origin. It was a warm night: any child in those free-living parts might be expected to play truant from bed. He found a kind of camaraderie even among grown-up people; he might have been a neighbour's child as he went quickly by, but they weren't going to tell on him, they'd been young once themselves. He picked up a protective coating of dust from the pavements, of smuts from the trains which passed along the backs in a spray of fire. Once he was caught in a knot of children running away from something or somebody, laughing as they ran; he was whirled with them round a turning and abandoned, with a sticky fruit-drop in his hand.

He couldn't have been more lost, but he hadn't the stamina to keep on. At first he feared that someone would stop him; after an hour he hoped that someone would. He couldn't find his way back, and in any case he was afraid of arriving home alone; he was afraid of Mrs Baines, more afraid than he had ever been.

Baines was his friend, but something had happened which gave
Mrs Baines all the power. He began to loiter on purpose to be
noticed, but no one noticed him. Families were having a last
breather on the doorsteps, the refuse bins had been put out
and bits of cabbage stalks soiled his slippers. The air was full
of voices, but he was cut off; these people were strangers
and would always now be strangers; they were marked by
Mrs Baines and he shied away from them into a deep class-
consciousness. He had been afraid of policemen, but now he
wanted one to take him home; even Mrs Baines could do
nothing against a policeman. He sidled past a constable who
was directing traffic, but he was too busy to pay him any attention. Philip sat down against a wall and cried.

It hadn't occurred to him that that was the easiest way, that
all you had to do was to surrender, to show you were beaten
and accept kindness ... It was lavished on him at once by two
women and a pawnbroker. Another policeman appeared, a
young man with a sharp incredulous face. He looked as if he
noted everything he saw in pocket-books and drew conclusions.
A woman offered to see Philip home, but he didn't trust her: she
wasn't a match for Mrs Baines immobile in the hall. He
wouldn't give his address; he said he was afraid to go home. He
had his way; he got his protection. 'I'll take him to the station,'
the policeman said, and holding him awkwardly by the hand (he
wasn't married; he had his career to make) he led him round the
corner, up the stone stairs into the little bare over-heated room
where Justice lived.

5

Justice waited behind a wooden counter on a high stool; it wore
a heavy moustache; it was kindly and had six children ('three of
them nippers like yourself'); it wasn't really interested in Philip,
but it pretended to be, it wrote the address down and sent a
constable to fetch a glass of milk. But the young constable was
interested; he had a nose for things.

'Your home's on the telephone, I suppose,' Justice said. 'We'll ring them up and say you are safe. They'll fetch you very soon. What's your name, sonny?'

'Philip.'

'Your other name?'

'I haven't got another name.' He didn't want to be fetched; he wanted to be taken home by someone who would impress even Mrs Baines. The constable watched him, watched the way he drank the milk, watched him when he winced away from questions.

'What made you run away? Playing truant, eh?'

'I don't know.'

'You oughtn't to do it, young fellow. Think how anxious your father and mother will be.'

'They are away.'

'Well, your nurse.'

'I haven't got one.'

'Who looks after you, then?' The question went home. Philip saw Mrs Baines coming up the stairs at him, the heap of black cotton in the hall. He began to cry.

'Now, now, now,' the sergeant said. He didn't know what to do; he wished his wife were with him; even a policewoman might have been useful.

'Don't you think it's funny,' the constable said, 'that there hasn't been an inquiry?'

'They think he's tucked up in bed.'

'You are scared, aren't you?' the constable said. 'What scared you?'

'I don't know.'

'Somebody hurt you?'

'No.'

'He's had bad dreams,' the sergeant said. 'Thought the house was on fire, I expect. I've brought up six of them. Rose is due back. She'll take him home.'

'I want to go home with you,' Philip said; he tried to smile at the constable, but the deceit was immature and unsuccessful.

'I'd better go,' the constable said. 'There may be something wrong.'

'Nonsense,' the sergeant said. 'It's a woman's job. Tact is what you need. Here's Rose. Pull up your stockings, Rose. You're a disgrace to the Force. I've got a job of work for you.' Rose shambled in: black cotton stockings drooping over her boots, a gawky Girl Guide manner, a hoarse hostile voice. 'More tarts, I suppose.'

'No, you've got to see this young man home.' She looked at him owlishly.

'I won't go with her,' Philip said. He began to cry again. 'I don't like her.'

'More of that womanly charm, Rose,' the sergeant said. The telephone rang on his desk. He lifted the receiver. 'What? What's that?' he said. 'Number 48? You've got a doctor?' He put his hand over the telephone mouth. 'No wonder this nipper wasn't reported,' he said. 'They've been too busy. An accident. Woman slipped on the stairs.'

'Serious?' the constable asked. The sergeant mouthed at him; you didn't mention the word death before a child (didn't he know? he had six of them), you made noises in the throat, you grimaced, a complicated shorthand for a word of only five letters anyway.

'You'd better go, after all,' he said, 'and make a report. The doctor's there.'

Rose shambled from the stove; pink apply-dapply cheeks, loose stockings. She stuck her hands behind her. Her large morgue-like mouth was full of blackened teeth. 'You told me to take him and now just because something interesting . . . I don't expect justice from a man . . .'

'Who's at the house?' the constable asked.

'The butler.'

'You don't think,' the constable said, 'he saw . . .'

'Trust me,' the sergeant said. 'I've brought up six. I know 'em through and through. You can't teach me anything about children.'

'He seemed scared about something.'

'Dreams,' the sergeant said.

'What name?'

'Baines.'

'This Mr Baines,' the constable said to Philip, 'you like him, eh? He's good to you?' They were trying to get something out of him; he was suspicious of the whole roomful of them; he said 'yes' without conviction because he was afraid at any moment of more responsibilities, more secrets.

'And Mrs Baines?'

'Yes.'

They consulted together by the desk. Rose was hoarsely aggrieved; she was like a female impersonator, she bore her womanhood with an unnatural emphasis even while she scorned it in her creased stockings and her weather-exposed face. The charcoal shifted in the stove; the room was over-heated in the mild late summer evening. A notice on the wall described a body found in the Thames, or rather the body's clothes: wool vest, wool pants, wool shirt with blue stripes, size ten boots, blue serge suit worn at the elbows, fifteen and a half celluloid collar. They couldn't find anything to say about the body, except its measurements, it was just an ordinary body.

'Come along,' the constable said. He was interested, he was glad to be going, but he couldn't help being embarrassed by his company, a small boy in pyjamas. His nose smelt something, he didn't know what, but he smarted at the sight of the amusement they caused: the pubs had closed and the streets were full again of men making as long a day of it as they could. He hurried through the less frequented streets, chose the darker pavements, wouldn't loiter, and Philip wanted more and more to loiter, pulling at his hand, dragging with his feet. He dreaded the sight of Mrs Baines waiting in the hall: he knew now that she was dead. The sergeant's mouthing had conveyed that; but she wasn't buried, she wasn't out of sight; he was going to see a dead person in the hall when the door opened.

The light was on in the basement, and to his relief the constable made for the area steps. Perhaps he wouldn't have to see Mrs Baines at all. The constable knocked on the door because it was too dark to see the bell, and Baines answered. He stood there in the doorway of the neat bright basement room and you could see the sad complacent plausible sentence he had prepared wither at the sight of Philip; he hadn't expected Philip to return like that in the policeman's company. He had to begin thinking all over again; he wasn't a deceptive man. If it hadn't been for Emmy he would have been quite ready to let the truth lead him where it would.

'Mr Baines?' the constable asked.

He nodded; he hadn't found the right words; he was daunted by the shrewd knowing face, the sudden appearance of Philip there.

'This little boy from here?'

'Yes,' Baines said. Philip could tell that there was a message he was trying to convey, but he shut his mind to it. He loved Baines, but Baines had involved him in secrets, in fears he didn't understand. That was what happened when you loved – you got involved; and Philip extricated himself from life, from love, from Baines.

'The doctor's here,' Baines said. He nodded at the door, moistened his mouth, kept his eyes on Philip, begging for something like a dog you can't understand, 'There's nothing to be done. She slipped on these stone basement stairs. I was in here. I heard her fall.' He wouldn't look at the notebook, at the constable's spidery writing which got a terrible lot on one page.

'Did the boy see anything?'

'He can't have done. I thought he was in bed. Hadn't he better go up? It's a shocking thing. O,' Baines said, losing control, 'it's a shocking thing for a child.'

'She's through there?' the constable asked.

'I haven't moved her an inch,' Baines said.

'He'd better then – '

'Go up the area and through the hall,' Baines said, and again he begged dumbly like a dog: one more secret, keep this secret, do this for old Baines, he won't ask another.

'Come along,' the constable said. 'I'll see you up to bed. You're a gentleman. You must come in the proper way through the front door like the master should. Or will you go along with him, Mr Baines, while I see the doctor?'

'Yes,' Baines said, 'I'll go.' He came across the room to Philip, begging, begging, all the way with his old soft stupid expression: this is Baines, the old Coaster; what about a palm-oil chop, eh?; a man's life; forty niggers; never used a gun; I tell you I couldn't help loving them; it wasn't what we call love, nothing we could understand. The messages flickered out from the last posts at the border, imploring, beseeching, reminding: this is your old friend Baines; what about an elevenses; a glass of ginger pop won't do you any harm; sausages; a long day. But the wires were cut, the messages just faded out into the vacancy of the scrubbed room in which there had never been a place where a man could hide his secrets.

'Come along, Phil, it's bedtime. We'll just go up the steps ...' Tap, tap, tap, at the telegraph; you may get through, you can't tell, somebody may mend the right wire. 'And in at the front door.'

'No,' Philip said, 'no. I won't go. You can't make me go. I'll fight. I won't see her.'

The constable turned on them quickly. 'What's that? Why won't you go?'

'She's in the hall,' Philip said. 'I know she's in the hall. And she's dead. I won't see her.'

'You moved her then?' the constable said to Baines. 'All the way down here? You've been lying, eh?' That means you had to tidy up ... Were you alone?'

'Emmy,' Philip said, 'Emmy.' He wasn't going to keep any more secrets: he was going to finish once and for all with everything, with Baines and Mrs Baines and the grown-up life beyond him. 'It was all Emmy's fault,' he protested with a quaver which reminded Baines that after all he was only a child; it had been hopeless to expect help there; he was a child; he didn't understand what it all meant; he couldn't read this short-hand of terror; he'd had a long day and he was tired out. You could see him dropping asleep where he stood against the dresser, dropping back into the comfortable nursery peace. You couldn't blame him. When he woke in the morning, he'd hardly remember a thing.

'Out with it,' the constable said, addressing Baines with professional ferocity, 'who is she?' just as the old man sixty years later startled his secretary, his only watcher, asking, 'Who is she? Who is she?' dropping lower and lower to death, passing on the way perhaps the image of Baines: Baines hopeless, Baines letting his head drop, Baines 'coming clean'.

1936

A CHANCE FOR MR LEVER

MR LEVER knocked his head against the ceiling and
swore. Rice was stored above, and in the dark the rats began to
move. Grains of rice fell between the slats on to his Revelation
suitcase, his bald head, his cases of tinned food, the little square
box in which he kept his medicines. His boy had already set up
the camp-bed and mosquito-net, and outside in the warm damp
dark his folding table and chair. The thatched pointed huts
streamed away towards the forest and a woman went from hut
to hut carrying fire. The glow lit her old face, her sagging
breasts, her tattooed diseased body.

It was incredible to Mr Lever that five weeks ago he had been
in London.

He couldn't stand upright; he went down on hands and knees
in the dust and opened his suitcase. He took out his wife's
photograph and stood it on the chop-box; he took out a writing-
pad and an indelible pencil: the pencil had softened in the heat
and left mauve stains on his pyjamas. Then, because the light of
the hurricane lamp disclosed cockroaches the size of black-
beetles flattened against the mud wall, he carefully closed the
suitcase. Already in ten days he had learnt that they'd eat anything – socks, shirts, the laces out of your shoes.

Mr Lever went outside; moths beat against his lamp, but
there were no mosquitoes; he hadn't seen or heard one since he
landed. He sat in a circle of light carefully observed. The blacks
squatted outside their huts and watched him; they were
friendly, interested, amused, but their strict attention irritated
Mr Lever. He could feel the small waves of interest washing
round him, when he began to write, when he stopped writing,
when he wiped his damp hands with a handkerchief. He
couldn't touch his pocket without a craning of necks.

Dearest Emily, he wrote, *I've really started now. I'll send this
letter back with a carrier when I've located Davidson. I'm very*

well. Of course everything's a bit strange. Look after yourself, my dear, and don't worry.

'Massa buy chicken,' his cook said, appearing suddenly between the huts. A small stringy fowl struggled in his hands.

'Well,' Mr Lever said, 'I gave you a shilling, didn't I?'

'They no like,' the cook said. 'These low bush people.'

'Why don't they like? It's good money.'

'They want king's money,' the cook said, handing back the Victorian shilling. Mr Lever had to get up, go back into his hut, grope for his money-box, search through twenty pounds of small change: there was no peace.

He had learnt that very quickly. He had to economize (the whole trip was a gamble which scared him); he couldn't afford hammock carriers. He would arrive tired out after seven hours of walking at a village of which he didn't know the name and not for a minute could he sit quietly and rest. He must shake hands with the chief, he must see about a hut, accept presents of palm wine he was afraid to drink, buy rice and palm oil for the carriers, give them salts and aspirin, paint their sores with iodine. They never left him alone for five minutes on end until he went to bed. And then the rats began, rushing down the walls like water when he put out the light, gambolling among his cases.

I'm too old, Mr Lever told himself, I'm too old, writing damply, indelibly, *I hope to find Davidson tomorrow. If I do, I may be back almost as soon as this letter. Don't economize on the stout and milk, dear, and call in the doctor if you feel bad. I've got a premonition this trip's going to turn out well. We'll take a holiday, you need a holiday,* and staring ahead past the huts and the black faces and the banana trees towards the forest from which he had come, into which he would sink again next day, he thought, Eastbourne, Eastbourne would do her a world of good; and he continued to write the only kind of lies he had ever told Emily, the lies which comforted. *I ought to draw at least three hundred in commission and expenses.* But it wasn't the sort of place where he'd been accustomed to sell heavy machinery; thirty years of it, up and down Europe and in the States, but never anything like this. He could hear his filter dripping in the hut, and somewhere somebody was playing something (he was so lost he hadn't got the simplest terms to his hands), something monotonous, melancholy, superficial, a twanging of palm fibres which seemed to convey that you weren't happy, but it didn't matter, everything would always be the same.

Look after yourself, Emily, he repeated. It was almost the only thing he found himself capable of writing to her; he couldn't describe the narrow, steep, lost paths, the snakes sizzling away like flames, the rats, the dust, the naked diseased bodies. He was unbearably tired of nakedness. *Don't forget* – It was like living with a lot of cows.

'The chief,' his boy whispered, and between the huts under a waving torch came an old stout man wearing a robe of native cloth and a battered bowler hat. Behind him his men carried six bowls of rice, a bowl of palm oil, two bowls of broken meat. 'Chop for the labourers,' the boy explained, and Mr Lever had to get up and smile and nod and try to convey without words that he was pleased, that the chop was excellent, that the chief would get a good dash in the morning. At first the smell had been almost too much for Mr Lever.

'Ask him,' he said to his boy, 'if he's seen a white man come through here lately. Ask him if a white man's been digging around here. Damn it,' Mr Lever burst out, the sweat breaking on the backs of his hands and on his bald head, 'ask him if he's seen Davidson?'

'Davidson?'

'Oh, hell,' Mr Lever said, 'you know what I mean. The white man I'm looking for.'

'White man?'

'What do you imagine I'm here for, eh? White man? Of course white man. I'm not here for my health.' A cow coughed, rubbed its horns against the hut and two goats broke through between the chief and him, upsetting the bowls of meat scraps; nobody cared, they picked the meat out of the dust and dung.

Mr Lever sat down and put his hands over his face, fat white well-cared-for hands with wrinkles of flesh over the rings. He felt too old for this.

'Chief say no white man been here long time.'

'How long?'

'Chief say not since he pay hut tax.'

'How long's that?'

'Long long time.'

'Ask him how far is it to Greh, tomorrow.'

'Chief say too far.'

'Nonsense,' Mr Lever said.

'Chief say too far. Better stay here. Fine town. No humbug.'

Mr Lever groaned. Every evening there was the same trouble. The next town was always too far. They would invent any excuse to delay him, to give themselves a rest.

'Ask the chief how many hours – ?'

'Plenty, plenty.' They had no idea of time.

'This fine chief. Fine chop. Labourers tired. No humbug.'

'We are going on,' Mr Lever said.

'This fine town. Chief say – '

He thought: if this wasn't the last chance, I'd give up. They nagged him so, and suddenly he longed for another white man (not Davidson, he daren't say anything to Davidson) to whom he could explain the desperation of his lot. It wasn't fair that a man, after thirty years' commercial travelling, should need to go from door to door asking for a job. He had been a good traveller, he had made money for many people, his references were excellent, but the world had moved on since his day. He wasn't streamlined; he certainly wasn't streamlined. He had been ten years retired when he lost his money in the depression.

Mr Lever walked up and down Victoria Street showing his references. Many of the men knew him, gave him cigars, laughed at him in a friendly way for wanting to take on a job at his age ('I can't somehow settle at home. The old warhorse you know . . .'), cracked a joke or two in the passage, went back that night to Maidenhead silent in the first-class carriage, shut in with age and ruin and how bad things were and poor devil his wife's probably sick.

A CHANCE FOR MR LEVER

It was in the rather shabby little office off Leadenhall Street that Mr Lever met his chance. It called itself an engineering firm, but there were only two rooms, a typewriter, a girl with gold teeth and Mr Lucas, a thin narrow man with a tic in one eyelid. All through the interview the eyelid flickered at Mr Lever. Mr Lever had never before fallen so low as this.

But Mr Lucas struck him as reasonably honest. He put 'all his cards on the table'. He hadn't got any money, but he had expectations; he had the handling of a patent. It was a new crusher. There was money in it. But you couldn't expect the big trusts to change over their machinery now. Things were too bad. You'd got to get in at the start, and that was where – why, that was where this chief, the bowls of chop, the nagging and the rats and the heat came in. They called themselves a republic, Mr Lucas said, he didn't know anything about that, they were not as black as they were painted, he supposed (ha, ha, nervously, ha, ha); anyway, this company had slipped agents over the border and grabbed a concession: gold and diamonds. He could tell Mr Lever in confidence that the trust was frightened of what they'd found. Now an enterprising man could just slip across (Mr Lucas liked the word slip, it made everything sound easy and secret) and introduce this new crusher to them: it would save them thousands when they started work, there'd be a fat commission, and afterwards, with that start ... There was a fortune for them all.

'But can't you fix it up in Europe?'

Tic, tic, went Mr Lucas's eyelid. 'A lot of Belgians; they are leaving all decisions to the man on the spot. An Englishman called Davidson.'

'How about expenses?'

'That's the trouble,' Mr Lucas said. 'We are only beginning. What we want is a partner. We can't afford to send a man. But if you like a gamble ... Twenty per cent commission.'

'Chief say excuse him.' The carriers squatted round the basins and scooped up the rice in their left hands. 'Of course. Of course,' Mr Lever said absent-mindedly. 'Very kind, I'm sure.'

He was back out of the dust and dark, away from the stink of

146

goats and palm oil and whelping bitches, back among the rotarians and lunch at Stone's, 'the pint of old', and the trade papers; he was a good fellow again, finding his way back to Golders Green just a bit lit; his masonic emblem rattled on his watch-chain, and he bore with him from the tube station to his house in Finchley Road a sense of companionship, of broad stories and belches, a sense of bravery.

He needed all his bravery now; the last of his savings had gone into the trip. After thirty years he knew a good thing when he saw it, and he had no doubts about the new crusher. What he doubted was his ability to find Davidson. For one thing there weren't any maps; the way you travelled in the Republic was to write down a list of names and trust that someone in the villages you passed would understand and know the route. But they always said 'Too far'. Good fellowship wilted before the phrase.

'Quinine,' Mr Lever said. 'Where's my quinine?' His boy never remembered a thing; they just didn't care what happened to you; their smiles meant nothing, and Mr Lever, who knew better than anyone the value of a meaningless smile in business, resented their heartlessness, and turned towards the dilatory boy an expression of disappointment and dislike.

'Chief say white man in bush five hours away.'

'That's better,' Mr Lever said. 'It must be Davidson. He's digging for gold?'

'Ya. White man dig for gold in bush.'

'We'll be off early tomorrow,' Mr Lever said.

'Chief say better stop this town. Fever humbug white man.'

'Too bad,' Mr Lever said, and he thought with pleasure: my luck's changed. He'll want help. He won't refuse me a thing. A friend in need is a friend indeed, and his heart warmed towards Davidson, seeing himself arrive like an answer to prayer out of the forest, feeling quite biblical and vox humana. He thought: Prayer. I'll pray tonight, that's the kind of thing a fellow gives up, but it pays, there's something in it, remembering the long agonizing prayer on his knees, by the sideboard, under the decanters, when Emily went to hospital.

'Chief say white man dead.'

Mr Lever turned his back on them and went into his hut. His sleeve nearly overturned the hurricane lamp. He undressed quickly, stuffing his clothes into a suitcase away from the cockroaches. He wouldn't believe what he had been told; it wouldn't pay him to believe. If Davidson were dead, there was nothing he could do but return; he had spent more than he could afford; he would be a ruined man. He supposed that Emily might find a home with her brother, but he could hardly expect her brother – he began to cry, but you couldn't have told in the shadowy hut the difference between sweat and tears. He knelt down beside his camp-bed and mosquito-net and prayed on the dust of the earth floor. Up till now he had always been careful never to touch ground with his naked feet for fear of jiggers; there were jiggers everywhere, they only waited an opportunity to dig themselves in under the toe-nails, lay their eggs and multiply.

'O God,' Mr Lever prayed, 'don't let Davidson be dead; let him be just sick and glad to see me.' He couldn't bear the idea that he might not any longer be able to support Emily. 'O God, there's nothing I wouldn't do.' But that was an empty phrase; he had no real notion as yet of what he would do for Emily. They had been happy together for thirty-five years; he had never been more than momentarily unfaithful to her when he was lit after a rotarian dinner and egged on by the boys; whatever skirt he'd been with in his time, he had never for a moment imagined that he could be happy married to anyone else. It wasn't fair if, just when you were old and needed each other most, you lost your money and couldn't keep together.

But of course Davidson wasn't dead. What would he have died of? The blacks were friendly. People said the country was unhealthy, but he hadn't so much as heard a mosquito. Besides, you didn't die of malaria; you just lay between the blankets and took quinine and felt like death and sweated it out of you. There was dysentery, but Davidson was an old campaigner; you were safe if you boiled and filtered the water. The water was poison even to touch; it was unsafe to wet your feet because of guinea worm, but you didn't die of guinea worm.

Mr Lever lay in bed and his thoughts went round and round and he couldn't sleep. He thought: you don't die of a thing like guinea worm. It makes a sore on your foot, and if you put your foot in water you can see the eggs dropping out. You have to find the end of the worm, like a thread of cotton, and wind it round a match and wind it out of your leg without breaking; it stretches as high as the knee. I'm too old for this country, Mr Lever thought.

Then his boy was beside him again. He whispered urgently to Mr Lever through the mosquito-net. 'Massa, the labourers say they go home.'

'Go home?' Mr Lever asked wearily; he had heard it so often before. 'Why do they want to go home? What is it now?' but he didn't really want to hear the latest squabble: that the Bande men were never sent to carry water because the headman was a Bande, that someone had stolen an empty treacle tin and sold it in the village for a penny, that someone wasn't made to carry a proper load, that the next day's journey was 'too far'. He said, 'Tell 'em they can go home. I'll pay them off in the morning. But they won't get any dash. They'd have got a good dash if they'd stayed.' He was certain it was just another try-on; he wasn't as green as all that.

'Yes, massa. They no want dash.'

'What's that?'

'They frightened fever humbug them like white man.'

'I'll get carriers in the village. They can go home.'

'Me too, massa.'

'Get out,' Mr Lever said; it was the last straw; 'get out and let me sleep.' The boy went at once, obedient even though a deserter, and Mr Lever thought: sleep, what a hope. He lifted the net and got out of bed (bare-footed again: he didn't care a damn about the jiggers) and searched for his medicine box. It was locked, of course, and he had to open his suitcase and find the key in a trouser pocket. His nerves were more on edge than ever by the time he found the sleeping tablets and he took three of them. That made him sleep, heavily and dreamlessly, though when he woke he found that something had made him fling out his arms and open the net. If there had been a single mosquito in the place, he'd have been bitten, but of course there wasn't one.

He could tell at once that the trouble hadn't blown over. The village – he didn't know its name – was perched on a hill-top; east and west the forest flowed out beneath the little plateau; to the west it was a dark unfeatured mass like water, but in the east you could already discern the unevenness, the great grey cotton trees lifted above the palms. Mr Lever was always called before dawn, but no one had called him. A few of his carriers sat outside a hut sullenly talking; his boy was with them. Mr Lever went back inside and dressed; he thought all the time, I must be firm, but he was scared, scared of being deserted, scared of being made to return.

When he came outside again the village was awake: the women were going down the hill to fetch water, winding silently past the carriers, past the flat stones where the chiefs were buried, the little grove of trees where the rice birds, like green and yellow canaries, nested. Mr Lever sat down on his folding chair among the chickens and whelping bitches and cow dung and called his boy. He took 'a strong line'; but he didn't know what was going to happen. 'Tell the chief I want to speak to him,' he said.

There was some delay; the chief wasn't up yet, but presently he appeared in his blue and white robe, setting his bowler hat straight. 'Tell him,' Mr Lever said, 'I want carriers to take me to the white man and back. Two days.'

'Chief no agree,' the boy said.

Mr Lever said furiously, 'Damn it, if he doesn't agree, he won't get any dash from me, not a penny.' It occurred to him immediately afterwards how hopelessly dependent he was on these people's honesty. There in the hut for all to see was his money-box; they had only to take it. This wasn't a British or French colony; the blacks on the coast wouldn't bother, could do nothing if they did bother, because a stray Englishman had been robbed in the interior.

'Chief say how many?'

'It's only for two days,' Mr Lever said. 'I can do with six.'

'Chief say how much?'

'Sixpence a day and chop.'

'Chief no agree.'

'Ninepence a day then.'

'Chief say too far. A shilling.'

'All right, all right,' Mr Lever said, 'A shilling then. You others can go home if you want to. I'll pay you off now, but you won't get any dash, not a penny.'

He had never really expected to be left, and it gave him a sad feeling of loneliness to watch them move sullenly away (they were ashamed of themselves) down the hill to the west. They hadn't any loads, but they weren't singing; they drooped silently out of sight, his boy with them, and he was alone with his pile of boxes and the chief who couldn't talk a word of English. Mr Lever smiled tremulously.

It was ten o'clock before his new carriers were chosen; he could tell that none of them wanted to go, and they would have to walk through the heat of the middle day if they were to find Davidson before it was dark. He hoped the chief had explained properly where they were going; he couldn't tell; he was completely shut off from them, and when they started down the eastward slope, he might just as well have been alone.

They were immediately caught up in the forest. Forest conveys a sense of wildness and beauty, of an active natural force, but this Liberian forest was simply a dull green wilderness. You passed, on the path a foot or so wide, through an endless back garden of tangled weeds; it didn't seem to be growing round you, so much as dying. There was no life at all, except for a few large birds whose wings creaked overhead through the invisible sky like an unoiled door. There was no view, no way out for the eyes, no change of scene. It wasn't the heat that tired, so much as the boredom; you had to think of things to think about; but even Emily failed to fill the mind for more than three minutes at a time. It was a relief, a distraction, when the path was flooded and Mr Lever had to be carried on a man's back. At first he had disliked the strong bitter smell (it reminded him of a breakfast food he was made to eat as a child), but he soon got over that. Now he was unaware that they smelt at all; any more than he was aware that the great swallow-tailed butterflies, which clustered at the water's edge and rose in green clouds round his waist, were beautiful. His senses were dulled and registered very little except his boredom.

But they did register a distinct feeling of relief when his leading carrier pointed to a rectangular hole dug just off the path. Mr Lever understood. Davidson had come this way. He stopped and looked at it. It was like a grave dug for a small man, but it went down deeper than graves usually do. About twelve feet below there was black water, and a few wooden props which held the sides from slipping were beginning to rot; the hole must have been dug since the rains. It didn't seem enough, that hole, to have brought out Mr Lever with his plans and estimates for a new crusher. He was used to big industrial concerns, the sight of pitheads, the smoke of chimneys, the dingy rows of cottages back to back, the leather armchair in the office, the good cigar, the masonic hand-grips, and again it seemed to him, as it had seemed in Mr Lucas's office, that he had fallen very low. It was as if he was expected to do business beside a hole a child had dug in an overgrown and abandoned back garden; percentages wilted in the hot damp air. He shook his head; he mustn't be discouraged; this was an old hole. Davidson had probably done better since. It was only common sense to suppose that the gold rift which was mined at one end in Nigeria, at the other in Sierra Leone, would pass through the republic. Even the biggest mines had to begin with a hole in the ground. The company (he had talked to the directors in Brussels) were quite confident: all they wanted was the approval of the man on the spot that the crusher was suitable for local conditions. A signature, that was all he had to get, he told himself, staring down into the puddle of black water.

Five hours, the chief had said, but after six hours they were still walking. Mr Lever had eaten nothing; he wanted to get to Davidson first. All through the heat of the day he walked. The forest protected him from the direct sun, but it shut out the air, and the occasional clearings, shrivelled though they were in the vertical glare, seemed cooler than the shade because there was a little more air to breathe. At four o'clock the heat diminished, but he began to fear they wouldn't reach Davidson before dark. His foot pained him; he had caught a jigger the night before; it was as if someone were holding a lighted match to his toe. Then at five they came on a dead black.

Another rectangular hole in a small cleared space among the dusty greenery had caught Mr Lever's eye. He peered down and was shocked to see a face return his stare, white eyeballs like phosphorus in the black water. The black had been bent almost double to fit him in; the hole was really too small to be a grave, and he had swollen. His flesh was like a blister you could prick with a needle. Mr Lever felt sick and tired; he might have been tempted to return if he could have reached the village before dark, but now there was nothing to do but go on; the carriers luckily hadn't seen the body. He waved them forward and stumbled after them among the roots, fighting his nausea. He fanned himself with his sun helmet; his wide fat face was damp and pale. He had never seen an uncared-for body before; his parents he had seen carefully laid out with closed eyes and washed faces; they 'fell asleep' quite in accordance with their epitaphs, but you couldn't think of sleep in connection with the white eyeballs and the swollen face. Mr Lever would have liked very much to say a prayer, but prayers were out of place in the dead drab forest; they simply didn't 'come'.

With the dusk a little life did waken: something lived in the dry weeds and brittle trees, if only monkeys. They chattered and screamed all round you, but it was too dark to see them; you were like a blind man in the centre of a frightened crowd who wouldn't say what scared them. The carriers too were frightened. They ran under their fifty-pound loads behind the dipping light of the hurricane lamp, their huge flat carriers' feet flapping in the dust like empty gloves. Mr Lever listened nervously for mosquitoes; you would have expected them to be out by now, but he didn't hear one.

Then at the top of a rise above a small stream they came on

153

Davidson. The ground had been cleared in a square of twelve feet and a small tent pitched; he had dug another hole; the scene came dimly into view as they climbed the path; the chop-boxes piled outside the tent, the syphon of soda water, the filter, an enamel basin. But there wasn't a light, there wasn't a sound, the flaps of the tent were not closed, and Mr Lever had to face the possibility that after all the chief might have told the truth.

Mr Lever took the lamp and stooped inside the tent. There was a body on the bed. At first Mr Lever thought Davidson was covered with blood, but then he realized it was a black vomit which stained his shirt and khaki shorts, the fair stubble on his chin. He put out a hand and touched Davidson's face, and if he hadn't felt a slight breath on his palm he would have taken him for dead; his skin was so cold. He moved the lamp closer, and now the lemon-yellow face told him all he wanted to know: he hadn't thought of that when his boy said fever. It was quite true that a man didn't die of malaria, but an odd piece of news read in New York in '98 came back to mind: there had been an outbreak of yellow jack in Rio and ninety-four per cent of the cases had been fatal. It hadn't meant anything to him then, but it did now. While he watched, Davidson was sick, quite effortlessly; he was like a tap out of which something flowed.

It seemed at first to Mr Lever to be the end of everything, of his journey, his hopes, his life with Emily. There was nothing he could do for Davidson, the man was unconscious, there were times when his pulse was so low and irregular that Mr Lever thought that he was dead until another black stream spread from his mouth; it was no use even cleaning him. Mr Lever laid his own blankets over the bed on top of Davidson's because he was so cold to the touch, but he had no idea whether he was doing the right, or even the fatally wrong, thing. The chance of survival, if there were any chance at all, depended on neither of them. Outside his carriers had built a fire and were cooking the rice they had brought with them. Mr Lever opened his folding chair and sat by the bed. He wanted to keep awake: it seemed right to keep awake. He opened his case and found his unfinished letter to Emily. He sat by Davidson's side and tried to write, but he could think of nothing but what he had already written too often: *Look after yourself. Don't forget that stout and milk.*

He fell asleep over his pad and woke at two and thought that Davidson was dead. But he was wrong again. He was very thirsty and missed his boy. Always the first thing his boy did at the end of a march was to light a fire and put on a kettle; after that, by the time his table and chair were set up, there was water ready for the filter. Mr Lever found half a cup of soda water left in Davidson's syphon; if it had been only his health at stake he would have gone down to the stream, but he had Emily to remember. There was a typewriter by the bed, and it occurred to Mr Lever that he might just as well begin to write his report of failure now; it might keep him awake; it seemed disrespectful to the dying man to sleep. He found paper under some letters which had been typed and signed but not sealed. Davidson must have been taken ill very suddenly. Mr Lever wondered whether it was he who had crammed the black into the hole; his boy perhaps, for there was no sign of a servant. He balanced the typewriter on his knee and headed the letter 'In Camp near Greh'.

It seemed to him unfair that he should have come so far, spent so much money, worn out a rather old body to meet his inevitable ruin in a dark tent beside a dying man, when he could have met it just as well at home with Emily in the plush parlour. The thought of the prayers he had uselessly uttered on his knees by the camp-bed among the jiggers, the rats and the cockroaches made him rebellious. A mosquito, the first he had heard, went humming round the tent. He slashed at it savagely; he wouldn't have recognized himself among the rotarians. He was lost and he was set free. Moralities were what enabled a man to live happily and successfully with his fellows, but Mr Lever wasn't happy and he wasn't successful, and his only fellow in the little stuffy tent wouldn't be troubled by Untruth in Advertising or by Mr Lever coveting his neighbour's oxen. You couldn't keep your ideas intact when you discovered their geographical nature. The Solemnity of Death: death wasn't solemn; it was a lemon-yellow skin and a black vomit. Honesty is the Best Policy: he saw quite suddenly how false that was. It was an anarchist who sat happily over the typewriter, an anarchist who recognized nothing but one personal relationship, his affection for Emily. Mr Lever began to type: *I have examined the plans and estimates of the new Lucas crusher* . . .

Mr Lever thought with savage happiness: I win. This letter would be the last the company would hear from Davidson. The junior partner would open it in the dapper Brussels office; he would tap his false teeth with a Waterman pen and go in to talk to M. Golz. *Taking all these factors into consideration I recommend acceptance* . . . They would telegraph to Lucas. As for Davidson, that trusted agent of the company would have died of yellow fever at some never accurately determined date. Another agent would come out, and the crusher . . . Mr Lever carefully copied Davidson's signature on a spare sheet of paper. He wasn't satisfied. He turned the original upside-down and copied it that way, so as not to be confused by his own idea of how a letter should be formed. That was better, but it didn't satisfy him. He searched until he found Davidson's own pen and began again to copy and copy the signature. He fell asleep copying it and woke again an hour later to find the lamp was out; it had burnt up all the oil. He sat there beside Davidson's bed till daylight; once he was bitten by a mosquito in the ankle and clapped his hand to the place too late: the brute went humming out. With the light Mr Lever saw that Davidson was dead. 'Dear, dear,' he said. 'Poor fellow.' He spat out with the words, quite delicately in a corner, the bad morning taste in his mouth. It was like a little sediment of his conventionality.

Mr Lever got two of his carriers to cram Davidson tidily into his hole. He was no longer afraid of them or of failure or of separation. He tore up his letter to Emily. It no longer represented his mood in its timidity, its secret fear, its gentle fussing phrases, *Don't forget the stout. Look after yourself.* He would be home as soon as the letter, and they were going to do things together now they'd never dreamt of doing. The money for the crusher was only the beginning. His ideas stretched farther now than Eastbourne, they stretched as far as Switzerland; he had a feeling that, if he really let himself go, they'd stretch as far as the Riviera. How happy he was on what he thought of as 'the trip home'. He was freed from what had held him back through a long pedantic career, the fear of a conscious fate that notes the dishonesty, notes the skirt in Piccadilly, notes the glass too many of Stone's special. Now he had said Boo to that goose . . .

But you who are reading this, who know so much more than Mr Lever, who can follow the mosquito's progress from the dead swollen black to Davidson's tent, to Mr Lever's ankle, you may possibly believe in God, a kindly god tender towards human frailty, ready to give Mr Lever three days of happiness, three days off the galling chain, as he carried back through the forest his amateurish forgeries and the infection of yellow fever in the blood. The story might very well have encouraged my faith in that loving omniscience if it had not been shaken by personal knowledge of the drab forest through which Mr Lever now went so merrily, where it is impossible to believe in any spiritual life, in anything outside the nature dying round you, the shrivelling of the weeds. But of course, there are two opinions about everything; it was Mr Lever's favourite expression, drinking beer in the Ruhr, Pernod in Lorraine, selling heavy machinery.

1936

BROTHER

THE Communists were the first to appear. They walked quickly, a group of about a dozen, up the boulevard which runs from Combat to Ménilmontant; a young man and a girl lagged a little way behind because the man's leg was hurt and the girl was helping him along. They looked impatient, harassed, hopeless, as if they were trying to catch a train which they knew already in their hearts they were too late to catch.

The proprietor of the café saw them coming when they were still a long way off; the lamps at that time were still alight (it was later that the bullets broke the bulbs and dropped darkness over all that quarter of Paris), and the group showed up plainly in the wide barren boulevard. Since sunset only one customer had entered the café, and very soon after sunset firing could be heard from the direction of Combat; the Metro station had closed hours ago. And yet something obstinate and undefeatable in the proprietor's character prevented him from putting up the shutters; it might have been avarice; he could not himself have told what it was as he pressed his broad yellow forehead against the glass and stared this way and that, up the boulevard and down the boulevard.

But when he saw the group and their air of hurry he began immediately to close the café. First he went and warned his only customer who was practising billiard shots, walking round and round the table, frowning and stroking a thin moustache between shots, a little green in the face under the low diffused lights.

'The Reds are coming,' the proprietor said, 'you'd better be off. I'm putting up the shutters.'

'Don't interrupt. They won't harm me,' the customer said. 'This is a tricky shot. Red's in baulk. Off the cushion. Screw on spot.' He shot his ball straight into a pocket.

'I knew you couldn't do anything with that,' the proprietor

said, nodding his bald head. 'You might just as well go home.
Give me a hand with the shutters first. I've sent my wife away.'
The customer turned on him maliciously, rattling the cue between his fingers. 'It was your talking that spoilt the shot.
You've cause to be frightened, I dare say. But I'm a poor man.
I'm safe. I'm not going to stir.' He went across to his coat and
took out a dry cigar. 'Bring me a bock.' He walked round the
table on his toes and the balls clicked and the proprietor padded
back to the bar, elderly and irritated. He did not fetch the beer
but began to close the shutters; every move he made was slow
and clumsy. Long before he had finished the group of Communists was outside.

He stopped what he was doing and watched them with furtive
dislike. He was afraid that the rattle of the shutters would attract their attention. If I am very quiet and still, he thought,
they may go on, and he remembered with malicious pleasure
the police barricade across the Place de la République. That
will finish them. In the meanwhile I must be very quiet, very
still, and he felt a kind of warm satisfaction at the idea that
worldly wisdom dictated the very attitude most suited to his
nature. So he stared through the edge of a shutter, yellow,
plump, cautious, hearing the billiard balls crackle in the other
room, seeing the young man come limping up the pavement on
the girl's arm, watching them stand and stare with dubious faces
up the boulevard towards Combat.

But when they came into the café he was already behind the
bar, smiling and bowing and missing nothing, noticing how they
had divided forces, how six of them had begun to run back the
way they had come.

The young man sat down in a dark corner above the cellar
stairs and the others stood round the door waiting for something to happen. It gave the proprietor an odd feeling that they
should stand there in his café not asking for a drink, knowing
what to expect, when he, the owner, knew nothing, understood
nothing. At last the girl said 'Cognac', leaving the others and
coming to the bar, but when he poured it out for her, very
careful to give a fair and not a generous measure, she simply

took it to the man sitting in the dark and held it to his mouth.

'Three francs,' the proprietor said. She took the glass and sipped a little and turned it so that the man's lips might touch the same spot. Then she knelt down and rested her forehead against the man's forehead and so they stayed.

'Three francs,' the proprietor said, but he could not make his voice bold. The man was no longer visible in his corner, only the girl's back, thin and shabby in a black cotton frock, as she knelt, leaning forward to find the man's face. The proprietor was daunted by the four men at the door, by the knowledge that they were Reds who had no respect for private property, who would drink his wine and go away without paying, who would rape his women (but there was only his wife, and she was not there), who would rob his bank, who would murder him as soon as look at him. So with fear in his heart he gave up the three francs as lost rather than attract any more attention.

Then the worst that he contemplated happened.

One of the men at the door came up to the bar and told him to pour out four glasses of cognac. 'Yes, yes,' the proprietor said, fumbling with the cork, praying secretly to the Virgin to send an angel, to send the police, to send the Gardes Mobiles, now, immediately, before the cork came out, 'that will be twelve francs.'

'Oh, no,' the man said, 'we are all comrades here. Share and share alike. Listen,' he said, with earnest mockery, leaning across the bar, 'all we have is yours just as much as it's ours, comrade,' and stepping back a pace he presented himself to the proprietor, so that he might take his choice of stringy tie, of threadbare trousers, of starved features. 'And it follows from that, comrade, that all you have is ours. So four cognacs. Share and share alike.'

'Of course,' the proprietor said, 'I was only joking.' Then he stood with bottle poised, and the four glasses tingled upon the counter. 'A machine-gun,' he said, 'up by Combat,' and smiled to see how for the moment the men forgot their brandy, as they fidgeted near the door. Very soon now, he thought, and I shall be quit of them.

'A machine-gun,' the Red said incredulously, 'they're using machine-guns?'

'Well,' the proprietor said, encouraged by this sign that the Gardes Mobiles were not very far away, 'you can't pretend that you aren't armed yourselves.' He leant across the bar in a way that was almost paternal. 'After all, you know, your ideas – they wouldn't do in France. Free love.'

'Who's talking of free love?' the Red said.

The proprietor shrugged and smiled and nodded at the corner. The girl knelt with her head on the man's shoulder, her back to the room. They were quite silent and the glass of brandy stood on the floor beside them. The girl's beret was pushed back on her head and one stocking was laddered and darned from knee to ankle.

'What, those two? They aren't lovers.'

'I,' the proprietor said, 'with my bourgeois notions would have thought ...'

'He's her brother,' the Red said.

The men came clustering round the bar and laughed at him, but softly as if a sleeper or a sick person were in the house. All the time they were listening for something. Between their shoulders the proprietor could look out across the boulevard; he could see the corner of the Faubourg du Temple.

'What are you waiting for?'

'For friends,' the Red said. He made a gesture with open palm as if to say: You see, we share and share alike. We have no secrets.

Something moved at the corner of the Faubourg du Temple.

'Four more cognacs,' the Red said.

'What about those two?' the proprietor asked.

'Leave them alone. They'll look after themselves. They're tired.'

How tired they were. No walk up the boulevard from Ménilmontant could explain the tiredness. They seemed to have come farther and fared a great deal worse than their companions. They were more starved; they were infinitely more hopeless, sitting in their dark corner away from the friendly gossip, the amicable voices which now confused the proprietor's brain, until for a moment he believed himself to be a host entertaining friends.

He laughed and made a broad joke directed at the two of them, but they made no sign of understanding. Perhaps they were to be pitied cut off from the camaraderie round the counter; perhaps they were to be envied for their deeper comradeship. The proprietor thought for no reason at all of the bare grey trees of the Tuileries like a series of exclamation marks drawn against the winter sky. Puzzled, disintegrated, with all his bearings lost, he stared out through the door towards the Faubourg.

It was as if they had not seen each other for a long while, and would soon again be saying good-bye. Hardly aware of what he was doing he filled four glasses with brandy. They stretched out worn blunted fingers for them.

'Wait,' he said. 'I've got something better than this'; then paused, conscious of what was happening across the boulevard. The lamplights splashed down on blue steel helmets; the Gardes Mobiles were lining out across the entrance to the Faubourg, and a machine-gun pointed directly at the café windows.

So, the proprietor thought, my prayers are answered. Now I must do my part, not look, not warn them, save myself. Have they covered the side door?

'I will get the other bottle. Real Napoleon brandy. Share and share alike.' He felt a curious lack of triumph as he opened the trap of the bar and came out. He tried not to walk quickly back towards the billiard room. Nothing that he did must warn these men; he tried to spur himself with the thought that every slow casual step he took was a blow for France, for his café, for his savings. He had to step over the girl's feet to pass her; she was asleep. He noted the sharp shoulder blades thrusting through the cotton, and raised his eyes and met her brother's, filled with pain and despair.

He stopped. He found he could not pass without a word. It was as if he needed to explain something, as if he belonged to the wrong party. With false bonhomie he waved the corkscrew he carried in the other's face. 'Another cognac, eh?'

'It's no good talking to them,' the Red said, 'they're German. They don't understand a word.'

'German?'

'That's what's wrong with his leg. A concentration camp.'

The proprietor told himself that he must be quick, that he must put a door between him and them, that the end was very close, but he was bewildered by the hopelessness in the man's gaze. 'What's he doing here?' Nobody answered him. It was as if his question were too foolish to need a reply. With his head sunk upon his breast the proprietor went past, and the girl slept on. He was like a stranger leaving a room where all the rest are friends. A German. They don't understand a word; and up, up through the heavy darkness of his mind, through the avarice and the dubious triumph, a few German words remembered from the very old days climbed like spies into the light: a line from the *Lorelei* learnt at school, *Kamerad* with its wartime suggestion of fear and surrender, and oddly from nowhere the phrase *mein Bruder*. He opened the door of the billiard room and closed it behind him and softly turned the key.

'Spot in baulk,' the customer explained and leant across the great green table, but while he took aim, wrinkling his narrow peevish eyes, the firing started. It came in two bursts with a rip of glass between. The girl cried out something, but it was not one of the words he knew. Then feet ran across the floor, the trap of the bar slammed. The proprietor sat back against the table and listened for any further sound; but silence came in under the door and silence through the keyhole.

'The cloth. My God, the cloth,' the customer said, and the proprietor looked down at his own hand which was working the corkscrew into the table.

'Will this absurdity never end?' the customer said. 'I shall go home.'

'Wait,' the proprietor said, 'wait.' He was listening to voices and footsteps in the other room. They were voices he did not recognize. Then a car drove up and presently drove away again. Somebody rattled the handle of the door.

'Who is it?' the proprietor called.

'Who are you? Open that door.'

'Ah,' the customer said with relief, 'the police. Where was I now? Spot in baulk.' He began to chalk his cue. The proprietor opened the door. Yes, the Gardes Mobiles had arrived; he was safe again, though his windows were smashed. The Reds had vanished as if they had never been. He looked at the raised trap, at the smashed electric bulbs, at the broken bottle which dripped behind the bar. The café was full of men, and he remembered with odd relief that he had not had time to lock the side door.

'Are you the owner?' the officer asked. 'A bock for each of these men and a cognac for myself. Be quick about it.'

The proprietor calculated, 'Nine francs fifty,' and watched closely with bent head the coins rattle upon the counter.

'You see,' the officer said with significance, 'we pay.' He nodded towards the side door. 'Those others: did they pay?'

No, the proprietor admitted, they had not paid, but as he counted the coins and slipped them into the till, he caught himself silently repeating the officer's order – 'A bock for each of these men.' Those others, he thought, one's got to say that for them, they weren't mean about the drink. It was four cognacs with them. But, of course, they did not pay. 'And my windows,' he complained aloud with sudden asperity, 'what about my windows?'

'Never you mind,' the officer said, 'the government will pay. You have only to send in your bill. Hurry up now with my cognac. I have no time for gossip.'

'You can see for yourself,' the proprietor said, 'how the bottles have been broken. Who will pay for that?'

'Everything will be paid for,' the officer said.

'And now I must go to the cellar to fetch more.'

He was angry at the reiteration of the word pay. They enter my café, he thought, they smash my windows, they order me about and think that all is well if they pay, pay, pay. It occurred to him that these men were intruders.

'Step to it,' the officer said, and turned and rebuked one of the men who had leant his rifle against the bar.

At the top of the cellar stairs the proprietor stopped. They were in darkness, but by the light from the bar he could just make out a body half-way down. He began to tremble violently, and it was some seconds before he could strike a match. The young German lay head downwards, and the blood from his head had dropped on to the step below. His eyes were open and stared back at the proprietor with the old despairing expression of life. The proprietor would not believe that he was dead. 'Kamerad,' he said, bending down, while the match singed his fingers and went out, trying to recall some phrase in German, but he could only remember, as he bent lower still, 'mein Bruder'. Then suddenly he turned and ran up the steps, waved the match-box in the officer's face, and called out in a low hysterical voice to him and his men and to the customer stooping under the low green shade, 'Salauds! Salauds!'

'What was that? What was that?' the officer exclaimed. 'Did you say that he was your brother? It's impossible,' and he frowned incredulously at the proprietor and rattled the coins in his pocket.

1936

JUBILEE

MR CHALFONT ironed his trousers and his tie. Then he folded up his ironing-board and put it away. He was tall and he had preserved his figure; he looked distinguished even in his pants in the small furnished bed-sitting room he kept off Shepherd's Market. He was fifty, but he didn't look more than forty-five; he was stony broke, but he remained unquestionably Mayfair.

He examined his collar with anxiety; he hadn't been out of doors for more than a week, except to the public-house at the corner to eat his morning and evening ham roll, and then he always wore an overcoat and a soiled collar. He decided that it wouldn't damage the effect if he wore it once more; he didn't believe in economizing too rigidly over his laundry, you had to spend money in order to earn money, but there was no point in being extravagant. And somehow he didn't believe in his luck this cocktail time; he was going out for the good of his morale, because after a week away from the restaurants it would have been so easy to let everything slide, to confine himself to his room and his twice daily visit to the public-house.

The Jubilee decorations were still out in the cold windy May. Soiled by showers and soot the streamers blew up across Piccadilly, draughty with desolation. They were the reminder of a good time Mr Chalfont hadn't shared; he hadn't blown whistles or thrown paper ribbons; he certainly hadn't danced to any harmoniums. His neat figure was like a symbol of Good Taste as he waited with folded umbrella for the traffic lights to go green; he had learned to hold his hand so that one frayed patch on his sleeve didn't show, and the rather exclusive club tie, freshly ironed, might have been bought that morning. It wasn't lack of patriotism or loyalty which had kept Mr Chalfont indoors all through Jubilee week. Nobody drank the toast of the King more sincerely than Mr Chalfont so long as someone else was standing the drink, but an instinct deeper than good form had warned him not to be about. Too many people whom he had once known (so he explained it) were coming up from the country; they might want to look him up, and a fellow just couldn't ask them back to a room like this. That explained his discretion; it didn't explain his sense of oppression while he waited for the Jubilee to be over.

Now he was back at the old game.

He called it that himself, smoothing his neat grey military moustache. The old game. Somebody going rapidly round the corner into Berkeley Street nudged him playfully and said, 'Hullo, you old devil,' and was gone again, leaving the memory of many playful nudges in the old days, of Merdy and the Boob. For he couldn't disguise the fact that he was after the ladies. He didn't want to disguise it. It made his whole profession appear even to himself rather gallant and carefree. It disguised the fact that the ladies were not so young as they might be and that it was the ladies (God bless them!) who paid. It disguised the fact that Merdy and the Boob had long ago vanished from his knowledge. The list of his acquaintances included a great many women but hardly a single man; no one was more qualified by a long grimy experience to tell smoking-room stories, but the smoking-room in which Mr Chalfont was welcome did not nowadays exist.

Mr Chalfont crossed the road. It wasn't an easy life, it exhausted him nervously and physically, he needed a great many sherries to keep going. The first sherry he had always to pay for himself; that was the thirty pounds he marked as expenses on his income-tax return. He dived through the entrance, not looking either way, for it would never do for the porter to think that he was soliciting any of the women who moved heavily like seals through the dim aquarium light of the lounge. But his usual seat was occupied.

He turned away to look for another chair where he could exhibit himself discreetly: the select tie, the tan, the grey distinguished hair, the strong elegant figure, the air of a retired Governor from the Colonies. He studied the woman who sat in his chair covertly: he thought he'd seen her somewhere, the

167

mink coat, the overblown figure, the expensive dress. Her face was familiar but unnoted, like that of someone you pass every day at the same place. She was vulgar, she was cheerful, she was undoubtedly rich. He couldn't think where he had met her.

She caught Mr Chalfont's eye and winked. He blushed, he was horrified, nothing of this sort had ever happened to him before; the porter was watching and Mr Chalfont felt scandal at his elbow, robbing him of his familiar restaurant, his last hunting ground, turning him perhaps out of Mayfair altogether into some bleak Paddington parlour where he couldn't keep up the least appearance of gallantry. Am I so obvious, he thought, so obvious? He went hastily across to her before she could wink again. 'Excuse me,' he said, 'you must remember me. What a long time . . .'

'Your face is familiar, dear,' she said. 'Have a cocktail.'

'Well,' Mr Chalfont said, 'I should certainly not mind a sherry, Mrs – Mrs – I've quite forgotten your surname.'

'You're a sport,' the woman said, 'but Amy will do.'

'Ah,' Mr Chalfont said, 'you are looking very well, Amy. It gives me much pleasure to see you sitting there again after all these – months – why, years it must be. The last time we met . . .'

'I don't remember you clearly, dear, though of course when I saw you looking at me . . . I suppose it was in Jermyn Street.'

'Jermyn Street,' Mr Chalfont said. 'Surely not Jermyn Street. I've never . . . Surely it must have been when I had my flat in Curzon Street. Delectable evenings one had there. I've moved since then to a rather humbler abode where I wouldn't dream of inviting you . . . But perhaps we could slip away to some little nest of your own. Your health, my dear. You look younger than ever.'

'Happy days,' Amy said. Mr Chalfont winced. She fingered her mink coat. 'But you know – I've retired.'

'Ah, lost money, eh,' Mr Chalfont said. 'Dear lady, I've suffered in that way too. We must console each other a little. I suppose business is bad. Your husband – I seem to recall a trying man who did his best to interfere with our idyll. It was quite an idyll, wasn't it, those evenings in Curzon Street?'

'You've got it wrong, dear. I never was in Curzon Street. But if you date back to the time I tried that husband racket, why that goes years back, to the mews off Bond Street. Fancy your remembering. It was wrong of me. I can see that now. And it never really worked. I don't think he looked like a husband. But now I've retired. Oh, no,' she said, leaning forward until he could smell the brandy on her plump little lips, 'I haven't lost money; I've made it.'

'You're lucky,' Mr Chalfont said.

'It was all the Jubilee,' Amy explained.

'I was confined to my bed during the Jubilee,' Mr Chalfont said. 'I understand it all went off very well.'

'It was lovely,' Amy said. 'Why, I said to myself, everyone ought to do something to make it a success. So I cleaned up the streets.'

'I don't quite understand,' Mr Chalfont said. 'You mean the decorations?'

'No, no,' Amy said, 'that wasn't it at all. But it didn't seem to me nice, when all these Colonials were in London, for them to see the girls in Bond Street and Wardour Street and all over the place. I'm proud of London, and it didn't seem right to me that we should get a reputation.'

'People must live.'

'Of course they must live. Wasn't I in the business myself, dear?'

'Oh,' Mr Chalfont said, 'you were in the business?' It was quite a shock to him; he looked quickly this way and that, fearing that he might have been observed.

'So you see I opened a House and split with the girls. I took all the risk, and then of course I had my other expenses. I had to advertise.'

'How did you – how did you get it known?' He couldn't help having a kind of professional interest.

'Easy, dear. I opened a tourist bureau. Trips to the London underworld. Limehouse and all that. But there was always an old fellow who wanted the guide to show him something privately afterwards.'

'Very ingenious,' Mr Chalfont said.

'And loyal too, dear. It cleaned up the streets properly. Though of course I only took the best. I was very select. Some of them jibbed, because they said they did all the work, but as I said to them, it was My Idea.'

'So now you're retired?'

'I made five thousand pounds, dear. It was really my jubilee as well, though you mightn't think it to look at me. I always had the makings of a business woman, and I saw, you see, how I could extend the business. I opened at Brighton too. I cleaned up England in a way of speaking. It was ever so much nicer for the Colonials. There's been a lot of money in the country these last weeks. Have another sherry, dear, you are looking poorly.'

'Really, really you know I ought to be going.'

'Oh, come on. It's Jubilee, isn't it? Celebrate. Be a sport.'

'I think I see a friend.'

He looked helplessly around: a friend: he couldn't even think of a friend's name. He wilted before a personality stronger than his own. She bloomed there like a great dressy autumn flower. He felt old: my jubilee. His frayed cuffs showed; he had forgotten to arrange his hand. He said, 'Perhaps. Just one. It ought really to be on me,' and as he watched her bang for the waiter in the dim genteel place and dominate his disapproval when he came, Mr Chalfont couldn't help wondering at the unfairness of her confidence and her health. He had a touch of neuritis, but she was carnival; she really seemed to belong to the banners and drinks and plumes and processions. He said quite humbly, 'I should like to have seen the procession, but I wasn't up to it. My rheumatism,' he excused himself. His little withered sense of good taste could not stand the bright plebeian spontaneity. He was a fine dancer, but they'd have outdanced him on the pavements; he made love attractively in his formal well-bred way, but they'd have outloved him, blind and drunk and crazy and happy in the park. He had known that he would be out of place, he'd kept away; but it was humiliating to realize that Amy had missed nothing.

'You look properly done, dear,' Amy said. 'Let me lend you a couple of quid.'

'No, no,' Mr Chalfont said. 'Really I couldn't.'

'I expect you've given me plenty in your time.'

But had he? He couldn't remember her; it was such a long time since he'd been with a woman except in the way of business. He said, 'I couldn't. I really couldn't.' He tried to explain his attitude while she fumbled in her bag.

'I never take money – except, you know, from friends.' He admitted desperately, 'or except in business.' But he couldn't take his eyes away. He was broke and it was cruel of her to show him a five-pound note. 'No. Really.' It was a long time since his market price had been as high as five pounds.

'I know how it is, dear,' Amy said, 'I've been in the business myself, and I know just how you feel. Sometimes a gentleman would come home with me, give me a quid and run away as if he was scared. It was insulting. I never did like taking money for nothing.'

'But you're quite wrong,' Mr Chalfont said. 'That's not it at all. Not it at all.'

'Why, I could tell almost as soon as you spoke to me. You don't need to keep up pretences with me, dear,' Amy went inexorably on, while Mayfair faded from his manner until there remained only the bed-sitting room, the ham rolls, the iron heating on the stove. 'You don't need to be proud. But if you'd rather (it's all the same to me, it doesn't mean a thing to me) we'll go home, and let you do your stuff. It's all the same to me, dear, but if you'd rather – I know how you feel,' and presently they went out together arm-in-arm into the decorated desolate street.

'Cheer up, dear,' Amy said, as the wind picked up the ribbons and tore them from the poles and lifted the dust and made the banners flap, 'a girl likes a cheerful face.' And suddenly she became raucous and merry, slapping Mr Chalfont on his back, pinching his arm, saying, 'Let's have a little Jubilee spirit, dear,'

taking her revenge for a world of uncongenial partners on old
Mr Chalfont. You couldn't call him anything else now but old
Mr Chalfont.

1936

A DAY SAVED

I HAD stuck closely to him, as people say like a shadow. But that's absurd. I'm no shadow. You can feel me, touch me, hear me, smell me. I'm Robinson. But I had sat at the next table, followed twenty yards behind down every street, when he went upstairs I waited at the bottom, and when he came down I passed out before him and paused at the first corner. In that way I was really like a shadow, for sometimes I was in front of him and sometimes I was behind him.

Who was he? I never knew his name. He was short and ordinary in appearance and he carried an umbrella; his hat was a bowler, and he wore brown gloves. But this was his importance to me: he carried something I dearly, despairingly wanted. It was beneath his clothes, perhaps in a pouch, a purse, perhaps dangling next to his skin. Who knows how cunning the most ordinary man can be? Surgeons can make clever insertions. He may have carried it even closer to his heart than the outer skin.

What was it? I never knew. I can only guess, as I might guess at his name, calling him Jones or Douglas, Wales, Canby, Fotheringay. Once in a restaurant I said 'Fotheringay' softly to my soup and I thought he looked up and round about him. I don't know. This is the horror I cannot escape: knowing nothing, his name, what it was he carried, why I wanted it so, why I followed him.

Presently we came to a railway bridge and underneath it he met a friend. I am using words again very inexactly. Bear with me. I try to be exact. I pray to be exact. All I want in the world is to know. So when I say he met a friend, I do not know that it was a friend, I know only that it was someone he greeted with apparent affection. The friend said to him, 'When do you leave?' He said, 'At two from Dover.' You may be sure I felt my pocket to make sure the ticket was there.

Then his friend said, 'If you fly you will save a day.'

173

He nodded, he agreed, he would sacrifice his ticket, he would save a day.

I ask you, what does a day saved matter to him or to you? A day saved from what? for what? Instead of spending the day travelling, you will see your friend a day earlier, but you cannot stay indefinitely,you will travel home twenty-four hours sooner, that is all. But you will fly home and again save a day? Save it from what, for what? You will begin work a day earlier, but you cannot work on indefinitely. It only means that you will cease work a day earlier. And then, what? You cannot die a day earlier. So you will realize perhaps how rash it was of you to save a day, when you discover how you cannot escape those twenty-four hours you have so carefully preserved; you may push them forward and push them forward, but some time they must be spent, and then you may wish you had spent them as innocently as in the train from Ostend.

But this thought never occurred to him. He said, 'Yes, that's true. It would save a day. I'll fly.' I nearly spoke to him then. The selfishness of the man. For that day which he thought he was saving might be his despair years later, but it was my despair at the instant. For I had been looking forward to the long train journey in the same compartment. It was winter, and the train would be nearly empty, and with the least luck we should be alone together. I had planned everything. I was going to talk to him. Because I knew nothing about him, I should begin in the usual way by asking whether he minded the window being raised a little or a little lowered. That would show him that we spoke the same language and he would probably be only too ready to talk, feeling himself in a foreign country; he would be grateful for any help I might be able to give him, translating this or that word.

Of course I never believed that talk would be enough. I should learn a great deal about him, but I believed that I should have to kill him before I knew all. I should have killed him, I think, at night, between the two stations which are the farthest parted, after the customs had examined our luggage and our passports had been stamped at the frontier, and we had pulled

down the blinds and turned out the light. I had even planned
what to do with his body, with the bowler hat and the umbrella
and the brown gloves, but only if it became necessary, only if in
no other way he would yield what I wanted. I am a gentle
creature, not easily roused.

But now he had chosen to go by aeroplane and there was
nothing that I could do. I followed him, of course, sat in the
seat behind, watched his tremulousness at his first flight, how he
avoided for a long while the sight of the sea below, how he kept
his bowler hat upon his knees, how he gasped a little when the
grey wing tilted up like the arm of a windmill to the sky and the
houses were set on edge. There were times, I believe, when he
regretted having saved a day.

We got out of the aeroplane together and he had a small
trouble with the customs. I translated for him. He looked at me
curiously and said, 'Thank you.' He was – again I suggest that I
know when all I mean is I assume by his manner and his conversation – stupid and good-natured, but I believe for a
moment he suspected me, thought he had seen me somewhere,
in a tube, in a bus, in a public baths, below the railway bridge,
on how many stairways. I asked him the time. He said, 'We put
our clocks back an hour here,' and beamed with an absurd
pleasure because he had saved an hour as well as a day.

I had a drink with him, several drinks with him. He was
absurdly grateful for my help. I had beer with him at one
place, gin at another, and at a third he insisted on my sharing a
bottle of wine. We became for the time being friends. I felt
more warmly towards him than towards any other man I have
known, for, like love between a man and a woman, my affection
was partly curiosity. I told him that I was Robinson; he meant
to give me a card, but while he was looking for one he drank
another glass of wine and forgot about it. We were both a little
drunk. Presently I began to call him Fotheringay. He never
contradicted me and it may have been his name, but I seem to
remember also calling him Douglas, Wales and Canby without
correction. He was very generous and I found it easy to talk
with him; the stupid are often companionable. I told him that I

was desperate and he offered me money. He could not understand what I wanted.

I said, 'You've saved a day. You can afford to come with me tonight to a place I know.'

He said, 'I have to take a train tonight.' He told me the name of the town, and he was not surprised when I told him that I was coming too.

We drank together all that evening and went to the station together. I was planning, if it became necessary, to kill him. I thought in all friendliness that perhaps after all I might save him from having saved a day. But it was a small local train; it crept from station to station, and at every station people got out of the train and other people got into the train. He insisted on travelling third class and the carriage was never empty. He could not speak a word of the language and he simply curled up in his corner and slept; it was I who remained awake and had to listen to the weary painful gossip, a servant speaking of her mistress, a peasant woman of the day's market, a soldier of the Church, and a man who, I believe, was a tailor of adultery, wire-worms and the harvest of three years ago.

It was two o'clock in the morning when we reached the end of our journey. I walked with him to the house where his friends lived. It was quite close to the station and I had not time to plan or carry out any plan. The garden gate was open and he asked me in. I said no. I would go to the hotel. He said his friends would be pleased to put me up for the remainder of the night, but I said no. The lights were on in a downstairs room and the curtains were not drawn. A man was asleep in a chair by a great stove and there were glasses on a tray, a decanter of whisky, two bottles of beer and a long thin bottle of Rhine wine. I stepped back and he went in and almost immediately the room was full of people. I could see his welcome in their eyes and in their gestures. There was a woman in a dressing-gown and a girl who sat with thin knees drawn up to her chin and three men, two of them old. They did not draw the curtains, though he must surely have guessed that I was watching them. The garden was cold; the winter beds were furred with weeds. I laid my hand on some prickly bush. It was as if they gave a deliberate display of their unity and companionship. My friend – I call him my friend, but he was really no more than an acquaintance and was my friend only for so long as we both were drunk – sat in the middle of them all, and I could tell from the way his lips were moving that he was telling them many things which he had never told me. Once I thought I could detect from his lip movements, 'I have saved a day.' He looked stupid and good-natured and happy. I could not bear the sight for long. It was an impertinence to display himself like that to me. I have never ceased to pray from that moment that the day he saved may be retarded and retarded until eventually he suffers its eighty-six thousand four hundred seconds when he has the most desperate need, when he is following another as I followed him, closely as people say like a shadow, so that he has to stop, as I have had to stop, to reassure himself: you can smell me, you can touch me, you can hear me, I am not a shadow: I am Fotheringay, Wales, Canby, I am Robinson.

1935

I SPY

CHARLIE STOWE waited until he heard his mother snore before he got out of bed. Even then he moved with caution and tiptoed to the window. The front of the house was irregular, so that it was possible to see a light burning in his mother's room. But now all the windows were dark. A searchlight passed across the sky, lighting the banks of cloud and probing the dark deep spaces between, seeking enemy airships. The wind blew from the sea, and Charlie Stowe could hear behind his mother's snores the beating of the waves. A draught through the cracks in the window-frame stirred his night-shirt. Charlie Stowe was frightened.

But the thought of the tobacconist's shop which his father kept down a dozen wooden stairs drew him on. He was twelve years old, and already boys at the County School mocked him because he had never smoked a cigarette. The packets were piled twelve deep below, Gold Flake and Player's, De Reszke, Abdulla, Woodbines, and the little shop lay under a thin haze of stale smoke which would completely disguise his crime. That it was a crime to steal some of his father's stock Charlie Stowe had no doubt, but he did not love his father; his father was unreal to him, a wraith, pale, thin, indefinite, who noticed him only spasmodically and left even punishment to his mother. For his mother he felt a passionate demonstrative love; her large boisterous presence and her noisy charity filled the world for him; from her speech he judged her the friend of everyone, from the rector's wife to the 'dear Queen', except the 'Huns', the monsters who lurked in Zeppelins in the clouds. But his father's affection and dislike were as indefinite as his movements. Tonight he had said he would be in Norwich, and yet you never knew. Charlie Stowe had no sense of safety as he crept down the wooden stairs. When they creaked he clenched his fingers on the collar of his night-shirt.

At the bottom of the stairs he came out quite suddenly into the little shop. It was too dark to see his way, and he did not dare touch the switch. For half a minute he sat in despair on the bottom step with his chin cupped in his hands. Then the regular movement of the searchlight was reflected through an upper window and the boy had time to fix in memory the pile of cigarettes, the counter, and the small hole under it. The footsteps of a policeman on the pavement made him grab the first packet to his hand and dive for the hole. A light shone along the floor and a hand tried the door, then the footsteps passed on, and Charlie cowered in the darkness.

At last he got his courage back by telling himself in his curiously adult way that if he were caught now there was nothing to be done about it, and he might as well have his smoke. He put a cigarette in his mouth and then remembered that he had no matches. For a while he dared not move. Three times the searchlight lit the shop, as he muttered taunts and encouragements. 'May as well be hung for a sheep,' 'Cowardy, cowardy custard,' grown-up and childish exhortations oddly mixed.

But as he moved he heard footfalls in the street, the sound of several men walking rapidly. Charlie Stowe was old enough to feel surprise that anybody was about. The footsteps came nearer, stopped; a key was turned in the shop door, a voice said: 'Let him in,' and then he heard his father, 'If you wouldn't mind being quiet, gentlemen. I don't want to wake up the family.' There was a note unfamiliar to Charlie in the undecided voice. A torch flashed and the electric globe burst into blue light. The boy held his breath; he wondered whether his father would hear his heart beating, and he clutched his night-shirt tightly and prayed, 'O God, don't let me be caught.' Through a crack in the counter he could see his father where he stood, one hand held to his high stiff collar, between two men in bowler hats and belted mackintoshes. They were strangers.

'Have a cigarette,' his father said in a voice dry as a biscuit. One of the men shook his head. 'It wouldn't do, not when we are on duty. Thank you all the same.' He spoke gently, but without kindness: Charlie Stowe thought his father must be ill.

'Mind if I put a few in my pocket?' Mr Stowe asked, and when the man nodded he lifted a pile of Gold Flake and Players from a shelf and caressed the packets with the tips of his fingers.

'Well,' he said, 'there's nothing to be done about it, and I may as well have my smokes.' For a moment Charlie Stowe feared discovery, his father stared round the shop so thoroughly; he might have been seeing it for the first time. 'It's a good little business,' he said, 'for those that like it. The wife will sell out, I suppose. Else the neighbours'll be wrecking it. Well, you want to be off. A stitch in time. I'll get my coat.'

'One of us'll come with you, if you don't mind,' said the stranger gently.

'You needn't trouble. It's on the peg here. There, I'm all ready.'

The other man said in an embarrassed way, 'Don't you want to speak to your wife?' The thin voice was decided, 'Not me. Never do today what you can put off till tomorrow. She'll have her chance later, won't she?'

'Yes, yes,' one of the strangers said and he became very cheerful and encouraging. 'Don't you worry too much. While there's life . . .' and suddenly his father tried to laugh.

When the door had closed Charlie Stowe tiptoed upstairs and got into bed. He wondered why his father had left the house again so late at night and who the strangers were. Surprise and awe kept him for a little while awake. It was as if a familiar photograph had stepped from the frame to reproach him with neglect. He remembered how his father had held tight to his collar and fortified himself with proverbs, and he thought for the first time that, while his mother was boisterous and kindly, his father was very like himself, doing things in the dark which frightened him. It would have pleased him to go down to his father and tell him that he loved him, but he could hear through the window the quick steps going away. He was alone in the house with his mother, and he fell asleep.

1930

PROOF POSITIVE

THE tired voice went on. It seemed to surmount enormous obstacles to speech. The man's sick, Colonel Crashaw thought, with pity and irritation. When a young man he had climbed in the Himalayas, and he remembered how at great heights several breaths had to be taken for every step advanced. The five-foot-high platform in the Music Rooms of The Spa seemed to entail for the speaker some of the same effort. He should never have come out on such a raw afternoon, thought Colonel Crashaw, pouring out a glass of water and pushing it across the lecturer's table. The rooms were badly heated, and yellow fingers of winter fog felt for cracks in the many windows. There was little doubt that the speaker had lost all touch with his audience. It was scattered in patches about the hall – elderly ladies who made no attempt to hide their cruel boredom, and a few men, with the appearance of retired officers, who put up a show of attention.

Colonel Crashaw, as president of the local Psychical Society, had received a note from the speaker a little more than a week before. Written by a hand which trembled with sickness, age or drunkenness, it asked urgently for a special meeting of the society. An extraordinary, a really impressive, experience was to be described while still fresh in the mind, though what the experience had been was left vague. Colonel Crashaw would have hesitated to comply if the note had not been signed by a Major Philip Weaver, Indian Army, retired. One had to do what one could for a brother officer; the trembling of the hand must be either age or sickness.

It proved principally to be the latter when the two men met for the first time on the platform. Major Weaver was not more than sixty, thin, and dark, with an ugly obstinate nose and satire in his eye, the most unlikely person to experience anything un-explainable. What antagonized Crashaw most was that Weaver

181

used scent; a white handkerchief which drooped from his breast pocket exhaled as rich and sweet an odour as a whole altar of lilies. Several ladies prinked their noses, and General Leadbitter asked loudly whether he might smoke.

It was quite obvious that Weaver understood. He smiled provocatively and asked very slowly, 'Would you mind not smoking? My throat has been bad for some time.' Crashaw murmured that it was terrible weather; influenza throats were common. The satirical eye came round to him and considered him thoughtfully, while Weaver said in a voice which carried half-way across the hall, 'It's cancer in my case.'

In the shocked vexed silence that followed the unnecessary intimacy he began to speak without waiting for any intro- duction from Crashaw. He seemed at first to be in a hurry. It was only later that the terrible impediments were placed in the way of his speech. He had a high voice, which sometimes broke into a squeal, and must have been peculiarly disagreeable on the parade-ground. He paid a few compliments to the local society; his remarks were just sufficiently exaggerated to be irritating. He was glad, he said, to give them the chance of hearing him; what he had to say might alter their whole view of the relative values of matter and spirit.

Mystic stuff, thought Crashaw.

Weaver's high voice began to shoot out hurried platitudes. The spirit, he said, was stronger than anyone realized; the physi- ological action of heart and brain and nerves were subordinate to the spirit. The spirit was everything. He said again, his voice squeaking up like bats into the ceiling, 'The spirit is so much stronger than you think.' He put his hand across his throat and squinted sideways at the window-panes and the nuzzling fog, and upwards at the bare electric globe sizzling with heat and poor light in the dim afternoon. 'It's immortal,' he told them very seriously, and they shifted, restless, uncomfortable and weary, in their chairs.

It was then that his voice grew tired and his speech impeded. The knowledge that he had entirely lost touch with his audience may have been the cause. An elderly lady at the back had taken her knitting from a bag, and her needles flashed along the walls when the light caught them, like a bright ironic spirit. Satire for a moment deserted Weaver's eyes. and Crashaw saw the vacancy it left, as though the ball had turned to glass.

'This is important,' the lecturer cried to them. 'I can tell you a story – ' His audience's attention was momentarily caught by his promise of something definite, but the stillness of the lady's needles did not soothe him. He sneered at them all: 'Signs and wonders,' he said.

Then he lost the thread of his speech altogether.

His hand passed to and fro across his throat and he quoted Shakespeare, and then St Paul's Epistle to the Galatians. His speech, as it grew slower, seemed to lose all logical order, though now and then Crashaw was surprised by the shrewdness in the juxtaposition of two irrelevant ideas. It was like the conversation of an old man which flits from subject to subject, the thread a subconscious one. 'When I was at Simla,' he said, bending his brows as though to avoid the sunflash on the barrack square, but perhaps the frost, the fog, the tarnished room broke his memories. He began to assure the wearied faces all over again that the spirit did not die when the body died, but that the body only moved at the spirit's will. One had to be obstinate, to grapple . . .

Pathetic, Crashaw thought, the sick man's clinging to his belief. It was as if life were an only son who was dying and with whom he wished to preserve some form of communication . . .

A note was passed to Crashaw from the audience. It came from a Dr Brown, a small alert man in the third row; the society cherished him as a kind of pet sceptic. The note read: 'Can't you make him stop? The man's obviously very ill. And what good is his talk, anyway?'

Crashaw turned his eyes sideways and upwards and felt his pity vanish at sight of the roving satirical eyes that gave the lie to the tongue, and at the smell, overpoweringly sweet, of the scent in which Weaver had steeped his handkerchief. The man was an 'outsider'; he would look up his record in the old Army Lists when he got home.

'Proof positive,' Weaver was saying, sighing a shrill breath of exhaustion between the words. Crashaw laid his watch upon the table, but Weaver paid him no attention. He was supporting himself on the rim of the table with one hand. 'I'll give you,' he said, speaking with increasing difficulty, 'proof pos ...' His voice scraped into stillness, like a needle at a record's end, but the quiet did not last. From an expressionless face, a sound which was more like a high mew than anything else, jerked the audience into attention. He followed it up, still without a trace of any emotion or understanding, with a succession of incomprehensible sounds, a low labial whispering, an odd jangling note, while his fingers tapped on the table. The sounds brought to mind innumerable séances, the bound medium, the tambourine shaken in mid-air, the whispered trivialities of ghosts in the darkness, the dinginess, the airless rooms.

Weaver sat down slowly in his chair and let his head fall backwards. An old lady began to cry nervously, and Dr Brown scrambled on to the platform and bent over him. Colonel Crashaw saw the doctor's hand tremble as he picked the handkerchief from the pocket and flung it away from him. Crashaw, aware of another and more unpleasant smell, heard Dr Brown whisper, 'Send them all away. He's dead.'

He spoke with a distress unusual in a doctor accustomed to every kind of death. Crashaw, before he complied, glanced over Dr Brown's shoulder at the dead man. Major Weaver's appearance disquieted him. In a long life he had seen many forms of death, men shot by their own hand, and men killed in the field, but never such a suggestion of mortality. The body might have been one fished from the sea a long while after death; the flesh of the face seemed as ready to fall as an over-ripe fruit. So it was with no great shock of surprise that he heard Dr Brown's whispered statement: 'The man must have been dead a week.'

What the Colonel thought of most was Weaver's claim – 'Proof positive' – proof, he had probably meant, that the spirit

184

outlived the body, that it tasted eternity. But all he had certainly revealed was how, without the body's aid, the spirit in seven days decayed into whispered nonsense.

1930

THE SECOND DEATH

SHE found me in the evening under the trees that grew outside the village. I had never cared for her and would have hidden myself if I'd seen her coming. She was to blame, I'm certain, for her son's vices. If they were vices, but I'm very far from admitting that they were. At any rate he was generous, never mean, like others in the village I could mention if I chose.

I was staring hard at a leaf or she would never have found me. It was dangling from the twig, its stalk torn across by the wind or else by a stone one of the village children had flung. Only the green tough skin of the stalk held it there suspended. I was watching closely, because a caterpillar was crawling across the surface making the leaf sway to and fro. The caterpillar was aiming at the twig, and I wondered whether it would reach it in safety or whether the leaf would fall with it into the water. There was a pool underneath the trees, and the water always appeared red, because of the heavy clay in the soil.

I never knew whether the caterpillar reached the twig, for, as I've said, the wretched woman found me. The first I knew of her coming was her voice just behind my ear.

'I've been looking in all the pubs for you,' she said in her old shrill voice. It was typical of her to say 'all the pubs' when there were only two in the place. She always wanted credit for the trouble she hadn't really taken.

I was annoyed and I couldn't help speaking a little harshly. 'You might have saved yourself the trouble,' I said, 'you should have known I wouldn't be in a pub on a fine night like this.'

The old vixen became quite humble. She was always smooth enough when she wanted anything. 'It's for my poor son,' she said. That meant that he was ill. When he was well I never heard her say anything better than 'that dratted boy'. She'd make him be in the house by midnight every day of the week, as if there were any serious mischief a man could get up to in a

186

little village like ours. Of course we soon found a way to cheat her, but it was the principle of the thing I objected to – a grown man of over thirty ordered about by his mother, just because she hadn't a husband to control. But when he was ill, though it might be with only a small chill, it was 'my poor son'.

'He's dying,' she said, 'and God knows what I shall do without him.'

'Well, I don't see how I can help you,' I said. I was angry, because he'd been dying once before and she'd done everything but actually bury him. I imagined it was the same sort of dying this time, the sort a man gets over. I'd seen him about the week before on his way up the hill to see the big-breasted girl at the farm. I'd watched him till he was like a little black dot, which stayed suddenly by a square box in a field. That was the barn where they used to meet. I have very good eyes and it amuses me to try how far and how clearly they can see. I met him again some time after midnight and helped him get into the house without his mother knowing, and he was well enough then – only a little sleepy and tired.

The old vixen was at it again. 'He's been asking for you,' she shrilled at me.

'If he's as ill as you make out,' I said, 'it would be better for him to ask for a doctor.'

'Doctor's there, but he can't do anything.' That startled me for a moment, I'll admit it, until I thought, 'the old devil's malingering. He's got some plan or other.' He was quite clever enough to cheat a doctor. I had seen him throw a fit that would have deceived Moses.

'For God's sake come,' she said, 'he seems frightened.' Her voice broke quite genuinely, for I suppose in her way she was fond of him. I couldn't help pitying her a little, for I knew that he had never cared a mite for her and had never troubled to disguise the fact.

I left the trees and the red pool and the struggling caterpillar, for I knew that she would never leave me alone, now that her 'poor boy' was asking for me. Yet a week ago there was nothing she wouldn't have done to keep us apart. She thought me responsible for his ways, as though any mortal man could have kept him off a likely woman when his appetite was up.

I think it must have been the first time I had entered their cottage by the front door, since I came to the village ten years ago. I threw an amused glance at his window. I thought I could see the marks on the wall of the ladder we'd used the week before. We'd had a little difficulty in putting it straight, but his mother slept sound. He had brought the ladder down from the barn, and when he'd got safely in, I carried it up there again. But you could never trust his word. He'd lie to his best friend, and when I reached the barn I found the girl had gone. If he couldn't bribe you with his mother's money, he'd bribe you with other people's promises.

I began to feel uneasy directly I got inside the door. It was natural that the house should be quiet, for the pair of them never had any friends to stay, although the old woman had a sister-in-law living only a few miles away. But I didn't like the sound of the doctor's feet, as he came downstairs to meet us. He'd twisted his face into a pious solemnity for our benefit, as though there was something holy about death, even about the death of my friend.

'He's conscious,' he said, 'but he's going. There's nothing I can do. If you want him to die in peace, better let his friend go along up. He's frightened about something.'

The doctor was right. I could tell that as soon as I bent under the lintel and entered my friend's room. He was propped up on a pillow, and his eyes were on the door, waiting for me to come. They were very bright and frightened, and his hair lay across his forehead in sticky stripes. I'd never realized before what an ugly fellow he was. He had got sly eyes that looked at you too much out of the corners, but when he was in ordinary health, they held a twinkle that made you forget the slyness. There was something pleasant and brazen in the twinkle, as much as to say, 'I know I'm sly and ugly. But what does that matter? I've got guts.' It was that twinkle, I think, some women found attractive and stimulating. Now when the twinkle was gone, he looked a rogue and nothing else.

I thought it my duty to cheer him up, so I made a small joke out of the fact that he was alone in bed. He didn't seem to relish it, and I was beginning to fear that he, too, was taking a religious view of his death, when he told me to sit down, speaking quite sharply.

'I'm dying,' he said, talking very fast, 'and I want to ask you something. That doctor's no good – he'd think me delirious. I'm frightened, old man. I want to be reassured,' and then after a long pause, 'someone with common sense.' He slipped a little farther down in his bed.

'I've only once been badly ill before,' he said. 'That was before you settled here. I wasn't much more than a boy. People tell me that I was even supposed to be dead. They were carrying me out to burial, when a doctor stopped them just in time.'

I'd heard plenty of cases like that, and I saw no reason why he should want to tell me about it. And then I thought I saw his point. His mother had not been too anxious once before to see if he were properly dead, though I had little doubt that she made a great show of grief – 'My poor boy. I don't know what I shall do without him.' And I'm certain that she believed herself then, as she believed herself now. She wasn't a murderess. She was only inclined to be premature.

'Look here, old man,' I said, and I propped him a little higher on his pillow, 'you needn't be frightened. You aren't going to die, and anyway I'd see that the doctor cut a vein or something before they moved you. But that's all morbid stuff. Why, I'd stake my shirt that you've got plenty more years in front of you. And plenty more girls too,' I added to make him smile.

'Can't you cut out all that?' he said, and I knew then that he had turned religious. 'Why,' he said, 'if I lived, I wouldn't touch another girl. I wouldn't, not one.'

I tried not to smile at that, but it wasn't easy to keep a straight face. There's always something a bit funny about a sick man's morals. 'Anyway,' I said, 'you needn't be frightened.'

'It's not that,' he said. 'Old man, when I came round that other time, I thought that I'd been dead. It wasn't like sleep at all. Or rest in peace. There was someone there all round me,

189

who knew everything. Every girl I'd ever had. Even that young one who hadn't understood. It was before your time. She lived a mile down the road, where Rachel lives now, but she and her family went away afterwards. Even the money I'd taken from mother. I don't call that stealing. It's in the family. I never had a chance to explain. Even the thoughts I'd had. A man can't help his thoughts.'

'A nightmare,' I said.

'Yes, it must have been a dream, mustn't it? The sort of dream people do get when they are ill. And I saw what was coming to me too. I can't bear being hurt. It wasn't fair. And I wanted to faint and I couldn't, because I was dead.'

'In the dream,' I said. His fear made me nervous. 'In the dream,' I said again.

'Yes, it must have been a dream – mustn't it? – because I woke up. The curious thing was I felt quite well and strong. I got up and stood in the road, and a little farther down, kicking up the dust, was a small crowd, going off with a man – the doctor who had stopped them burying me.'

'Well?' I said.

'Old man,' he said, 'suppose it was true. Suppose I had been dead. I believed it then, you know, and so did my mother. But you can't trust her. I went straight for a couple of years. I thought it might be a sort of second chance. Then things got fogged and somehow ... It didn't seem really possible. It's not possible. Of course it's not possible. You know it isn't, don't you?'

'Why, no,' I said. 'Miracles of that sort don't happen nowadays. And anyway, they aren't likely to happen to you, are they? And here of all places under the sun.'

'It would be so dreadful,' he said, 'if it had been true, and I'd got to go through all that again. You don't know what things were going to happen to me in that dream. And they'd be worse now.' He stopped and then, after a moment, he added as though he were stating a fact: 'When one's dead there's no unconsciousness any more for ever.'

'Of course it was a dream,' I said, and squeezed his hand. He was frightening me with his fancies. I wished that he'd die quickly, so that I could get away from his sly, bloodshot and terrified eyes and see something cheerful and amusing, like the Rachel he had mentioned, who lived a mile down the road.

'Why,' I said, 'if there had been a man about working miracles like that, we should have heard of others, you may be sure. Even poked away in this God-forsaken spot,' I said.

'There were some others,' he said. 'But the stories only went round among the poor, and they'll believe anything, won't they? There were lots of diseased and crippled they said he'd cured. And there was a man, who'd been born blind, and he came and just touched his eyelids and sight came to him. Those were all old wives' tales, weren't they?' he asked me, stammering with fear, and then lying suddenly still and bunched up at the side of the bed.

I began to say, 'Of course, they were all lies,' but I stopped, because there was no need. All I could do was to go downstairs and tell his mother to come up and close his eyes. I wouldn't have touched them for all the money in the world. It was a long time since I thought of that day, ages and ages ago, when I felt a cold touch like spittle on my lids and opening my eyes had seen a man like a tree surrounded by other trees walking away.

1929

THE END OF THE PARTY

PETER MORTON woke with a start to face the first light. Rain tapped against the glass. It was January the fifth.

He looked across a table on which a night-light had guttered into a pool of water, at the other bed. Francis Morton was still asleep, and Peter lay down again with his eyes on his brother. It amused him to imagine it was himself whom he watched, the same hair, the same eyes, the same lips and line of cheek. But the thought palled, and the mind went back to the fact which lent the day importance. It was the fifth of January. He could hardly believe a year had passed since Mrs Henne-Falcon had given her last children's party.

Francis turned suddenly upon his back and threw an arm across his face, blocking his mouth. Peter's heart began to beat fast, not with pleasure now but with uneasiness. He sat up and called across the table, 'Wake up.' Francis's shoulders shook and he waved a clenched fist in the air, but his eyes remained closed. To Peter Morton the whole room seemed to darken, and he had the impression of a great bird swooping. He cried again, 'Wake up,' and once more there was silver light and the touch of rain on the windows. Francis rubbed his eyes. 'Did you call out?' he asked.

'You are having a bad dream,' Peter said. Already experience had taught him how far their minds reflected each other. But he was the elder, by a matter of minutes, and that brief extra interval of light, while his brother still struggled in pain and darkness, had given him self-reliance and an instinct of protection towards the other who was afraid of so many things.

'I dreamed that I was dead,' Francis said.

'What was it like?' Peter asked.

'I can't remember,' Francis said.

'You dreamed of a big bird.'

'Did I?'

The two lay silent in bed facing each other, the same green eyes, the same nose tilting at the tip, the same firm lips, and the same premature modelling of the chin. The fifth of January, Peter thought again, his mind drifting idly from the image of cakes to the prizes which might be won. Egg-and-spoon races, spearing apples in basins of water, blind man's buff.

'I don't want to go,' Francis said suddenly. 'I suppose Joyce will be there ... Mabel Warren.' Hateful to him, the thought of a party shared with those two. They were older than he. Joyce was eleven and Mabel Warren thirteen. The long pigtails swung superciliously to a masculine stride. Their sex humiliated him, as they watched him fumble with his egg, from under lowered scornful lids. And last year ... he turned his face away from Peter, his cheeks scarlet.

'What's the matter?' Peter asked.

'Oh, nothing. I don't think I'm well. I've got a cold. I oughtn't to go to the party.' Peter was puzzled. 'But Francis, is it a bad cold?'

'It will be a bad cold if I go to the party. Perhaps I shall die.'

'Then you mustn't go,' Peter said, prepared to solve all difficulties with one plain sentence, and Francis let his nerves relax, ready to leave everything to Peter. But though he was grateful he did not turn his face towards his brother. His cheeks still bore the badge of a shameful memory, of the game of hide and seek last year in the darkened house, and of how he had screamed when Mabel Warren put her hand suddenly upon his arm. He had not heard her coming. Girls were like that. Their shoes never squeaked. No boards whined under the tread. They slunk like cats on padded claws.

When the nurse came in with hot water Francis lay tranquil leaving everything to Peter. Peter said, 'Nurse, Francis has got a cold.'

The tall starched woman laid the towels across the cans and said, without turning, 'The washing won't be back till tomorrow. You must lend him some of your handkerchiefs.'

'But, Nurse,' Peter asked, 'hadn't he better stay in bed?'

'We'll take him for a good walk this morning,' the nurse said.

193

'Wind'll blow away the germs. Get up now, both of you,' and she closed the door behind her.

'I'm sorry,' Peter said. 'Why don't you just stay in bed? I'll tell mother you felt too ill to get up.' But rebellion against destiny was not in Francis's power. If he stayed in bed they would come up and tap his chest and put a thermometer in his mouth and look at his tongue, and they would discover he was malingering. It was true he felt ill, a sick empty sensation in his stomach and a rapidly beating heart, but he knew the cause was only fear, fear of the party, fear of being made to hide by himself in the dark, uncompanioned by Peter and with no night-light to make a blessed breach.

'No, I'll get up,' he said, and then with sudden desperation, 'But I won't go to Mrs Henne-Falcon's party. I swear on the Bible I won't.' Now surely all would be well, he thought. God would not allow him to break so solemn an oath. He would show him a way. There was all the morning before him and all the afternoon until four o'clock. No need to worry when the grass was still crisp with the early frost. Anything might happen. He might cut himself or break his leg or really catch a bad cold. God would manage somehow.

He had such confidence in God that when at breakfast his mother said, 'I hear you have a cold, Francis,' he made light of it. 'We should have heard more about it,' his mother said with irony, 'if there was not a party this evening,' and Francis smiled, amazed and daunted by her ignorance of him. His happiness would have lasted longer if, out for a walk that morning, he had not met Joyce. He was alone with his nurse, for Peter had leave to finish a rabbit-hutch in the woodshed. If Peter had been there he would have cared less; the nurse was Peter's nurse also, but now it was as though she were employed only for his sake, because he could not be trusted to go for a walk alone. Joyce was only two years older and she was by herself.

She came striding towards them, pigtails flapping. She glanced scornfully at Francis and spoke with ostentation to the nurse. 'Hello, Nurse. Are you bringing Francis to the party this evening? Mabel and I are coming.' And she was off again down the street in the direction of Mabel Warren's home, consciously alone and self-sufficient in the long empty road. 'Such a nice girl,' the nurse said. But Francis was silent, feeling again the jump-jump of his heart, realizing how soon the hour of the party would arrive. God had done nothing for him, and the minutes flew.

They flew too quickly to plan any evasion, or even to prepare his heart for the coming ordeal. Panic nearly overcame him when, all unready, he found himself standing on the doorstep, with coat-collar turned up against a cold wind, and the nurse's electric torch making a short trail through the darkness. Behind him were the lights of the hall and the sound of a servant laying the table for dinner, which his mother and father would eat alone. He was nearly overcome by the desire to run back into the house and call out to his mother that he would not go to the party, that he dared not go. They could not make him go. He could almost hear himself saying those final words, breaking down for ever the barrier of ignorance which saved his mind from his parents' knowledge. 'I'm afraid of going. I won't go. I daren't go. They'll make me hide in the dark, and I'm afraid of the dark. I'll scream and scream and scream.' He could see the expression of amazement on his mother's face, and then the cold confidence of a grown-up's retort.

'Don't be silly. You must go. We've accepted Mrs Henne-Falcon's invitation.' But they couldn't make him go; hesitating on the doorstep while the nurse's feet crunched across the frost-covered grass to the gate, he knew that. He would answer: 'You can say I'm ill. I won't go. I'm afraid of the dark.' And his mother: 'Don't be silly. You know there's nothing to be afraid of in the dark.' But he knew the falsity of that reasoning; he knew how they taught also that there was nothing to fear in death, and how fearfully they avoided the idea of it. But they couldn't make him go to the party. 'I'll scream. I'll scream.'

'Francis, come along.' He heard the nurse's voice across the dimly phosphorescent lawn and saw the yellow circle of her torch wheel from tree to shrub. 'I'm coming,' he called with despair; he couldn't bring himself to lay bare his last secrets and end reserve between his mother and himself, for there was still in the last resort a further appeal possible to Mrs Henne-Falcon. He comforted himself with that, as he advanced steadily across the hall, very small, towards her enormous bulk. His heart beat unevenly, but he had control now over his voice, as he said with meticulous accent, 'Good evening, Mrs Henne-Falcon. It was very good of you to ask me to your party.' With his strained face lifted towards the curve of her breasts, and his polite set speech, he was like an old withered man. As a twin he was in many ways an only child. To address Peter was to speak to his own image in a mirror, an image a little altered by a flaw in the glass, so as to throw back less a likeness of what he was than of what he wished to be, what he would be without his unreasoning fear of darkness, footsteps of strangers, the flight of bats in dusk-filled gardens.

'Sweet child,' said Mrs Henne-Falcon absent-mindedly, before, with a wave of her arms, as though the children were a flock of chickens, she whirled them into her set programme of entertainments: egg-and-spoon races, three-legged races, the spearing of apples, games which held for Francis nothing worse than humiliation. And in the frequent intervals when nothing was required of him and he could stand alone in corners as far removed as possible from Mabel Warren's scornful gaze, he was able to plan how he might avoid the approaching terror of the dark. He knew there was nothing to fear until after tea, and not until he was sitting down in a pool of yellow radiance cast by the ten candles on Colin Henne-Falcon's birthday cake did he become fully conscious of the imminence of what he feared. He heard Joyce's high voice down the table, 'After tea we are going to play hide and seek in the dark.'

'Oh, no,' Peter said, watching Francis's troubled face, 'don't let's. We play that every year.'

'But it's in the programme,' cried Mabel Warren. 'I saw it myself. I looked over Mrs Henne-Falcon's shoulder. Five o'clock tea. A quarter to six to half past, hide and seek in the dark. It's all written down in the programme.'

Peter did not argue, for if hide and seek had been inserted in

196

Mrs Henne-Falcon's programme, nothing which he could say would avert it. He asked for another piece of birthday cake and sipped his tea slowly. Perhaps it might be possible to delay the game for a quarter of an hour, allow Francis at least a few extra minutes to form a plan, but even in that Peter failed, for children were already leaving the table in twos and threes. It was his third failure, and again he saw a great bird darken his brother's face with its wings. But he upbraided himself silently for his folly, and finished his cake encouraged by the memory of that adult refrain, 'There's nothing to fear in the dark.' The last to leave the table, the brothers came together to the hall to meet the mustering and impatient eyes of Mrs Henne-Falcon.

'And now,' she said, 'we will play hide and seek in the dark.'

Peter watched his brother and saw the lips tighten. Francis, he knew, had feared this moment from the beginning of the party, had tried to meet it with courage and had abandoned the attempt. He must have prayed for cunning to evade the game, which was now welcomed with cries of excitement by all the other children. 'Oh, do let's.' 'We must pick sides.' 'Is any of the house out of bounds?' 'Where shall home be?'

'I think,' said Francis Morton, approaching Mrs Henne-Falcon, his eyes focused unwaveringly on her exuberant breasts, 'it will be no use my playing. My nurse will be calling for me very soon.'

'Oh, but your nurse can wait, Francis,' said Mrs Henne-Falcon, while she clapped her hands together to summon to her side a few children who were already straying up the wide staircase to upper floors. 'Your mother will never mind.'

That had been the limit of Francis's cunning. He had refused to believe that so well prepared an excuse could fail. All that he could say now, still in the precise tone which other children hated, thinking it a symbol of conceit, was, 'I think I had better not play.' He stood motionless, retaining, though afraid, unmoved features. But the knowledge of his terror, or the reflection of the terror itself, reached his brother's brain. For the moment, Peter Morton could have cried aloud with the fear of bright lights going out, leaving him alone in an island of dark

THE END OF THE PARTY

surrounded by the gentle lappings of strange footsteps. Then he remembered that the fear was not his own, but his brother's. He said impulsively to Mrs Henne-Falcon, 'Please, I don't think Francis should play. The dark makes him jump so.' They were the wrong words. Six children began to sing, 'Cowardy cowardy custard,' turning torturing faces with the vacancy of wide sunflowers towards Francis Morton.

Without looking at his brother, Francis said, 'Of course I'll play. I'm not afraid, I only thought ...' But he was already forgotten by his human tormentors. The children scrambled round Mrs Henne-Falcon, their shrill voices pecking at her with questions and suggestions. 'Yes, anywhere in the house. We will turn out all the lights. Yes, you can hide in the cupboards. You must stay hidden as long as you can. There will be no home.'

Peter stood apart, ashamed of the clumsy manner in which he had tried to help his brother. Now he could feel, creeping in at the corners of his brain, all Francis's resentment of his championing. Several children ran upstairs, and the lights on the top floor went out. Darkness came down like the wings of a bat and settled on the landing. Others began to put out the lights at the edge of the hall, till the children were all gathered in the central radiance of the chandelier, while the bats squatted round on hooded wings and waited for that, too, to be extinguished.

'You and Francis are on the hiding side,' a tall girl said, and then the light was gone, and the carpet wavered under his feet with the sibilance of footfalls, like small cold draughts, creeping away into corners.

'Where's Francis?' he wondered. 'If I join him he'll be less frightened of all these sounds.' 'These sounds' were the casing of silence: the squeak of a loose board, the cautious closing of a cupboard door, the whine of a finger drawn along polished wood.

Peter stood in the centre of the dark deserted floor, not listening but waiting for the idea of his brother's whereabouts to enter his brain. But Francis crouched with fingers on his ears, eyes uselessly closed, mind numbed against impressions, and only a sense of strain could cross the gap of dark. Then a voice

called 'Coming', and as though his brother's self-possession had
been shattered by the sudden cry, Peter Morton jumped with his
fear. But it was not his own fear. What in his brother was a
burning panic was in him an altruistic emotion that left the
reason unimpaired. 'Where, if I were Francis, should I hide?'
And because he was, if not Francis himself, at least a mirror to
him, the answer was immediate. 'Between the oak bookcase on
the left of the study door, and the leather settee.' Between the
twins there could be no jargon of telepathy. They had been
together in the womb, and they could not be parted.

Peter Morton tiptoed towards Francis's hiding-place.
Occasionally a board rattled, and because he feared to be
caught by one of the soft questers through the dark, he bent and
untied his laces. A tag struck the floor and the metallic sound set
a host of cautious feet moving in his direction. But by that time
he was in his stockings and would have laughed inwardly at the
pursuit had not the noise of someone stumbling on his abandoned shoes made his heart trip. No more boards revealed Peter
Morton's progress. On stockinged feet he moved silently and
unerringly towards his object. Instinct told him he was near the
wall, and, extending a hand, he laid the fingers across his
brother's face.

Francis did not cry out, but the leap of his own heart revealed
to Peter a proportion of Francis's terror. 'It's all right,' he whispered, feeling down the squatting figure until he captured a
clenched hand. 'It's only me. I'll stay with you.' And grasping
the other tightly, he listened to the cascade of whispers his utter-
ance had caused to fall. A hand touched the book-case close to
Peter's head and he was aware of how Francis's fear continued
in spite of his presence. It was less intense, more bearable, he
hoped, but it remained. He knew that it was his brother's fear
and not his own that he experienced. The dark to him was only
an absence of light; the groping hand that of a familiar child.
Patiently he waited to be found.

He did not speak again, for between Francis and himself was
the most intimate communion. By way of joined hands thought
could flow more swiftly than lips could shape themselves round

words. He could experience the whole progress of his brother's emotion, from the leap of panic at the unexpected contact to the steady pulse of fear, which now went on and on with the regularity of a heart-beat. Peter Morton thought with intensity, 'I am here. You needn't be afraid. The lights will go on again soon. That rustle, that movement is nothing to fear. Only Joyce, only Mabel Warren.' He bombarded the drooping form with thoughts of safety, but he was conscious that the fear continued. 'They are beginning to whisper together. They are tired of looking for us. The lights will go on soon. We shall have won. Don't be afraid. That was someone on the stairs. I believe it's Mrs Henne-Falcon. Listen. They are feeling for the lights.' Feet moving on a carpet, hands brushing a wall, a curtain pulled apart, a clicking handle, the opening of a cupboard door. In the case above their heads a loose book shifted under a touch. 'Only Joyce, only Mabel Warren, only Mrs Henne-Falcon,' a crescendo of reassuring thought before the chandelier burst, like a fruit-tree, into bloom.

The voices of the children rose shrilly into the radiance. 'Where's Peter?' 'Have you looked upstairs?' 'Where's Francis?' but they were silenced again by Mrs Henne-Falcon's scream. But she was not the first to notice Francis Morton's stillness, where he had collapsed against the wall at the touch of his brother's hand. Peter continued to hold the clenched fingers in an arid and puzzled grief. It was not merely that his brother was dead. His brain, too young to realize the full paradox, wondered with an obscure self-pity why it was that the pulse of his brother's fear went on and on, when Francis was now where he had always been told there was no more terror and no more darkness.

1929

Graham Greene

THE COMEDIANS

'Greene arouses responses of curiosity and attention comparable to those set up by Malraux...Faulkner and Hemingway'
New Statesman

'Laughter is possible even in the dark night of Haiti...a vision that is at once comic and intensely serious...a major novel'
Roger Sharrock

Three men meet on a ship bound for Haiti, a world in the grip of the corrupt 'Papa Doc' and the Tontons Macoute, his sinister secret police. Brown the hotelier, Smith the innocent American and Jones the confidence man – these are the 'comedians' of Graham Greene's title. Hiding behind their actors' masks, they hesitate on the edge of life. And, to begin with, they are men afraid of love, afraid of pain, afraid of fear itself...

VINTAGE

Also available in Vintage

Graham Greene

DOCTOR FISCHER OF GENEVA OR THE BOMB PARTY

'Demonstrates once again Greene's talent
as a riveting storyteller'
Newsweek

'A brilliantly accomplished handling of the Russian roulette
theme, removing it from the sphere of self-indulgence and
broadening it into a parable about human greed, hate, com-
passion and salvation...a telling spiritual melodrama,
streaked with black farce'
Norman Shrapnel, *Guardian*

Doctor Fischer despises the human race. When the notori-
ous toothpaste millionaire decides to hold the last of his
famous parties - his own deadly version of the Book of
Revelations – Greene opens up a powerful vision of the
limitless greed of the rich. Black comedy and painful satire
combine in a totally compelling novel.

'Manages to say more about love, hate, happiness, grief,
immortality, greed and the disgustingly rich than most
contemporary English novels three times the length'
The Times

VINTAGE

Also available in Vintage

Graham Greene

THE HUMAN FACTOR

'As fine a novel as he has ever written...funny, shocking,
above all compassionate'
Anthony Burgess, *Observer*

A leak is traced to a small sub-section of SIS, sparking off the
inevitable security checks, tensions and suspicions. The sort
of atmosphere, perhaps, where mistakes could be made? For
Maurice Castle – dull, but brilliant with files – it is the end of
the line anyway, and time for him to retire to live peacefully
with his African wife, Sarah.

'Graham Greene's beautiful and disturbing novel is filled
with tenderness, humour, excitement and doubt'
The Times

'It is beautifully done, a pleasure to read, a succession of
deft, unobtrusive, yet masterly touches'
Guardian

VINTAGE

Also available in Vintage

Graham Greene

WAYS OF ESCAPE

'When I wrote a fragment of autobiography under the title *A Sort of Life* I closed the record at the age of about twenty-seven...I had tasted the pleasure of remembering and so I began a series of introductions to the Collected Edition of my books, looking back on the circumstances in which the books were conceived and written. They too were after all "a sort of life"'

Graham Greene

With superb skill and feeling, in *Ways of Escape* Graham Greene retraces the experiences and encounters of a long and extraordinary life; his travels around the world, seeking out people and political situations 'at the dangerous edge of things', his time in the British Secret Service in Africa and his brief involvement with Hollywood.

VINTAGE

BY GRAHAM GREENE
ALSO AVAILABLE FROM VINTAGE

☐ The Comedians	0099478374	£7.99
☐ Dr Fischer of Geneva	0099288494	£6.99
☐ The Human Factor	0099288524	£7.99
☐ The Honorary Consul	0099478382	£7.99
☐ A Sort of Life	0099282577	£6.99
☐ Travels With My Aunt	0099282585	£7.99